The Accidental MISTRESS

Also by Aya de León

THE BOSS

UPTOWN THIEF

The Accidental MISTRESS

AYA DE LEÓN

Kensington Publishing Corp.
www.kensingtonbooks.com

DAFINA BOOKS are published by

Kensington Publishing Corp.
119 West 40th Street
New York, NY 10018

To the extent that the image or images on the cover of this book depict a person or persons, such person or persons are merely models, and are not intended to portray any character or characters featured in the book.

All Kensington Titles, Imprints, and Distributed Lines are available at special quantity discounts for bulk purchases for sales promotions, premiums, fund-raising, and educational or institutional use. Special book excerpts or customized printings can also be created to fit specific needs. For details, write or phone the office of the Kensington special sales manager: Kensington Publishing Corp., 119 West 40th Street, New York, NY 10018, attn: Special Sales Department, Phone: 1-800-221-2647.

ISBN-13: 978-1-4967-1577-7
ISBN-10: 1-4967-1577-2
First Kensington Trade Edition: June 2018
First Kensington Mass Market Edition: May 2019

ISBN-13: 978-1-4967-1578-4 (e-book)
ISBN-10: 1-4967-1578-0 (e-book)

10 9 8 7 6 5 4 3 2 1

Printed in the United States of America

To Stuart, who lives at the intersection of Nigel and Cyril, with the occasional drive-by from Kingsley:
mi luv yuh . . .

Acknowledgments

Grateful as ever to my current and former agent/publishing team: Jenni Ferrari Adler, Esi Sogah, Claire Hill, Mercedes Fernandez, Lulu Martinez, and Dana Kaye. Also my family for ongoing support: Anna, Coco, Duy, Larry, Paci, Nina, Pam, and Carolina. My fabulous readers Brenda Burke and Rachel Aimee, who keep my story honest. To Kristina Mundera and my Lodestar fam who offered such great love and teaching that I could delegate some kidraising and write this book. To my West Indian ancestors, especially Diana Knight, may you be uplifted. And finally, to all the Justice Hustlers out there. Thank you for fighting for the world we want, need, and deserve, and for keeping the faith that we will win.

Prologue

November.

Lily had always been trouble. But Violet knew something was really wrong when she heard a strange man yelling her sister's name.

It was early afternoon, and Violet was standing out at the Manhattan Cruise Terminal, where some of their largest vessels came to dock. In front of her, a giant ship loomed, quiet and empty. On this unseasonably warm November day, Violet breathed in the briny smell of polluted water, and heard the swish and hiss of water sloshing around and below her.

Across the cream-colored bow, ELITE CRUISES was written in dark gold script. Along the lower half of the ship's side, dark windows dotted the outer wall like a triple strand of onyx beads. Above that, several stories of balconies stretched across the length of the ship.

A shirtless black man appeared at the railing. "Lily!" he bellowed.

Violet looked around but didn't see her sister. Much

farther down the ship's side, a hydraulic metal gangplank stretched from the belly of the vessel to the cement dock.

The man continued yelling. "Lily, but a wah di rass?!" He was dark and firmly muscled, cursing in Jamaican patois down at someone Violet couldn't see. "Lily, yu lossaz," he raged on. "A wah di bloodclaat dew yuh?"

Two days before, Violet had gotten a message from her sister via ship-to-shore call. Lily's voice had sounded bright and bubbly. She was coming to New York, and she gave the exact date, time, and location for Violet to meet her.

Spontaneous. Crazy. Practically no notice. Typical Lily. As kids, Violet had always chased after her reckless little sister and tried to keep her out of trouble. Violet had left for boarding school at fourteen. It had been twelve years since they had seen each other in person.

When Violet had left Trinidad, Lily was eleven and skinny, so it took Violet a moment to realize that the grown woman, nearly six feet tall and dark brown, headed her way was her sister. She had seen photos and even video chatted, but had never seen her full body. Now Lily was whizzing down the gangplank on a tandem bicycle.

Violet echoed the Jamaican man's curses, in US English. "What the fuck?"

Lily got closer. She was wearing a beige maid's uniform and flip-flops. She pulled up to Violet and screeched to a stop.

"Get on," Lily said, indicating the rear seat of the bicycle built for two. "If that crazy Yardie catches us, he'll kill me and you too for good measure."

In the distance, Violet saw the shirtless man running down the gangplank to give chase.

Violet was dressed for work, wearing wedge sandals

and a long A-line dress. She hiked the dress up in one fist and climbed onto the bike.

The sisters began to pedal. Violet's feet were unsteady in the high heels. Fortunately, cruise season was winding down, and there were few pedestrians. They only had to swing wide to avoid an elderly woman walking a dog.

At the corner, the light changed to green, and they turned onto a busy commercial Manhattan street. Unfortunately, the traffic was one-way and headed toward them.

"You're gonna get us killed!" Violet screamed, watching the line of vehicles bearing down on them. She shut her eyes, expecting to feel the impact of a delivery truck, crushing their bodies against a parked car or hurling them into the street.

But miraculously, Lily managed to avoid the line of swift cars.

Violet's eyes flew open as she could feel the bike leaning dangerously to the left. As they rounded a corner, she gripped the handles even tighter and clenched her body onto the bike. At least they were moving with traffic now, and the cars didn't look like potential executioners.

"Damn, Violet," her sister yelled over her shoulder, "will you pedal? I'm trying to put some space between me and that lunatic."

Violet began to pedal down the long block between two avenues. When this was over, if they didn't both get killed, she vowed to personally wring her sister's neck.

Stores and restaurants flashed by as they sped along a sidewalk crowded with pedestrians. Behind them, they heard a siren.

"Could that bastard have called the police?" Lily asked.

"Did you commit a crime?" Violet asked.

"Only jumping ship," Lily said. "But he knows if the police catch me without papers, I'll get deported."

"I don't fucking believe this," Violet said.

The police car turned down their block, but it got caught for a moment behind a garbage truck.

Lily turned the corner at the far end of the block.

"Brake!" she yelled to Violet.

Both women squeezed the hand brakes, and the bike stopped abruptly. Violet lurched into her sister's back, banging her ribs painfully on the handlebars.

Lily leaped up off the bike and yanked Violet behind her, as the bicycle clattered to the ground. Lily pulled Violet into the nearest storefront, which turned out to be a temporary Halloween costume shop.

It was November 1, so everything marked with an orange sticker was ninety-nine cents.

Violet leaned against the wall to catch her breath, but Lily grabbed a sexy witch costume and disappeared into one of the makeshift dressing rooms.

Violet's heart beat hard, and she sucked in the shop's stale air, which smelled of plastic. On one side of her were costumes for sexy witches, devils, and vampires. On the other side were men without heads, superheroes, and cartoon characters.

Through the plate-glass window, Violet saw a police car stop and two officers get out. They inspected the bicycle, and one of them talked into his radio.

Lily came out wearing the witch costume, her maid uniform balled up in her hand.

"Good," Lily said. "They're getting the bike."

She walked to the register and paid cash. Stopping at the full-length mirror, she set the pointy black hat on her head, pulling down its wide brim to cover her face.

"Lily, what the hell is going on?"

"I just immigrated," she said and strolled out the door.

Violet followed her, seething with fury, as they passed the two officers who were putting the tandem bike in the rear of their police SUV.

"I thought you were coming for a visit," Violet said.

"I feel at home already," Lily said. She looked around at the traffic roaring through the streets and the multitude of people striding purposefully past them.

A man in athletic gear was walking a pig on a leash. Lily exploded in delighted laughter. "Am I hallucinating after six weeks on a ship? A pig?"

"That's not important," Violet said. "Where will you stay in New York?"

"With you?" Lily asked.

"I can't," Violet said. "It's not just me. I live with my boyfriend. If you'd said something in your message—"

"I understand," Lily said. "Can I use your phone?"

Lily proceeded to go online to look up the number for a health clinic. She called and asked for a woman named Tyesha who worked there—a friend from when Lily had lived in New York before. She left a message with the receptionist.

"Can I . . . get you an AirBnB room or something?" Violet asked.

Lily waved the idea away. She pulled a scrap of paper out of her maid's uniform and called a man she had met on the cruise. They made a date for that evening.

"I can't believe how short you are!" Lily said, when she handed back the phone.

"I'm not short," Violet said. "You've just become a giant."

Even in her high heels, Violet still was several inches

shorter than her sister in the flip-flops. But they had a large gene pool to pull from. Their mother was short and dark. Violet had met their father only once, when she was four, but she remembered that he was unfathomably tall, a black and South Asian mix. Lily had her father's height and her mother's dark skin. Violet was shorter and lighter.

"Lily, you can't just come to New York with no visa," Violet said. "What about work? A place to live?"

"I did it before," Lily laughed. "I can always find work. And I have a place for the night with my new friend. Don't worry. I'm not a child anymore. I been doing fine since you left Trinidad. I got that cruise ship job. I made it back to New York."

"What are you gonna do until you meet your friend?" Violet asked.

Lily shrugged. "Wander through the city. Get lost, then get found again. Unless you want to show me around."

"I'm sorry," Violet said. "I've got to get back to work." Tears pricked her eyes. Her sister hadn't even been a teen when Violet had left Port of Spain for boarding school. Now she had men calling her back to ships and offering to share their bed with her.

Violet pulled her sister into a tight hug. "I'll talk to my boyfriend about you staying," she said.

"No rush," Lily said. "I like this guy. I wasn't able to get to know him thanks to Kingsley, Mr. Jealous Jamaican. I won't be needing a place for a few nights at least."

Hearing Lily's Trinidadian lilt, Violet's own voice began to sound strange to her. She'd worked so hard to sound American during that first year at boarding school.

"How can I get in touch with you?" Violet asked.

"I'll get a phone this week," Lily said. "Meanwhile, I have your number memorized."

They hugged, and Violet watched the tall, pointy hat until it disappeared into the Manhattan foot traffic.

Chapter 1

Late May

A year and a half after her sister jumped ship, Violet was planning her wedding to Quentin. Her phone was constantly ringing with wedding planning as well as work calls. She was the assistant to one of New York's top makeup artists. That particular day, they were making up the actress Delia Borbon.

Violet reached into the makeup case and handed her boss the smallest, most delicate brush to line Borbon's left eye. Her boss asked for the black liner, but Violet handed her the navy. Her boss might be the makeup artist to the stars, but she worked mostly with white people. Violet knew Caribbean skin tones. Intuitively, Violet knew the slight blue tint would bring out the copper in the skin of the Puerto Rican actress.

"I love this," Borbon said, in her rich, throaty voice. "It's not quite black, is it?"

Her boss looked closer. "No," she said, squinting. "Dark blue. Violet must have picked the wrong one. A happy accident. It looks great on you."

Violet smiled and nodded, but Borbon gave her a subtle wink.

Back home in Trinidad, Violet's mother had taught her and her sister about makeup. The clients had run the gamut of skin shades. "Everyone is so preoccupied with how dark or light the skin," her mother had said. "But the key to good makeup is to focus on the tones. Do you want to bring out red, gold, or blue, you know?" Their mother had worked hard to de-emphasize color issues in their family, as Violet was much fairer-skinned than Lily.

Her boss was making up Delia Borbon for a weekly magazine wedding shoot. Late May morning light filtered in through the high windows of the Chelsea loft studio. The forty-something star sat in her beige slip, looking utterly relaxed and at home, even with a dozen people running around her. In the magazine, Borbon would have her signature hourglass shape, but now, a roll in her soft belly pressed against the fabric of the slip. On a hanger nearby, a huge, poofy-skirted dress hung beside a full complement of shapewear.

"Violet's getting married on Labor Day," her boss confided to the star, explaining that Violet's soon-to-be mother-in-law had recommended her for the job.

"You're marrying into the Ross family?" Borbon asked. "They're practically African American royalty."

"I had no idea who he was when we met," Violet said. "I'm not from the US."

"Speaking of royalty," Violet's boss said, "I need you to be sure to get that call from Henri. Well, Mr. Delacroix to you." She turned to Borbon. "The French designer. His son is marrying a member of the British royal family. I'm making her up tomorrow."

"You'll certainly be using paler shades than today," Borbon said. "I've seen that girl. Have they checked for a pulse?" She turned to Violet. "Will your family be coming in for the wedding?"

"My mother has a heart condition, unfortunately," Violet said. "She's not able to fly."

"Such a shame," her boss said. "I thought you had a sister in town."

"Nope, it's just me," Violet lied.

Speeding below midtown on the downtown train, she heard her name.

"Violet? Violet Johnson, is that you?"

She turned to see a young man she recognized. She recalled the high cheekbones and full lips but couldn't conjure his name.

"Nigel McDaniels, from Harvard," he said, a smile splitting his dark brown face.

"From the theater department," she said. "How's it going? I haven't seen you since we did *The Wiz.*"

"Really glad to see you," he said. "I was thinking of you and didn't have your number. I've been doing this Caribbean Circus show, and we need a new set and makeup designer. I wondered if you would consider working with us."

"I wish I could," she said. "I actually landed a full-time job." She offered her card with the name of her boss's company, Facing Manhattan.

"Fancy," he said.

"But she's got me running like a lunatic," Violet confided.

"Jump, colored girl!" Nigel said, and Violet laughed.

"Practically. Plus I've got other projects going on."

"I'm glad you're doing well," he said. "I always hoped you'd do something creative, even though you were an economics major."

"You know how it is," she said. "You're Jamaican, right? I'm sure your family is less than thrilled that you're an artist."

"You should hear my mother," he said. " 'Oh, Goooohd,' " he mimicked in her Jamaican English. "We did not send our son to Harvard so he could perform in a circus! So rude and disobedient. No respect!' "

Violet laughed. "My mother is a makeup artist," she said, "so you'd think she'd be happy about it. But she says she expected 'more' from me. Although it's gotten a little better lately, since tomorrow we'll be making up a member of the British royal family."

Nigel laughed out loud. "I'm sure she'll be bragging to all her friends."

A triangle of brown skin kept peeking out from a torn spot in the collar of his Caribbean Circus T-shirt. She could see the curve of his muscle into his collarbone, and it distracted her. Most of the men she interacted with these days wore suits and ties. The only skin visible was on their hands and faces. But she could see the pull of his broad shoulders against the cotton fabric and the length of his strong arms extending from the short sleeves. The easy grace of Nigel's body in the torn shirt reminded her of men back home.

"God, it's great to see you," she said.

"You, too," he said. "Hey, are you still dating that black American guy—what was his name?"

"Quentin," Violet said.

"Quentin Ross," Nigel said. "The Harvard legacy."

"Actually, that's my big personal project. We're getting married." She pulled her hand down from the subway bar and showed him the diamond engagement ring.

"Whoa, that's quite a—"

The train gave a sudden lurch while Violet's hand

was off the overhead bar. She crashed into Nigel. As the two pressed together, she noticed that he smelled familiar. Some sort of soap or aftershave or something that men used back in the West Indies. Slowly, she caught herself and straightened up.

"See, you go flashing that big ring, you get into trouble," he said.

"Flashing?" she asked, turning the rock under to the palm side of her hand. "Are you kidding me? Most of the time I hide it so nobody tries to rob me." She gripped the bar overhead to steady herself.

He reached up and touched the gold bangle on her wrist. "Now, this is the jewelry I remember you always wearing. You had this in college, right?"

"Yeah," she said. "Since I was little."

Her mother had curved the precious gold bracelet tight around her wrist when she was seven and had stretched it wider as she grew.

Nigel smiled at her. "Violet Johnson. Well, congratulations on both counts. The wedding and the big job."

"I hope things go great with the circus," she said. "This is my stop."

"Here's my card," he said. "So we can stay in touch."

When Violet got out of the subway, she wasn't sure where she was going, only that she needed to find her sister. Their mother was worried. Lily's phone was disconnected, and their mother couldn't get hold of her.

Violet wasn't surprised that Lily's phone had been turned off. The big shock was that Lily had managed to keep from being deported and finally gotten her papers somehow.

But if her mother was worried, then she had to check on Lily. Violet had gone by Lily's apartment, but the building manager said she'd moved out with no forwarding address. He did, however, have a work address from her rental application.

Several years earlier—the first time Lily had moved to New York—Violet had still been living in Boston. From time to time, she would get distress calls from her younger sister. Usually Lily needed money. But once, Lily had put Violet down as a reference for a waitressing job. Could Violet vouch for her if the lady called?

"Absolutely not," Violet had said, exasperated. "I can't lie to this woman for you."

"But I do have waitressing experience," Lily said. "Back in Trinidad. She said I needed someone in the states to vouch for me. I told her I did some catering for you, and gave her your number."

"Without asking me?" Violet asked, her anger rising.

"I had to improvise," Lily said. "Yours is the only number in the US that I know by heart."

So Violet had reluctantly agreed, and Lily had gotten the job. She'd promised Violet unlimited free drinks when she and Quentin came to Manhattan. But Violet had never made it from Boston to New York City in the two years that Lily had lived there. Then Lily had moved back to Trinidad, and the two of them had very little contact until the day Violet met her sister at the cruise ship docks.

Now, Violet walked down a street in Lower Manhattan with Lily's work address in her hand. The One-Eyed King. Was this the bar where she'd helped her sister get a job?

When Violet arrived at the location, she double-checked the address. The One-Eyed King was worse than the dive bar Violet had been imagining. A strip club? Lily worked at a Manhattan strip club? She knew

Lily had played a stripper on Broadway. That was bad enough, but actually stripping?

She walked to the door, where a young woman with blue hair looked her up and down. She took in Violet's modest sheath dress, shoulder-length pressed hair, and light makeup. But above all, she observed her tight expression of distaste.

"Can I help you?" the young woman asked.

Violet explained that she was Lily's sister. The girl said that they usually didn't give out information, but she knew Lily's phone was cut off, and they did look a lot alike.

Yes, Lily did work there, but she wasn't scheduled for that day. She might be found volunteering at a health center nearby. The girl offered to give her walking or subway directions to the Maria de la Vega Community Health Clinic.

"No, thanks," Violet said, but she copied down the name and phone number for the health center and texted it to her mother.

There. She'd located Lily to the best of her ability. Not dead. Not deported. Not in the hospital. Let her mother take it from here. Now Violet could finally start her weekend.

She didn't want to be picked up in front of the strip club, so she walked down a couple of doors to a national café franchise.

The day was hot and muggy, but she hated waiting in the arctic interior of the overly air-conditioned coffee shop. Humid East Coast summers reminded her of Trinidad in weather only, but unless she was in Brooklyn, the similarities ended there. Manhattan held none of the rhythms of Trinidad. Even in the most crowded part of downtown Port of Spain, there was some touch of nature, some reminder of the sea or the island's rural history.

She had just finished texting her location to Quentin when a young woman tapped her on the shoulder. She wore a too-tight yellow dress and asked to borrow Violet's cell phone. She had left hers at home and needed to check in with her babysitter.

Violet unlocked her phone and handed it over.

The young woman dialed a number. "Hello, Mrs. Ramirez. Just want to make sure everything's okay."

As the girl listened and nodded, Violet noticed that she was pretty but had on too much makeup. The lipstick was too dark. It should have been brighter. And the eyes were overly lined above and below. Especially on a light-skinned girl like her, all that black just looked heavy. What was she? Black? Indian? Latina? On a warm day like today, she should have just lined the upper lid and done mascara.

At the curb, Quentin's limo beeped.

Violet retrieved the phone from the young woman, who smiled and thanked her profusely.

"No worries," Violet said and slid into the limo next to Quentin.

He greeted her with a soft kiss on the lips. "How was your day, future Mrs. Ross?" Quentin wasn't exactly handsome as much as he was charismatic. The planes of his face didn't inspire art, but Violet was attracted to the confidence with which he carried himself.

When he had asked her on a date in college, she was shocked. Her? The editor of *The Crimson*, the president of the Black Students Association, the hotshot in the Delphic Club was interested in her? Over time, she came to find his looks intensely attractive, as he showed the world his power but was always soft with her.

"My day was—" Violet began.

"No, baby," Quentin said with a chuckle. "We talked about this. If you're gonna marry into this family, you need to start learning to refer to yourself in the third person."

"Right," Violet laughed. "The future Mrs. Ross spent her morning fetching and carrying for her mistress and is now waiting for an important phone call from Henri Delacroix."

"The French fashion designer?" Quentin asked.

"The very one," Violet said. "His son is marrying some young royal from England, and we're making her up tomorrow. My boss is thrilled to add royalty to her list of clients. And the fact that Delacroix asked her personally has her beside herself. He's supposed to call me when he gets into Manhattan, and my boss wants me to ask him personally if everything is okay."

"Can't his hotel concierge do that?"

"Why contract out when you've got your own hired help?" Violet asked. "Don't worry, honey, it's just gonna be one phone call. He should be landing soon. Once he arrives, I turn off the cell and we can practice for our honeymoon."

"Why wait?" Quentin asked and pulled her into a more aggressive kiss.

Violet glanced up at the limo driver and raised the privacy partition.

They couple was still making out five minutes later when Violet's phone rang.

"Hold on," she said, adjusting her blouse.

The number came up blocked, but she answered the phone.

"Violet Johnson," she said. The phone was staticky in her ear, but there seemed to be a voice cutting in and out. She heard "today" then "plane"—or could it have been "feign"? Then the phone dropped the call.

"Hello? Hello?" Her phone had several bars of service and a full charge.

It rang again, and Violet was greeted with the same static. "We seem to have a bad connection," she said. "Who's calling, please?"

The phone crackled, and she could hear a male voice talking in what sounded like a distant tunnel. She couldn't make out any of the words.

"Can you speak up?" she asked. "Perhaps increase the volume on your phone?"

Quentin turned on the limo's TV and flipped channels until he found CNN.

She waved for him to turn it down, but Quentin didn't seem to notice. She plugged her other ear with her finger and hunched down to listen closely. On the phone, a man was speaking in a distant, muffled voice. She could only make out a sense of urgency in his tone.

"I still can't hear you," she said. "My signal is fine. Is there anything you can do on your end?"

She thought she heard the voice say "Damn!" and then a minute of static before the call dropped again.

"Quentin, can you please turn off the volume on the TV?" she asked. "Or at least wear the headphones?"

Quentin lifted the remote and muted the TV, picking up his earbuds. "Was it Delacroix?" he asked.

"I couldn't tell," Violet said. "With my boss, I never know who she'll have calling me. Maybe I should check in with her."

"Don't worry about it," Quentin said, sliding a hand onto her hip. "There's obviously nothing you can do . . ."

The phone rang a third time, and Violet picked up for the same blocked number.

"Can you hear me?" she asked. "Is this Mr. Delacroix?"

"I can hear you," came the response. At the same time her own voice echoed back to her.

"Kitty, is that you?" Delacroix asked.

Violet had expected his accent to be French. "Not Kitty. Violet," she said. "The assistant at Facing Manhattan."

"I'm in Manhattan," Delacroix said.

"Already?" Violet asked. "Didn't you just land at JFK?"

"What are you talking about?" Delacroix asked. "Honey, don't play with me."

"Excuse me?" Violet asked.

"I said don't play with me," he said. "When are you coming, Kitty? Big Daddy needs his pussycat."

"Mr. Delacroix!" Violet sat up straight in her seat. "That's not appropriate."

"Dela-who?" the man asked, his voice now hard, suspicious. "Is this Kitty?"

"This is not Kitty," Violet said. "You have the wrong number. Goodbye."

"What happened?" Quentin asked.

"I don't know," Violet said. "I can't tell if it was a wrong number or an obscene phone call."

He slid a hand onto her hip. "Can I whisper something obscene in your ear?"

She lifted his hand up off her. "Please, Quentin. The only thing that's less of a turn-on than an obscene phone call is your boyfriend joking about it."

"Fiancé," he corrected and turned to the stock reports on CNN, putting the earbuds into his ears.

Violet dozed. She woke up briefly to see spindly trees passing the window. She fell asleep again.

She woke up as the limo was pulling to a stop in front of a stunning five-story hotel.

It had a stately stone façade, but the lobby was decidedly modern.

"Pretty gorgeous, huh?" Quentin asked.

Violet glanced down at her phone to make sure she didn't have any missed calls. "Amazing," she said, and kissed him.

The hotel was even more impressive inside, with a huge hall that had a wall of windows that opened onto the sea.

Quentin took both her hands in his. "I know my mother picked the place, but I think she has pretty good taste. Even though the invitations went out months ago . . . if you don't like it, say the word. We can honeymoon somewhere else. As long as we get married, okay? It's just so hard to get away from the office right now. I don't want to spend two days flying. It's a short helicopter ride from Midtown. What do you say?"

Violet looked out at the evening sky, the blue of the ocean, the line of foam at the sand's edge. "It's beautiful, Quentin. I love it." She kissed him deeply. "Lots of women would be thrilled to have a mother-in-law handle so much of her wedding. Especially when she's paying."

"Technically," Quentin said, kissing her again, "my dad is paying."

"I'd like to take you up to the bedroom and make you pay a little," she said.

"Oh, future Mrs. Ross," Quentin said, "have your way with me."

Twenty minutes later, he was lying back on the king-size bed, and she was on top, thrusting slowly up and down. His body sank down into the Egyptian cotton sheets.

She felt the pleasure of him between her legs, but her eyes were focused on the ocean out the window, barely visible in the gathering dusk.

"Yes!" he moaned, and grabbed her hips tighter, thrusting up into her until he climaxed.

He lingered inside her, running his hands down along her ass, and gazing up into her eyes. "I love you," he said.

"I love you, too," she said, and rolled off of him.

Later that same night, Violet's sister, Lily, was called up to the stage at the Nuyorican Poets Café. The moment the emcee called her name, some of the women in the audience began to yell, "Ninety-nine!"

Lily shook her head and made her way between the tables and chairs to the small stage, a 4-inch x 4-inch notebook in hand. The club was packed extra tight, because they had an all-star feature lineup of poets. The hem of her dark maxi skirt caught on the hinge of a folding chair, and she pulled it loose. She had on a tight flowered crop tank, and her belly ring showed.

Finally, she made it to the stage, which was empty except for a mic on a stand and a tall stool.

When she got up to the mic, she leaned down into it and said, "I'm gonna do some new shit." With the dip of her head, several of her micro-braid extensions fell forward, and she tucked them behind her ear.

"Come on, Lily!" a woman shouted from the back. She was leaning against the exposed brick wall and had a beer in her hand. "We wanna hear about stripper problems!"

Lily laughed. "That poem is over a year old. Can't a girl write something new?" She opened the notebook and flipped through the pages.

"Not tonight," another woman called, her voice familiar. Lily peered through the dim room to a table about halfway back. The heckler was her friend Tyesha, a young African American woman in a tight blue dress. She was sitting with a Latina woman in her early forties who had on jeans and a green surplice blouse. Her long dark hair was pulled back into a sloppy bun.

Lily's eyes widened. "Nuyorican Café," she said. "We have a local legend in the building. Marisol Rivera, the founder of the Maria de la Vega health clinic, anti-gentrification warrior, empowerer of women, and all-around badass."

Marisol shook her head and waved the compliment away.

"And seated next to her, my girl Tyesha Couvillier, the current executive director of the clinic."

Tyesha grinned and did a mock British royal wave. As she turned from side to side, nodding to her subjects, her bone-straight weave slid across her shoulders.

"And for anyone who doesn't know," Lily went on, "the clinic provides holistic health services to sex workers, so in honor of Marisol, I guess I will be reading my poem '99 Problems but a Pimp Ain't One.' "

Several women in the audience screamed with delight.

Lily set her notebook down on the stool and adjusted the mic to her full height of six feet. She knew this piece from memory.

She closed her eyes and took a breath, then launched into the poem:

I got ninety-nine problems, but a pimp ain't one.
You got money problems, I feel bad for you, hon,
'Cause I got ninety-nine problems, but a pimp
ain't one.

Her voice rang strong and confident through the room.

You look and see some kind of opportunity
To make cash from an ass that belongs to me.
I got the flavor you savor, but I ain't doing you
no favor.
You think these charms come natural? Nah, this is
sexual labor.
I got these guys nearly jizzin' when I'm quizzing
them, "Boo?
Do you like it like that? Do I do it for you?"
And you blew it for true when you asked me on
a date.
But way too fucking curious about the money I
make.
Thanks for the dinner and the drinks, it was fun.
I got ninety-nine problems, but a pimp ain't one.

That line got a laugh.

Yeah, ninety-nine problems, but a pimp ain't one.
While the owners of this club got a scheme they
tryna run.
They took the dressing room out, put in a VIP
With a king-size bed and I'm like, "Excuse me?"
They jack up the fees and expand our dance sets.
It's like I'll have to blow your buddies just to pay
my rent.

If I wanted to sell sex I wouldn't be here
In a poorly run strip club with watered-down beer.
I came to dance, so let me be clear.
I don't need your help to develop my career.

I'm wearing eight-inch heels, but my ass is bare.
I'm hanging upside down on a pole in mid-air,
Where I can jiggle my ass, make it bounce, make it clap.
Funny how I think I should make money for that.
These assholes tryna get paid from work that I've done.
I got ninety-nine problems, but a pimp ain't one.
Pay me!

I got ninety-nine problems but a pimp ain't one.
I got black stripper problems at that intersection.
So about that fat ass, which you know you want,
You see it from any angle, even from the front.
But my ass and me hit a glass ceiling
With these club managers and their shady dealing.
Cause the stripping industry has a problem with race.
See, they want my black ass, but not my black face.
They want light bright chicks in the VIP
Where the big spenders are with the fat money.
VIP rappers picking me to dance on their lap.
Club promoters tryna block and keep it whiter than that.
And in spite of the fact that I please every time,
I can't get a pass with a skintone like mine,
Though I'm glowing like an African Caribbean sun
With ninety-nine black problems, but a pimp ain't one.

She took the mic off the stand and began to prowl across the front of the stage:

One thing I've learned in the industry
Is that sex work is work and freedom ain't free.
The one job where women earn more than men.
Every time I turn around some dick's exploiting us again.
So we organized to fight the bosses,
And the shady investors had to cut their losses
'Cause we won the fight, and now I'm pleased to say
We got a living wage and sick leave pay
And health insurance as backup to ACA,
Plus matching funds for our 401(k).

That's right, motherfuckers, we got a stripper un-ION.
'Cause I got:

She took the mic and held it out to the audience. They roared back:

"NINETY-NINE PROBLEMS, BUT A PIMP AIN'T ONE!"

She jammed the mic back on the stand and jumped off the edge of the stage, as the crowd erupted in cheers. She snatched her notebook off the stool and strutted back to her seat. Tyesha, Marisol, and several other women in the audience were on their feet.

Violet and Quentin were lying in a half doze, tangled in the hotel bedsheets, when Violet's phone rang again. "Don't answer it," Quentin said, sliding his hands around her waist to stop her.

She stumbled out of bed, nearly tripping over the comforter that they had pushed onto the floor. "I have to. It might be Mr. Delacroix."

She grabbed the phone, and picked up to an unfamiliar number with a 212 area code.

"Hello?"

"Stay away from my husband, you tacky little slut."

"Excuse me?" Violet said.

"I know you're sleeping with him." The voice was a woman's. American accent, crystal clear, and furious. "Believe me, he's never gonna marry a piece of trash like you."

"You have the wrong number," Violet said, and hung up.

The phone rang again, almost instantly.

"Was it the obscene phone guy?" Quentin asked.

"No, a woman," Violet said. She looked at the phone to see the same 212 number.

"Allow me," Quentin said.

"But what if—" Violet began.

Quentin held up a finger and picked it up. "Hello?"

From across the room, Violet could hear the same woman's voice. "Don't try to disguise your voice, bitch. I know it's you."

"No, actually," Quentin said. "It's the bitch's fiancé. The future Mr. Bitch. May I help you?"

Violet busted up laughing, but the voice coming through the phone was cold and serious.

"Maybe you think it's funny that your little whore is cheating on you with my husband, but I don't."

"Well, maybe you'll think it's funny when I hang up on you," he said, and did so.

"Honey, are you by any chance cheating on me with a married man?" Quentin asked, laughing.

"Absolutely not," Violet said. "That woman is crazy."

Quentin pulled her close to him. "When we get married, let's not have affairs, okay?"

The phone rang again. "Looks like the same number," he said. "Turn the ringer off."

"I can't until after Delacroix calls," she said.

After twenty-three calls in the next hour, she called Delacroix's assistant and gave him the hotel landline number.

By midnight, Delacroix had called, and they had turned off all phones and made love again. Violet's phone had fifty-three missed calls, and her voice mail was full.

Chapter 2

Delacroix was staying at Le Fleur Hotel in Midtown. Their smallest conference room seated fifty, and Violet was the last to arrive.

There were maybe two-dozen people, clustered down at one end of the antique oak table.

"I am so sorry," Violet murmured as she slipped into the room with her boss's style book.

Her boss waved the concern away and motioned for Violet to sit in the empty seat beside her. Around the table were Delacroix, his handsome son, and the young royal whom he'd be marrying. The son was swarthy, but the bride-to-be was as pale as ever. The wedding team surrounded them. Violet recognized the petite blonde as the wedding planner. The only other face Violet recognized was a plump, gray-haired woman, Dilani Mara, the dress designer.

She was showing several of her empire-waist dress styles. The duchess was curvy but wanted a modest look.

Against her hip, Violet's phone vibrated. She glanced at it below the table.

It was a text from her mother:

Are you with the royals? Can you send a photo?

Violet rolled her eyes and shut off the phone.

Dilani Mara's assistant had just pulled out several fabric swatches when someone burst into the room. She was a gorgeous African American woman in her forties, built like a lingerie model. She scanned the room with narrowed eyes.

"You can't—" the wedding planner began, but the woman shoved her back. The room gasped, and the angry woman rested her gaze on Violet.

"You!" she said. "You're the little slut who's been messing with my husband!"

Violet recognized the voice from the phone call.

"Get away from me," Violet yelled, backing up as the woman came toward her. "I don't know you or your husband."

"I'm calling security!" the wedding planner said, scrambling for the hotel phone.

"Yes!" Violet said. "Please! This woman is crazy."

Before the woman could get all the way around the table to Violet, two guards came into the room.

The woman put her hands up with a shrug. "No need. I'm going." On her way out, she turned to the startled young royal. "You should be more careful about who you have on your wedding team. This girl's a homewrecker. And him"—she turned to the caterer—"he did my wedding." She wrinkled her nose. "The crab cakes were a little dry."

The young royal turned to a member of her entourage. A woman in her fifties with a tight graying bun stood up. She asked for "a word" with Violet and her boss in the hallway.

"I'm so sorry," Violet said. "I don't know what that woman is talking about."

Her boss shushed her.

In the hallway, the elderly woman explained that the royal family, of course, could not be associated with any sort of scandal. They would, of course, understand.

"But it's not my fault," Violet began.

Her boss silenced her with a withering look.

"Of course," her boss said graciously. "I hope the young couple has a lovely wedding."

The British woman went back in and left the two of them sitting in the hallway.

"She can't really—" Violet began.

"You're fired," her boss said flatly.

"What?" Violet asked. "I didn't do anything."

"It doesn't matter," her now ex-boss said. "We do makeup. Appearance is everything." She snatched her style book from Violet's hands and stalked out the door.

Still stunned, Violet walked into Quentin's office half an hour later.

"What are you doing here?" he asked, slightly irritated.

"I called you ten times," she said. "It kept ringing to voice mail."

"Because I'm in the middle of—"

"I got fired," she said. "That crazy woman who had been calling showed up at the meeting with Henri Delacroix. We lost the royal account, and my boss blamed me."

"I'm sorry, babe, but this isn't really the time," he said.

"Okay," Violet said. She felt stung, but she rallied. "We can talk later. I guess, on the bright side, I'll have more time for our own wedding planning."

"About that," Quentin said. "We're gonna need to postpone the wedding."

"What?" Violet asked. "Why?"

"Of course, your boss called my mother," he said. "Now she's all in a state. She refuses to pay for the wedding until she can find out more about this drama."

"But I have nothing to do with these people," Violet said.

"My mother won't be satisfied until she does some further investigation," he said. "We should be able to clear it up soon."

"But it's a case of mistaken identity," she said.

"Of course, but that's not the point," he said. "My parents are paying for the wedding."

Violet's earlier upset was turning to panic. She had worked so hard for this, and she could feel it beginning to dissolve, to slip away.

"Let's just have a small wedding, then," Violet suggested. "Invite your parents, and they can come or not. Better yet, we can go to Trinidad! Have it with my mom."

Quentin shook his head. "This kind of wedding is about establishing me, establishing us with all of my family's business connections. They see me as a kid, but I'll be a man, working at Dad's company, marrying a wonderful woman. This is our launch."

"Your mother never thought I was good enough for you," she said bitterly. "She's loving this."

"Don't worry, baby," Quentin said. "We're just postponing the wedding until all this dies down. My mother will do another round of background checking, and then she'll calm down and we can get married."

"But you believe me, right?" Violet asked.

"Sure," he said. "My family is just paranoid."

* * *

Violet had always recalled the day she met Quentin at Harvard with fondness; it was sort of the creation myth of their relationship. It was at her first Black Students Association meeting. But now, as she looked back on it, she recalled that Nigel had been there also. They had all walked over to the meeting from the freshman union dining hall—Violet, Shelby, Nigel, and a few other first-year students.

Quentin, who was a junior, spoke at the meeting. There had been a shooting of an unarmed black teen who was a student at a nearby university—Northeastern—in Boston. Quentin spoke passionately and implored the student community to come to a protest downtown.

"We act like these things can't touch us because we go to Harvard," he said. Then he stepped out from behind the podium and into the audience. "But how many of you have been stopped by the Harvard police and asked for your ID? Been told you looked like you didn't belong here?"

Several hands went up, including Nigel's.

"People tell me there are more black men in prison and on parole than there are in college," Quentin went on. "But this recent police murder proves that just because we made it to college doesn't mean we made it. Doesn't mean we're safe."

Every word he said resonated with Violet. She didn't feel safe. Being in these white institutions made her feel anxious and vulnerable.

After the meeting, she approached him. "I think I want to go to the protest," she said. "But I'm a little nervous. Will they be arresting people?"

"Nothing like that," Quentin said. "It's just a legal assembly."

And it had been. Just a group of people, mostly

black, marching in a circle and chanting slogans. Violet stood near Quentin in the small knot of Harvard students. Shelby didn't want to come, and Nigel had to work that day. So when the door of the police station opened and a group of officers walked out, she reached for Quentin's hand. The police simply walked past and didn't hassle them, but Quentin didn't let go.

The group of Harvard students rode the T back to campus. By then, Quentin had let her hand go, but he sat next to her on the train, their thighs touching.

By the time they got back to campus, it was dinnertime, and the group went to eat together at Adams House, Quentin's dorm. Afterward, a bunch of them retired up to his room and talked late into the night.

Mostly, they discussed and debated how, as Harvard students, they would be in the best position to make social change. Quentin talked about his plans to go to law school and his vision of doing corporate law to make money, but also doing pro-bono work for the community.

Eventually, everyone left but Violet. She was mesmerized by this charismatic young black man. And then he had kissed her. Before he had touched his lips to hers, she would never have imagined that she could be his choice. But it was actually happening. His lips were on hers. He wanted her, had chosen her. His arms were around her, pulling her close.

Violet was far too shy to do anything more than kiss that night. But they slept pressed together in his bed.

The next morning, they went to brunch together in the Adams House dining hall. Violet loaded up her plate with a blueberry waffle, eggs Benedict, and a bowl of fruit salad.

Quentin just ate a bagel and cream cheese for breakfast. He was already sitting at the table when Violet finished getting her food. He patted the empty chair next to him.

"Oh my god," his roommate Randall said. "A girl Quentin didn't kick out before dawn."

"How do you know he kicked them out?" Randall's girlfriend asked. Her name was Autumn. "Maybe Quentin's just been sleeping with vampires, and they had to get away before sunrise."

"Don't listen to them," Quentin had told Violet. "What they're trying to say is something you already know, that I'm really into you, and that I'm hoping you'll be around a lot more."

Violet smiled, almost shyly.

"Okay," Randall said. "Quentin and Violet? I guess your combined name would be *Quentinlet.*" The roommate turned to Violet. "Like the two of us, Randall and Autumn? Our combined name is *Random.*"

Violet laughed.

"Shorten it to *Quentlet,*" Quentin had suggested.

Violet thought both names sounded too much like *quintuplet.* Having five babies at once? Yikes.

"Sounds like piglet," his roommate had said. "Like a bunch of little mini Quentins running around. Quentlets."

"Piglet was totally cute," his girlfriend had said. "From Winnie the Pooh. Keep it."

"What do you think, Violet?" Quentin had asked.

Quentlet? The couple would be called *Violin* if her name went first. Violins were romantic: lovely to look at, smooth and curved to the touch, they made soulful music. Why hadn't any of them thought of that? In this name merger, did the guy's name have to always go first? Violet had no idea, so she had just shrugged it off.

She didn't really understand how it worked and didn't want to be presumptuous.

She had laughed it off. "It's not like anyone's going to be running around calling us that, right?"

Or would they? She would still occasionally find herself on the outside with groups of her peers in the US. Was it a joke? Was it something people really did? Was it referring to some pop culture thing that happened while she was a kid in Trinidad?

"People don't really go around using it," Autumn had said. "But it's sort of a couple thing. Do you think *Quentlet* is cute or no?"

A couple? Quentin was already talking about them as a couple? Violet liked that part. "I guess, *Quentlet* it is," she said and took a bite of her eggs Benedict.

They had stayed together all through college. Quentin had graduated and gone to Harvard Law School. Violet spent more time at his apartment off campus than she did in her own Harvard undergraduate dorm. They were inseparable until the summer after junior year, when he was locked down for a few months in Manhattan, preparing for the New York bar exam. While he studied, she stayed in his apartment. Without having to worry about rent, she was able to take an unpaid internship in Boston's financial district. She made a little money on the side doing makeovers in a downtown department store.

Quentin returned shortly after taking the bar, and they had a passionate reunion. They lay in bed that night, after enjoying a Thai food delivery.

"So is your internship really as bad as you've been hinting in your emails?" he asked. "Or were you just miserable because you missed me so much?"

"It was definitely that bad," Violet said. "Finance isn't for me. The whole . . . culture. People are totally obnoxious. But I've been having so much fun doing makeup."

"Makeup?" Quentin said. "Really?"

"My mother did makeup," Violet said. "I just love the art of it. I think I'll eventually be able put my business skills to good use. I want to start a makeup company."

"Really?" he said. "My mom knows someone in makeup. The woman who runs Facing Manhattan."

Violet's mouth fell open. "You've got to be kidding me."

"She's a good friend of my mom's," he said. "And she just went through a divorce. She might even come to Thanksgiving this year."

Which was how, over a plate of slow-smoked turkey and artisan heirloom cranberry sauce, Violet had scored a job in New York before she'd even finished the first semester of her senior year.

The evening after Violet got fired from Facing Manhattan, she sat in a booth at an uptown sushi bar with her best friend, the petite and glamorous Shelby.

"You know you have to pay for this," Violet said. "I'll need to save money since I got fired."

"Don't worry," Shelby said. "I know a few people who might need personal assistants. I'll put you in touch."

"None of them might happen to be top makeup artists, would they?"

"A job's a job," Shelby said, tapping the screen on her handheld. "First, let's get you an income source. Then we can work on the makeup career."

"I ran into Nigel from Harvard," Violet said.

"That hunky West Indian guy?" Shelby asked.

"I guess is he is a little bit of a hunk," Violet said. "He asked me to work on a Caribbean Circus project. I said I didn't have time with the job and the wedding. Now I've got nothing but time."

"Take him up on it temporarily," Shelby said, looking up from the device. "Meanwhile, here are five personal assistant prospects for you."

"Thanks, Shel," Violet said. "You're the best."

The two women had been friends since they had met at Harvard freshman year. Shelby was from Maryland, and she talked nonstop.

"Did you hear about this strip club mogul drama?" Shelby asked as their appetizers arrived. "It's trending right now. This guy had a string of clubs throughout the city. He was branching out into a more upscale brand and had gotten a bunch of investors. Now he's skipped town with a truckload of money, plus the dancers' pension fund."

"Pension fund?" Violet asked. "The strippers got a pension?" She thought of her sister. She definitely wasn't going to tell Shelby that Lily was stripping.

"Apparently, the strippers paid into a retirement fund, and the company matched it."

"Damn," Violet said. "Even strippers in this town have a brighter financial future than I do."

"Stop worrying, Vi," Shelby said. "Quentin is one of the richest black men in New York. This is all gonna blow over. Then you'll have your fairy-tale wedding and your happily ever after."

"Not with that mother-in-law, I won't," Violet said. "I can't believe she'd push Quentin to cancel our wedding because of a rumor. Am I back in high school?"

"High society? High school?" Shelby said. "There's definitely some overlap."

* * *

Violet and Shelby finished their meal, and Violet headed back to her apartment. Really, it was Quentin's family's apartment. Several of the neighbors were prominent politicians and businesspeople. The building had to be evacuated a couple of times a year due to bomb threats. There had been another one this week.

When she got to the front door, there were two men in suits standing in the foyer. "These gentlemen have been waiting for you," the doorman said.

"Violet Johnson?" one of the men asked.

"Yes?"

"We're with the FBI," he said. "We need you to come with us."

"There must be some mistake," she said. "I—"

"We just want to ask you some questions," the stony-faced agent said.

"Can I call my attorney?" she asked.

"Suit yourself," he said and escorted her into the back of the unmarked FBI sedan.

"Quentin!" she spoke urgently to his voice mail. "The FBI is taking me in for questioning. I have no idea what's going on. Please! Can you come help me?"

She got the address from the agent and hung up.

In the back of the car, her mind raced. Had there been another bomb threat? She was probably the only immigrant in the building. The only tenant who wasn't fabulously rich and well connected. Would she be the scapegoat now that she was no longer in Glenda Ross's good graces?

She was black, but her great-grandfather had been Indian and Muslim. Her mother's maiden last name was Khan. Was there some connection? Had the FBI dug into her past? Would she be seen as Muslim? Her parents hadn't actually been married. She had always gone by Johnson, but was Khan the legal name on her birth certificate? Would Glenda Ross find out?

When they finally brought her into an interview room, she sat up straight and pushed down the panic. She spoke clearly, with a confidence she didn't feel.

"I had absolutely nothing to do with any of the bomb threats in the building," she said in her clearest, most unaccented American English.

"This has nothing to do with a bomb threat," the agent said.

Violet blinked. "Then what is this about?"

Her phone buzzed, and there was a message from Quentin:

On my way. Say nothing until I get there.

"On second thought," she said, "I'd like to wait til my lawyer gets here. He's on his way."

"Suit yourself," the agent said.

Ten minutes later, the door opened, and Quentin rushed in.

"Quentin Ross," he said. "From Ross, Billingsley, and Hoyt. I'm Ms. Johnson's attorney."

Violet nodded.

"Welcome," the agent said. "We were just getting started. This does not, as Ms. Johnson suspected, have anything to do with a bomb threat in her building. Rather, we are investigating Teddy Hughes."

"The strip club king?" Quentin asked. "What does Vi– . . . Ms. Johnson have to do with him?"

"That's what we intended to ask her."

Quentin turned to Violet.

"Nothing," Violet said. "I just heard about him tonight. He's the guy who took some investors' money and some strippers' retirement, right?"

The other agent pushed some papers across the desk to her. "We have two-way call records to your cell phone the day before he left town."

"That's impossible," Violet said.

The agent pointed to a piece of paper in front of her on the table. He put a finger next to ten digits. "Is this your phone number?"

"Yes, but I never called him."

"We also have records of his wife calling you sixty-eight times."

"That crazy woman was Teddy Hughes's wife?"

"Is it true that Etta Hughes turned up at your place of employment and confronted you about having sex with her husband?"

"She was a lunatic," Violet said. "I've never met her husband."

"How do you explain the phone calls?" the agent poked the paper with a thick finger. "Friday afternoon: One call lasting thirty seconds at 4:13 PM. One lasting one minute, eighteen seconds at 4:16 PM. One lasting two minutes, eight seconds at 4:21 PM. Did the lunatic imagine these phone records?"

"Friday . . ." Violet said. "In the limo! Quentin, tell them! You were there when I got all those wrong number phone calls. It was a wrong number. We had a bad connection. I was expecting an important call for work. It took a while for me to figure it out because the connection kept breaking up. Quentin, tell them. You heard it all."

"You heard both sides of the conversation?" the FBI agent asked.

"I heard her side."

"And how do you explain the call from your phone to his earlier that same day?"

"I never called his phone," Violet said.

"Please, Ms. Johnson," the agent said taking back the papers. "These are your phone records we pulled from the cell company, and there's a call to his mobile phone on Friday afternoon."

"That's not possible," she said, bewildered.

"Was your phone out of your possession at any time?"

"No, I'm a personal assistant," she said, then caught herself. "I used to be a personal assistant. I was always on call."

"Did anyone else have access to your phone?"

"Only Quentin—" she broke off. "Wait! Around three-thirty! Did the call happen at three-thirty? I let a woman use my phone."

"Three thirty-seven PM," the agent said.

"Quentin," Violet said, "when you came to pick me up, I had to get my phone back from her."

"Did you actually witness this, Mr. Ross?"

Quentin shook his head slowly. "I never actually saw the young woman."

"It all makes sense now," Violet said. "I lent my phone to the wrong person. He obviously called back, looking for her. I don't know how the wife got the number, but jealous women snoop on men's phones all the time."

"One last question," the agent said. "Have you ever been to the One-Eyed King in Manhattan? It's one of the strip clubs that Teddy Hughes owned."

"No," Violet stammered. "I've never been . . . inside . . . that club."

The agent scrutinized Violet. "Whether or not you actually entered the premises, have you ever been to the One-Eyed King strip club?"

"I may have walked by—" Violet began, feeling her face flush.

"Let me refresh your memory," the FBI agent said. "A young woman working at the One-Eyed King identified you as having been there."

"I was looking for my sister," Violet said, her cheeks burning, unable to look either man in the eye.

"That's the first thing you've said that completely checks out," the agent said.

Quentin stood up. "My client has answered your questions satisfactorily. This is clearly a case of mistaken identity. She loaned a woman her phone. You know what they say—no good deed goes unpunished. My client is an immigrant from the third world. She's not always savvy about these things. I think we're done here." He nodded for Violet to stand.

"If you have any more questions, you know where to find her," he said.

Quentin stalked out, and Violet followed.

"You were amazing!" she said as he hailed a taxi.

"I don't like this," he said, climbing into the cab.

"I know," Violet said. "I didn't realize Lily was actually stripping, I thought she was just—"

"Not that," Quentin said. "The phone thing."

"I know. How insane is that?" she asked. "One wrong number, and I'm being questioned by the FBI. Like I would lie about loaning some woman my phone."

"That's what I mean, Violet," Quentin said. "I don't like only having your word for it. I did only hear your side of the conversation."

"What? Are you saying—" Violet began, but he cut her off.

"I'm saying that five days ago we were on one track, and now it's totally different. It was a scandal with my family when it was just some crazy woman harassing you. Now it's a major criminal matter, and the FBI is calling you in?" He shrugged his shoulder out from under her hand. "I'm an attorney. I look for hard evidence, not just circumstantial. This seems like a case of reasonable doubt."

"Stop thinking like an attorney, and think like the man who loves me," Violet said. "You know me. I would never cheat on you. Especially not with some strip club king. Please."

"I'm not sure," Quentin said through tight lips. "You know all about me. I'd never even met anyone from your family until I met your sister, Lily, only once."

"This is your mother talking, isn't it? That's exactly what she said to me when we announced our engagement. 'It seems sudden considering that we haven't even met your family.' "

"I'm just saying that I didn't expect this type of drama right before our wedding."

"And I didn't expect to be marrying a man who can't make up his own mind about the woman he loves," Violet said, feeling her face flush again. "Besides, your mother needs to decide which lie she's gonna make up about me. Am I the gold digger who's working day and night to worm my way into your family, or am I the low-class foreigner side piece for some old white strip club king."

"She never said—"

"They're both insulting, but the second one is downright offensive," Violet raged. "I did not come all the way from Trinidad after having worked my ass off to get a scholarship to a US boarding school, where I cried myself to sleep every night for the first year, get into Harvard, live through a dozen freezing East Coast winters, and spend the last nine months at the beck and call of the most obnoxious, self-centered white woman in the tristate area trying to get a leg up in the makeup business to become . . . the mistress of a strip club king? You have got to be kidding me."

"Are you done ranting?" he asked.

"For the moment," she said.

"Fine," Quentin said. "Because I need a little space right now."

Violet was stunned. "You're breaking up with me?" she asked.

"No," Quentin said hastily. "I still care about you. I want—I—let's just take a break. We'll let this whole thing blow over, then start from scratch. Figure out how to move forward."

Violet felt tears welling up, but she pushed them down.

"I'll move out of the apartment, then," Violet said, her syllables clipped.

"No need for that," Quentin said, waving a hand.

"I only agreed to stay there because we were getting married and your mother didn't think it would look good to have us living together before the wedding," Violet said.

"Suit yourself," Quentin said.

"You sound just like the FBI."

The multipurpose room of the Maria de la Vega Community Health Clinic was filled with the angry voices of various women. Loud, hard-working women who were pissed to find that their retirement money was gone.

"See?" a Trinidadian woman named Hibiscus said. "If we never had that union and put that money in the account, we would have it now."

"You cannot be serious right now," Lily said, outraged. "Before the union, the owner took out our dressing room to put in a sex room and jacked up the dance fees so high that we'd have to fuck guys in there to make a living."

"That wasn't him," Hibiscus scoffed. "That was his mob investors."

"Why are you defending him?" Tara asked. She was one of the union organizers, a curly-haired white girl with a lotus tattoo on her chest. "He seemed perfectly willing to let the mob run amok as long as the club was making money."

"Making money off our work," said Giselle, a brown skinned Latina.

"That's right," Lily said. "The club owner, Teddy Hughes, told his manager and his security guards not to lift a finger when the nephew of that mobster tried to drag one of us into the VIP room against her will. That's why we needed a union. Because they treat us as less than human."

"I think we asked for too much," Hibiscus said. "You get all high and mighty, and the mighty end up falling. That's all I'm saying."

"Enough of the debate," Giselle said. "Things were fucked up. We fought to form a union, and we got a pension fund. That was over a year ago."

"So that's it then?" a young blonde from Guadeloupe asked. "The money's just gone? He took it?"

"So here's what we know," Lily said. "Teddy Hughes, the owner, took the current accumulated profits, drained all of the operating accounts, and took our wages and our retirement fund."

"Plus the cash from the upscale investors," a girl called from across the room.

"Fuck them," another girl yelled back. "Don't nobody care about those investors. They probably didn't even have to work for that money."

"So Teddy Hughes took all the cash and skipped town," Tara added.

"And closed the clubs," another dancer said, referring to the chain of One-Eyed King clubs, one in each of New York City's boroughs. "So we can't even work to make up the money."

"Yeah," someone else said. "And there won't be enough work for all of us to make up our losses. If everybody rushes to other clubs, the market will be glutted, and we won't be able to get enough shifts."

"Well, wait a minute," Lily said. "It's not true that he closed the club. He just abandoned the club."

"And took all the operating money," Tara said.

"Tara," Lily said, "your girlfriend is one of the managers. She's got the keys, right? She has all the codes. She knows how to run the place. Why can't we open the club and work?"

"What about the rest of the staff?" Tara asked. "What about security? Those guys aren't gonna work for free, and we can't afford to tip them out."

Lily laughed. "Security? I know some badasses who would work for a lap dance. And be glad to kick the ass of some dick who got out of line."

"We could run it like a worker's collective," Tara said. "I'm game. What do we have to lose?"

"How about when it's time to pay rent and utilities?" Giselle asked. "Those bright lights aren't free."

"We'll cross that bridge when we come to it," Lily said. "We got over a week til rent is due. And maybe we can stall a bit after. That would give us time to earn enough to pay our own rent."

"Sounds good to me," Giselle said.

"Worst-case scenario," Tara said, "we dance and make tips for the next couple weeks while we look for other work."

"Okay," Lily said. "Let's put it to a vote."

As it turned out, everybody wanted to work, so the proposal passed, unanimously.

When Violet got to the Ross family apartment, she went straight to the closet. Behind the rack of designer dresses and above the shelf of high-fashion shoes was a battered cardboard box.

She pulled it off the shelf and brushed the dust off the top. Inside were stacks and stacks of 4-inch x 4-inch notebooks. She rummaged through until she found one that was only half filled with drawings. It ended with an unfinished sketch of a woman. She had luminous, longing eyes and the outline of an Afro with a pair of leaves in it. Violet dug through her purse for a pen. At the bottom, she found a blue ballpoint. She took the pen and notebook over to the breakfast alcove.

She hadn't drawn in years. Slowly, she began to sketch a new woman's face in the lower right-hand corner of the blank page. The woman's profile had a furrowed brow, slit eyes, and bared teeth. Instead of hair, her head was covered with flames. As was Violet's signature style, she filled up nearly every centimeter of the page. She created tone and texture with meticulous lines and shadings, even though it was monochrome. Two hours later, the woman glared up from the paper, a dark figure with her head ablaze.

Violet had occasionally sketched as a girl in Trinidad. As a parting gift, her uncle had given her the 4 x 4-inch notebook when she left for boarding school in New England.

She was fourteen. It was one of the things she carried in her single suitcase when she flew from Port of Spain to Boston.

The airline attendants on the flight to New York were all so nice and made her—a minor traveling unaccompanied—feel so welcome. They asked where she was going and encouraged her on this amazing adventure. Whether they were black, South Asian, or mixed, they all lit up when she said she was off to school. Her achievement was part of their Caribbean pride. They patted her hand, called her endearing nicknames, and wished her well.

When she landed at JFK, she waited for hours to clear customs. The agents searched through every scrap of her belongings. The way they looked at her, she felt like a criminal.

Finally, she was cleared. From JFK, she flew into Boston. The white flight attendants on the US airline made sure she had plenty of ginger ale but didn't ask where she was going.

On her way out of Boston's Logan International Airport, she asked a security guard for directions to the place she had been told to wait.

"Limousines?" she said it like a question.

He scoffed at her. "Limousines? You don't belong in any limousines. Where are you going?"

His words hit her like a slap. She stammered the name of the school.

His eyebrows rose, and his lip curled in scorn. "What?" he asked with a sneer. "They don't have enough maids there? You going to clean toilets? They can't hire Americans for these jobs? New Englanders? They gotta bring in smelly foreigners with ugly accents? Limousines? You need to go back to Africa or wherever you came from."

She stumbled back from his tirade, stunned. Tears

stung her eyes. She ducked into the women's room and cried.

She had felt so brave, so grown, so ready for this adventure. Now she felt tiny and terrified. How would she find her way to the school? Was everyone in America like this?

"Dear God," she prayed in a whisper in the stall, "please help me get to where I'm going."

When she came out and looked around, there was a table with a large sign that said GROUND TRANSPORTATION. A black woman with thick braids sat underneath it.

"I'm looking for limousines," Violet said, barely above a whisper.

"Sure, hon," the woman said. "Right out this way."

And then, in the direction of where she pointed, there was a Middle Eastern man with a sign that said VIOLET JOHNSON and the name of the school.

She felt flooded with relief, but a whine of anxiety persisted.

The man was friendly and had an accent, too. The school was almost a two-hour drive from Boston, and they chatted the whole way there. Violet slowly relaxed. The key to this country would be to talk to the brown people. She waved goodbye to the driver at the archway of the school entrance.

It took twenty-four hours for her to figure out that, at that elite boarding school, there weren't any brown people. No brown teachers. No brown administrators. She didn't even see any brown students for the first three days. Even the cleaning and food service staff was white.

All the teachers and students had flawlessly unaccented voices. They sounded like American actors or the Canadian newscasters she'd seen on television in

Trinidad. In contrast, the school's domestic and grounds staff had what she learned were New England accents, harsh and twangy. But nobody sounded foreign like her.

Smelly foreigner. Ugly accent.

She couldn't get the man from the airport out of her mind.

Every time she opened her mouth to speak, she was so self-conscious. She said as little as possible.

For the first six months after arriving in the US, Violet didn't speak beyond *yes, no, please,* and *thank you.* She did all her schoolwork—properly and on time. She obeyed all the rules. She sat quietly in whatever spot was designated. Her only form of expression was the small notebook from her uncle, in which she drew constantly.

She drew young black girls with haunted eyes who had hair made of plants. Their hair began as tropical leaves that reminded her of home. Palm fronds. Banana leaves. Birds of paradise. She checked botanical books out of the library and carefully, painstakingly copied the leaves from the flora back home. She sketched the veins and the scalloped edges. When she was on cafeteria duty and some carrots came with the tops on, she sketched faces with mohawks of green that swooped down in straight lines and exploded into leaves on the end.

When fall came, she watched maple leaves turn flaming colors and fall from trees. She used ninety-nine-cent nail polish to give the girls in her book afros of crimson and gold leaves scattering to the ground. In winter, the women in her drawings had gnarled, empty branches shooting up from their heads.

Her history teacher noticed one of the drawings and suggested to the counselor that she take art in the spring.

Violet loved the art class. She got to experiment with so many different supplies. Charcoal. Acrylic. Oil. Pastel. She began to use color beyond the nail polish. She had never seen so many different ways to draw on paper.

She also drew on canvas, fabric, wood. Her teacher encouraged her to try different sizes, but every picture, no matter the size of the canvas, was the same 4-inch square of her notebook. That, apparently, was the scale she worked in best.

The teacher also saw she had run out of pages in the notebook from her uncle. She had begun to draw on the front and back cover. One day, a stack of 4 x 4-inch notebooks showed up in her mailbox.

The art teacher was always so encouraging and supportive, without being prescriptive. *I like what you're trying with the red there. Keep going.* That was the thing she almost always ended with: *keep going.* Sometimes, Violet would be dissatisfied with what she drew.

"I don't like it," she ventured, more words than she'd said to anyone.

"Yeah," the teacher said. "Sometimes we try things, and we're not crazy about the results. So we get to try something else."

When Violet finally did speak—real sentences—she spoke to her art teacher. *Trying.* The teacher encouraged her to try. She was trying American English. She had been immersed in it for six months. It seemed like maybe she could make those sounds now.

"Aye wooould lyyyke tooo speeeak withowwwt unn ack sent," she told her teacher.

The woman shrugged. "Everyone has an accent," she said. "You mean you want to be able speak with an American accent?"

"Yesss, pleeease," Violet said.

So they practiced.

And eventually, she began to speak to other people.

She filled most of the notebooks while she was at boarding school. At Harvard, she tried to take an art class. It wasn't called art there, it was Visual and Environmental Studies. The teacher never said things like "keep going."

But she continued to sketch when she was stressed. Until she met Quentin. Shortly after they had gotten together, he was asleep on a Sunday morning. She had slid out of his bed and was sitting at his desk, sketching.

She had drawn the girl's face, eyes longing and fiery. She had sketched the shape of an Afro and had just begun to draw the fauna in her hair.

She didn't hear him slip out of bed and come up behind her.

"Whoa," he said, looking over her shoulder. "That's a pretty intense face. Is that you?" Then he began to laugh. "Are those leaves in her hair?"

"No," Violet said quickly. "It's a barrette. I didn't know you were awake." She closed the notebook. "Let's go to brunch."

She put the notebooks away in the cardboard box. It seemed like a small price to pay. Quentin Ross was her destiny.

Until a woman used her phone. And then he wasn't.

On May 30, Violet lugged two of her suitcases out of the Ross family's apartment. She wheeled them silently out onto the pile carpet in the high-ceilinged hallway.

A few yards ahead of her, the elevator dinged. When the door opened, she immediately recognized the attractive, forty-something black woman. It was Etta Hughes.

"What the hell are you doing here?" Violet asked.

"Looking for my man, you little gold digger," the wife said, pushing past her and into the apartment. She stormed around the place, looking into the empty closets and peering onto the fire escape.

"Gold digger?" Violet asked, outraged. "Look around you. This is one of the most exclusive addresses in Manhattan. And I live here because my fiancé comes from one of the wealthiest African American families in the country. They keep the apartment empty most of the time. Do you hear me? This place is the spare change his extended family keeps lying around. I was just supposed to live here until the wedding. A wedding that, incidentally, has been canceled since a crazy woman came to my job and lost her mind. Of course, that would be you. Do you see these suitcases? Gold digger? If it was gold I was digging for, I didn't need your sleazy little husband. Do you have any idea what my family back home would say if I was *marrying* a strip club king? Let alone living as *the mistress* of a married strip club king? I'm not the woman you're looking for. I'm just the woman whose phone she used, and then your husband called me back talking about 'Kitty, is that you?' To which I said, 'No, I'm not your goddamn Kitty.' "

"He said Kitty?"

"Oh my god," Violet exploded. "That's not the point."

"He used to call me Kitty," the wife said, deflated.

"The man runs a strip club empire! Did you really expect him to be faithful?"

The wife looked up and blinked at her, as if seeing her for the first time. "Of course not," she said. "He had a wife when we started screwing around. We had a deal." She slumped back against the wall. "He could fuck anyone. Just use a condom. Never more than once. And always come home to me."

"Well, he obviously didn't keep his end of the bargain."

The wife looked into the hollow apartment, realization dawning. "I'm sorry. I just fucking lost it. I didn't mean to take someone else's life down, too."

"It's a little late for sorry," Violet said.

For a moment, the two of them just stood there. Violet felt suddenly exhausted. Through the open window, the sounds of Manhattan drifted in and echoed off the hardwood floors and bare walls in the empty apartment.

"I wish I could find the girl who used my phone," Violet mumbled.

"It wouldn't matter," the wife said. "I remember how it was when the two of us were sneaking around back in the day. They would have been careful. We rarely used phones."

"The FBI has more resources than a jealous wife," Violet said. "If we could tell them who she was, they could prove it."

"We have photos of all the girls who work at the clubs," the wife said. "Why don't you come with me to the office? She's gotta be in there."

"I don't think so," Violet said bitterly. "You're the crazy woman who fucked up my life, remember? I'm not going anywhere with you."

"No," Etta said quietly. "I'm the wife of the guy whose mistress fucked up your life."

"You went after the wrong woman," Violet said.

The wife shook her head. "I can see that now," she said. "I'm so sorry. Let me help. Right now, you and I want the same thing: to find the two of them, so you can get your life back, and I can shoot them both in the face."

"Forget it," Violet said. "The FBI already suspects me

of conspiring to defraud or whatever. I'm not going to add accessory to murder."

"I was speaking metaphorically," the wife said.

"Then yes," Violet said. "Helping me is the least you can do." She closed the apartment door behind her. "And by the way, I'm not gonna get my life back. After the scene you made, my old boss isn't gonna rehire me. I'm sure she had a new assistant five minutes after she threw me out the door. I'm not getting back into Glenda Ross's good graces, either. I just want to be able to prove to my fiancé that I'm not cheating. If I can identify the real mistress for the FBI, then he'll have the ammunition he needs to stand up to his mother for me. If I can't salvage my whole life, at least I can salvage my relationship."

"I swear," the wife said, "I'll do everything I can to make it right."

"Are you serious that you won't shoot them?" Violet asked.

"Not in the face," the wife said.

"Are you crazy?" Violet asked.

"I'm joking," the wife said. "I've learned my lesson. When the man cheats, don't blame the woman. Blame him. So I'll only shoot him."

"You better be joking again," Violet said and pressed the down button for the elevator.

Violet had no idea that photos of strippers would be so monotonous. Glossy after glossy of darkly lined eyes, glistening teeth, moist lips, and miles and miles of hair. Hanging hair. Windblown hair. Swinging pony tails. Thousands of thighs wrapped around poles, straddling chairs, or spread eagle. The tops of breasts, the cleavage of breasts, the occasional bottoms of breasts. Navels with and without rings. Asses in thongs. Asses in booty shorts. Asses in skirts that weren't really skirts.

"They change their hair color all the time," the wife said. "You can't go by that." Her name was Etta, but in her mind, Violet kept thinking of her as "the wife." She was obviously apologetic and was trying to make up for her mistake by offering coffee, even espresso from an elaborate machine. Violet declined the offers. She just wanted to find the right picture and get out of there.

The woman who had used her phone had been honey blond. But the shade was unlikely to be natural. At least with her pecan-brown skin, they could skip the tens of thousands of photos of white women. Only the files of black, Latina, Asian (dark), and "exotic" files were relevant.

And after all the searching, she wasn't there. A few women looked similar, but upon closer inspection, perhaps a second shot from another angle or a closer look at the dancer's height, they weren't the right woman.

Finally, her eyes widened in recognition. A dark brown woman towering beside the pole, one leg up and coiled around it, half-yoga, half-stripper. Big teeth in her seductive smile. Peacock colors on her luminous brown eyes.

Her sister. Lily.

Looking at the photo, she had five thoughts at once.

How you gon show ya punany for the whole world to see?

Did you do your own makeup? It's amazing!

When did you get so flexible? Is that Pilates?

Our poor mother would have a heart attack if she saw this.

But above all, she felt a certainty. *I knew it. This is all your fault. You're the one who brought this awful woman into my life.*

Violet was distracted as she flipped through the rest

of the photos, but slowly she realized that they were all too dark to be the woman. In fact, the women in the photos seemed to be getting darker.

Violet blinked. She scanned back through the photos. Sure enough. They seemed to be arranged on some type of color spectrum. She didn't need to keep going. Clearly, the light brown woman who had used her phone wouldn't be any further back in the files.

She closed the folder and stood up. "I'm gonna go, then," Violet said.

"Go where?" Etta asked. "I thought you had to leave your place."

"I've got friends to stay with," she said, picking up her suitcases.

"You could stay here," Etta said. "We've got plenty of room."

"I'll pass," Violet said coolly. And went out to hail a cab.

Shelby lived in a one-bedroom co-op apartment in Park Slope. It was spacious, considering what she had paid for it, but so much smaller than the luxury apartment Quentin's family had put her up in.

Violet rolled her suitcase across the hardwood floor.

"Thanks so much for letting me stay, Shel," Violet said. She set the suitcase beside the fold-out couch that looked out through the bay window onto Prospect Park.

"Of course," Shelby said. "Stay as long as you want. But if it's more than a month, you might have to start paying rent." She looked up from the linen closet, where she was pulling out sheets for Violet. "Just kidding!"

"I am gonna try to get a job," Violet said. "Except none of your personal assistant contacts have gotten back to me."

"What about the hunky West Indian guy?" Shelby asked.

"Nigel?"

"Didn't he have some circus he wanted you to work for?"

"Seriously?" Violet asked. "Am I really desperate enough to work for a circus?"

"Here's what I know," Shelby said. "You want to be working. You want to look like you're in demand. Don't look like a slacker. So when Quentin comes around, he'll get jealous because you look like you're moving on."

"Quentin," Violet said. "I'm so through with him. No loyalty. "

"And as a bonus, if Quentin does come around, he'll see you with Mr. Hunky Trinidadian."

"He's Jamaican," Violet said.

"Whatever," Shelby said. "It's those shoulders that matter."

That night, the union from the One-Eyed King met again in the multipurpose room of the Maria de la Vega clinic. The dancers were cautiously optimistic. They had reopened the chain and were running the clubs like a worker co-op. The *Village Voice* had run a piece about them, "Renegade Strippers," and business was booming. The hip-hop artist Nashonna, a former stripper herself, had tweeted a video clip of herself rapping on stage at the One-Eyed King with the text:

Come see why liberated tits and ass are the hottest anywhere. Check my girls at @1EKnyc

Her tweet ended with several fire emojis. Then a

leading rap artist tweeted a GIF of himself with one of the dancers' asses in his face with the hashtag #UnionLapDance, and Twitter went crazy, with activists debating whether it was empowering for women or not.

So it looked like everyone would be able to pay their bills, at least for the month of June.

Lily called the meeting to order, as the women scrolled through selfies of men and women standing outside the chain of clubs on social media.

"So settle down everyone," Lily said. "We have a special guest tonight. Etta Hughes."

The room was suddenly hushed. If the strippers felt the sting of the owner's abrupt disappearance, they knew no one could be more hurt than his wife. They set their phones down as the honey blonde made her way to the front of the room.

She looked out at the women and tilted her head to the side. "So I'm Teddy Hughes's wife," she began. "But if I ever catch up with him, I'll be needing a status update to being his widow."

The girls laughed tentatively.

"I started out as a dancer myself at the One-Eyed King," she said. "More years ago than I care to admit to. So I have one piece of advice for all of you . . ."

The girls leaned in, expectant.

"Don't marry your goddamn boss," she said. The room erupted in laughter. Etta herself laughed long and hard, wiping tears away afterward. "And I mean that. But to the business at hand. First of all, I insisted Teddy make me a co-owner. That means that since he left, I'm in charge, and I support what you all are doing."

The dancers whistled and cheered.

"Maybe if we'd had a union when I was working here, I wouldn't have thought I needed to marry that dick in the first place."

More laughter.

"But here's the bad news," Etta went on. "We gotta come up with thirty thousand dollars in the next four days if we want to keep the club doors open another month."

"Thirty thousand?" one young woman asked.

"That'll just get us through the first half of the month," Etta said. "And only for this club. Brooklyn, Queens, and Staten Island, as you know, are much smaller clubs, and they're already closed. The Bronx rent isn't due til the fifteenth. If we keep going like you have the past few days, we'll be able to catch up in a month or two. But we can't stay open without operating capital. Teddy cleaned out all the accounts."

Giselle piped up. "I know a guy. Friend of my cousin's. A little rough, but a few months back, he said he had some money and was looking to open a strip club. Maybe we could get him to invest here."

"That sounds good," Etta said. "Tell your friend we'll pay with interest, and I have a contract lawyer who can do the promissory note so that we can guarantee he'll get his money."

"Can you get him on board in the next couple of days?" Lily asked.

"I think so," Giselle said.

"Sounds promising," Etta said. "And just know, we're working to recover all the shit that Teddy stole. Meanwhile, girls, keep doing what you're doing. We're gonna get through this."

The following day, Violet took the train across Brooklyn to the Caribbean Circus. It was a long hike from the station, along an industrial corridor. The building was located in a warehouse district, between a storage company and an import/export company that specialized in cheap plastic goods from China.

Walking in, she was greeted by the sight of a human tower—more than a dozen men and women standing on each other's shoulders. A petite woman was climbing onto the very top, as a crowd of enthusiastic schoolchildren clapped and squealed.

Violet sidled into the room and leaned against the back wall of the warehouse.

Nigel was one of the men on the bottom of the human tower. He stood shirtless and glistening. His torso was a literal triangle, from his broad shoulders to his narrow waist and his lower abdominal muscles, which tapered down into his low-slung pants.

Violet blinked and focused on the petite woman, as she steadied herself on the shoulders of two other women, then raised something up in the air. Violet was on the far end of the warehouse, so she couldn't quite make it out. Was it a flag? A scythe? Then, suddenly, the woman pulled out a lighter and lit it on fire.

Violet gasped along with the crowd. The object began to blaze with light. Violet found herself smiling with recognition. It was some kind of illuminated map of the Caribbean. All the islands flaming against a midnight-blue backdrop.

The children and their teachers applauded enthusiastically for what had apparently been the finale.

In an instant, the blazing Caribbean islands stopped burning, and the woman on top of the tower hooked the map to something above her head. Meanwhile, two women walked up to the base of the tower, and the petite woman flipped down into their arms.

The kids clapped some more, as the acrobats flipped

and leaped down. In spite of the excitement of the acrobatics, she found her eyes flitting frequently back to Nigel.

Then, after the last of the descending figures climbed off Nigel's shoulders, he turned to Violet and smiled. Had he noticed her entrance? She felt her skin flush at being seen. His grin was broad, with strong white teeth between his full lips.

Then he turned and joined the line of performers to take a bow. She felt exposed standing up, and found a seat near the back wall, where she felt less conspicuous.

She was still sitting there, ten minutes later, as the children filed out past her.

"Dante," a teacher's voice said, "we are not touching our friends' hair right now—hold on, Lucía—we're keeping our hands to ourselves, Dante, as we walk back to the subway."

She felt a soft hand on her shoulder and turned to see Nigel. He had a shirt on now and was toweling off his face.

"I can't believe you came by," he said, wearing the same grin.

"It turns out I do need a job, after all," she said.

"Seriously?" he said, putting a hand on her back and steering her to a cluttered dressing space. From the looks of the room, it might have been the office when the building was a factory or a warehouse. It had a bank of dirty windows and a chipped linoleum floor.

"It would be great if you could do makeup and set design for us," he said. "We can't pay anything like you're used to."

"Well, they fired me, so currently I'm getting nothing from them. A pittance would be a raise."

"Let me show you the makeup room," he said.

She looked at him expectantly.

"It was a joke," he said. "This is the everything room: office, makeup, dressing, kitchen."

"I'm sorry," she said. "Of course." She looked at the counter, which held a few rows of cosmetics: foundation in shades of bronze and brown, bright lipsticks and dark blushes, black liquid eyeliners and sparkling eye shadows.

"The big leagues got you spoiled," he said.

"Not anymore," she said. "I'm learning a lot about who my real friends are."

Chapter 3

Jimmy had always been the thin one. But since his brother's death, it was as if he was expanding to take his brother's place. When he walked in to the One-Eyed King, Lily took an instant dislike to him. It wasn't his body—she had a delicious flirtation going with a fat computer geek—but there was nothing delicious about Jimmy. It wasn't exactly his slicked-back hair or the tacky material on the shiny, button-down club shirt. She had seen those garish colors on other Caribbean men, and they worked. It was something about his humorlessness. He laughed a lot, but it was a sort of leering *heh-heh,* with a smile that didn't reach his eyes. He looked like a brown shark in party clothes.

Etta, her attorney, and the union leaders were sitting down with him. They had just explained the terms of the loan, the repayment, and the fifteen percent interest.

"What else do I get?" he asked. "I mean, basically I'm paying your rent, so this should be kinda my place too for the month."

"Sure," Giselle jumped in. "You can come by anytime to check on your investment."

Lily began, "I don't know—"

"Mr. Rios," Etta said, "are you looking to make some money or to have a VIP membership to this club? Because they cost several thousand."

"Nah," Jimmy said. "I don't need no VIP. I just wanna do what Gigi said. Come by from time to time and check on my investment."

Lily knew Giselle hated to be called Gigi and saw her mouth tighten at the unwelcome nickname.

After Etta and Jimmy had signed the contract, the big man stood up and shook everyone's hand, holding them much longer than necessary.

"I don't know if this was a good idea," Lily said after he'd left.

"I put an asshole provision into the contract," Etta said.

"What do you mean?" Lily asked.

"No penalty for early payment," Etta said. "So dance your asses off, and we can get rid of this dick as soon as possible."

"I was supposed to go to a poetry slam tonight," Lily said. "But I think I'm gonna pick up an extra shift instead. I wanna do my part to not owe him anything."

After Lily got off work, she was headed to the train station. Usually, she treated herself to Lyft, but tonight, she wanted all her extra money to go to paying their debt to Jimmy.

Just as she was about to slide her MetroCard, she got a text. It was from Cyril, the tech guy from California:

Just got out of my conference, and came to your job. They say you just left. Did I miss you?

Lily grinned and turned around. She texted back:

Perfect timing. Get a Lyft and meet me in front of the club;)

Cyril had first come into the One-Eyed King a month before. He was visiting with a group of guys from his tech firm in Silicon Valley. The crew was mostly young white guys, with a couple of South Asians. The rest of them seemed excited to be in a strip club, but Cyril was on his phone.

A few of the other guys in the crew came up and placed some five-dollar bills in her waistband, but he didn't even look up.

Lily didn't think any more about it until she walked across the club, taking another customer into the champagne room, and saw a Trinidadian flag on his shoulder bag.

An hour later, after he totally ignored her during another dance set, she came up to their table afterward.

"Young man," she said.

He snapped his head up.

"Yes, you," she said. "Does your mother know you're out in public acting so rude and disrespectful. One of your countrywomen is up here shaking her backside, trying to make a living, and you can't even be bothered to look up from your video game?"

He grinned. "It's not a video game. I'm reading about this place. Did you really curse out a reporter at a press conference?"

She grinned back. "Next time I'm up to dance," she said, "you come up with some bills, and maybe I'll tell you. And don't waste my time with singles. Make it worth my while."

The next time she went up to dance, he was sitting at the edge of the stage with a stack of fives.

"So," he asked, "did you have to work hard to develop that abrasive personal style or does it just come naturally?"

"What do you think?" she asked.

"Where in Trinidad are you from?" he asked.

"Tunapuna," she said. "You're from Port of Spain, right?"

"Originally, yes," he said.

"But you grew up here in the US," she said. "Am I right?"

"New Jersey," he said. "But I've lived in California for the last decade."

"And you miss abrasive West Indian women like me," she said, "don't you?"

He put a twenty in her waistband. "More than you could ever imagine."

She laughed and twirled away to a different customer on the other side of the stage.

Later that night, he approached her for a lap dance. She hooked a finger through the top of his button-down shirt and led him to the champagne room. In the corner was a free chair. She gave him a little push to sit him down.

He handed her the fee. "I don't really want a lap dance," he said. "Can we just talk?"

"Okay," she said. "But sit down, or it'll distract the other girls."

"Sure," he said and lowered himself into the chair.

She straddled him, her ass hovering just above his lap.

"Listen," he said. "I don't like strip clubs. Not my thing. I just came here with the guys from work. I don't want the fantasy that some woman likes me. Either she likes me or she doesn't. I'd like to take you out. Dinner. A movie. Some music. A club. Whatever you like to do. I'm not trying to take you to bed. But if you invite me, I certainly won't decline. I'm only in town one more night after this, and I'm not going to waste it in here. I'd rather be back in my hotel room reading a book. If you want to go out tomorrow, call me." He handed her a piece of paper with his number on it, and got up and left before the song even ended.

That was three months ago. She had taken him up on his date offer. He had taken her out to a delicious Caribbean/Asian fusion dinner, and afterward, he had taken her to an off-off-Broadway show by a Trinidadian playwright.

"I was on Broadway once," she said.

"I know," he said. "*Lap Dance.*"

"You googled me?" she asked.

"Of course," he said. "I work in Silicon Valley. The first thing you do before you take someone out is google them."

"What's it like out there?" she asked.

"I don't quite know how to answer that," he said. "On the one hand, it's an escape from everything here that used to bother me. Not a lot of energy and resources wasted on tradition. You don't have status because you're thus and so who came over on the Mayflower or your great-grandfather made a trillion dollars a hundred years ago. It's about now. Are you making waves today, right now? I like that. My mind is consistently engaged in ways I could never have imagined. I get to use the full range of my thinking."

"But . . ." Lily prompted.

"But the good stuff is all in my mind," he said. "That's why I don't like strip clubs. It's all about fantasy. I imagine things for a living. When I'm not at work, I want to know that everyone and everything around me is solid." He squeezed her hand.

"You're pretty solid," she said, pressing a bold hand on his thick belly.

"Yes, indeed," he said. "Lotta hours spent at the computer. Lotta takeout and not a lotta time at the gym. I need a good woman to cook for me and make me walk the dog."

Lily sucked her teeth. "There's gotta be some nice West Indian woman there to snatch up a successful guy like you."

He shrugged. "There's not much Caribbean community to speak of," he said. "On weekends, I go with my one West Indian friend to the Trini restaurant in San Jose. I'm making good money, but I'm trying to set myself up as a consultant. I want to move back to Trinidad when it's time to raise a family. If I can build up a roster of private clients in the next five years, I'll be able to make it work."

"And in the meantime?" Lily asked.

"In the meantime," he started to laugh, "I'm chasing after abrasive Trini strippers I meet while I'm at conferences in New York City."

They had talked and laughed late into the night. True to his word, he didn't pressure her for sex. Didn't even push for a goodnight kiss.

She liked him enough that she had given him her number, and he had called to tell her he was coming back into town this week.

* * *

When Lily walked back from the subway to the One-Eyed King, Cyril was waiting out front with a Lyft.

He pulled her into a hug. His body was pliant and welcoming. She sank into his belly and soft chest. Even in the warm evening, he felt solid. Familiar.

"So where to?" he asked.

"Is there a bar at your hotel?" she asked.

"If not, I'll make one," he said.

She laughed, and they climbed into the car.

An hour later, Lily was on top of Cyril. Her hands were buried in the tangled hair and flesh of his chest. His hands were cupping her breasts, stroking her nipples.

The rhythm of his thrusts inside her were savoring, unhurried.

She leaned forward and sank into his belly. He leaned forward and reached for her breasts, pressing them together and licking, sucking, nuzzling them insistently.

Lily moaned with the pleasure of it.

He grinned up at her and began to thrust harder.

She angled her hips at a sharper tilt to feel the shaft of him sliding along her clit.

"Yes," he murmured into her breast. He put one hand on her ass, pulling her harder into him, as the other hand held her nipple in his mouth.

Lily gasped with the pleasure of it.

"Don't," she rasped. "Don't stop—"

He began to thrust harder, faster.

Lily's mouth was open in a silent "O" as she felt her body on the verge of climax.

He smiled and gently bit her nipple, thrusting faster still.

And then she was gripping his shoulders, howling with the pleasure of the orgasm.

He grinned and took pleasure in her pleasure. Her head was thrown back, eyes closed. He was also glad that the hotel walls were solid. His co-workers in the next room couldn't hear him fucking.

Lily, on the other hand, if she had even been able to think about anything at that moment, wouldn't have given a fuck.

Chapter 4

The next morning, Violet was sitting on the couch watching a reality TV show on which women were competing to marry an oil tycoon.

"Those shows are really sick," Shelby said on her way out to work. She had on a tight pair of gray slacks with a low-cut charcoal blouse. "They're unhealthy to watch in the midst of a breakup. Don't do it, girl."

"I know," Violet said. "But there's something about watching these women make fools of themselves, falling all over this rich guy, that gives me some kind of consolation. Like I know I'm not them."

"I understand," Shelby said. "Those women are pathetic. But I've got some more empowering movies to watch, if you want."

Violet was halfway through *Living Out Loud* when she got a text from Etta:

I'm calling in reinforcements. Can you come meet them?

Through a haze of discouragement, Violet got up, took a shower, and headed downtown.

The address Etta had texted her seemed somehow

familiar. It turned out to be a storefront on the Lower East Side. The Maria de la Vega Community Health clinic. The same address the blue-haired girl at the strip club had given her. She entered with a silent curse toward her sister.

Inside, a dozen young women, mostly black and brown, lounged around the clinic lobby. By the door was a tall stack of the clinic's *Sexy Girl's Guide to Staying Safe and Healthy in NYC.* On the far wall was a poster that urged: USE CONDOMS . . . EVERY TIME.

Where the hell am I? Violet wondered.

In the background, a bassline thumped from the speakers of a wide-screen TV playing a video of the rapper Nashonna.

You didn't care what the stripper had to say
You let the pole get in the way . . .

Violet's eyes were drawn to the wall above the reception desk and a framed movie-style poster with the slogan "Live Nude Girls Unite!" and featuring three women styled as comic book heroes, half-naked, with a "Strippers Union" picket sign and a fist in the air.

She would probably run into Lily today.

She had just turned to walk out when Etta strode in. Beside her were two women—one Latina, one black. The black woman was young, maybe late twenties, and the Latina was older, late thirties or early forties. Both wore high-fashion business suits and tall shoes. The Latina had her hair pulled back into a tight French twist. The black girl had her hair in a bone-straight press. Had they been wearing other clothing, they might have looked like strippers themselves. Both had extreme hourglass shapes that the suits couldn't hide.

"You made it," Etta said with a smile and introduced Violet to the two women.

The black girl was Tyesha. Violet recalled that was the name of one of Lily's friends. They walked across the lobby, and Tyesha swiped a key card. The hallway to the stairwell opened, and the four women walked up a few flights of stairs to an outer office. At the desk, a petite young woman sat, her sandy brown hair escaping from a hastily pinned-back bun, as a trio of girls in their late teens scooped handfuls of condoms from a large glass punch bowl on the desk.

"Serena," the Latina woman called. She had been introduced as Marisol. "Can you join us in—" she broke off.

"My office," Tyesha finished the sentence.

The two women in suits laughed.

"Marisol was the original director," Tyesha said, explaining the inside joke.

"Old habits die hard," Marisol said.

"Yeah," Etta agreed. "Like sometimes I call Teddy 'my husband.' Instead of 'the dick that stole my life and all the strippers' money and ran off with some shady hoe.' "

"We don't use the word hoe in here as an insult," Tyesha said.

Etta nodded. "I can see that," she said. "Considering the clients."

Violet shuddered. Not just strippers but prostitutes? What had she gotten herself into?

The women moved into Tyesha's office, which was bright and beautifully decorated. It was done in mahogany-paneled walls and designer leather furniture, with a massive wooden desk. The warm indirect light sustained several plants.

Violet sat in a black leather armchair. Etta sat in the

twin chair, and the three women from the clinic sat on a matching leather couch opposite them.

With Marisol's prompting, Etta explained the situation to Tyesha and Serena, and pulled a laptop from her bag.

"I thought the FBI had seized his computer," Violet said.

"They took the one from his office, but I was out with his laptop when they did the house raid."

"You didn't check his home computer already?" Serena asked.

"I tried," Etta said. "He deleted all of his files, but I was able to get a bunch of photos that he had backed up on the hard drive. I was hoping we could just find her picture."

Etta had pulled up maybe five hundred photos and handed the laptop to Violet. Although these were mostly of young, hot women, they had more variety than the stripper promo shots. Women grinning with their faces pressed together in a nightclub. Women waving at the camera. Teddy Hughes with his arms draped around various women. Some were famous. Some were faces she recognized, perhaps from billboards or magazine covers. None of them was the woman who had borrowed her phone.

Violet set the laptop down on the coffee table and shook her head.

Tyesha and Marisol looked at Serena. The petite white girl picked up the laptop and pulled up several screens with mostly coded text on them.

"He deleted the main files," she said. "But there are backup files, plus some footprints where he synched the photos from his handheld."

"Can you pull those up?"

"I think so," Serena said. "But doing computer forensics takes a while. I should know something by tomorrow."

"I can't believe he would be with her all this time and not have a single photo," Etta said. "When he was cheating with me, he carried my picture in his wallet."

"Who's to say he didn't do that again?" Marisol asked.

"Girl," Etta said, "I checked that shit first thing." She closed the photo program on the computer.

Violet blinked at the screen saver. The face was unmistakable.

"That's her!" Violet said.

The other four women in the room crowded around the armchair as Violet pointed to a young woman sitting in profile with her butt on her stiletto-booted heels. She wore a black Halloween mask, and the photo caption read, "Unmask all your desires." The woman looked coyly at the camera through the mask, with heavily made-up eyes.

"I know the girl in that ad," Etta said. "She dances at the One-Eyed. I showed you her picture yesterday."

"No," Violet said, "I definitely didn't see her."

"Wait a minute," Serena said. She pulled the image from the screen saver and put it into another program.

"Are you sure you got a good look at this woman?" Etta asked.

"Listen," Violet said, "I have every incentive to look carefully. I'm telling you, I didn't see this woman yesterday."

On the screen, Serena blew up the image of the woman.

"Look!" she said. The woman's eyes were practically actual size on the screen.

"She has green eyes," Etta said. "So what?"

"The light in the eyes," Serena said. "It's not in the right place."

She zoomed back out. "See? Her shadow places the light source on the right. But in her eyes, the light source is reflected on the left."

Violet looked more closely.

"Son of a bitch," Etta said. "She looks a lot like the girl who posed for that promo, but you're right. That's not her face."

"He photoshopped his mistress's face onto this ad?" Violet said.

"What a dick," Tyesha said.

"In my own goddamn house," Etta said. "How many times did I look at that screen saver. Right into the eyes of the tramp ready to take my man."

"I need a copy of this to take to the FBI," Violet said.

"Don't go yet," Tyesha said. "You should find out what else is on that computer."

"The only other thing I found was this," Etta said. It was a credit card statement from Hughes's business account that covered the previous month.

Most of it looked pretty standard. Meals. Cab rides.

"He charged a massage," Serena pointed out.

"Probably with a happy ending," Etta said. "That fucker."

One line item caught Violet's attention. "Let me see that," she said.

She scanned down the page. "Hummingbirdwing.com!" Violet said.

"A cosmetics site," Etta said. "So what?"

Violet pulled up the website.

"This company specializes in makeup that stays on in heat and moisture," Violet said. "It's designed for tropical climates. It wicks the moisture to the surface, and you can blot it, but the makeup stays in place. It costs a fortune."

"High-tech makeup," Etta said. "So what?"

Tyesha looked at Violet. "So you're thinking they're going to a hot climate?"

"New York is hot enough this time of year," Etta said.

"But look how much she bought," Violet said, pointing out the amount that had been charged. "This isn't a supply for a couple months. This is a supply for a year. And I say that as a makeup professional."

Etta laughed bitterly. "I remember what that was like," she said. "You want to look made up twenty-four/seven. When you take a guy from his wife, you're always on the lookout for the next tramp who's gonna try to steal him from you."

"She had to be headed for someplace tropical," Violet said. "The only other explanation would be if she were on the international circuit dancing in a carnival."

"That bitch probably can't dance," Etta muttered.

"So she's somewhere hot trying to look hot," Tyesha said.

"And you can never pull it off," Etta said. "When you're the one who lives with him, eventually you become a real person. But these other chicks look picture-perfect for the five minutes he sees them. Or the one night they spend together."

"You gotta let it go, Etta," Marisol said.

Etta shook her head, and Violet could see her face pucker a bit as she held back tears.

"Let's see what else we can find on this laptop," Serena said. She and Violet scrolled through the laptop's backup files for the next hour.

"What's this?" Violet asked. She had searched for "Mexico," "Central America," "South America," "Caribbean," "Hawaii," and "Pacific," and finally got a hit with "British West Indies."

It was an escrow document for a tract of land in Trinidad.

Etta came over and leaned in to look. "What the fuck?" she muttered. "We sort of talked about maybe getting some land. I always had this fantasy of running a little bed and breakfast. Did that motherfucker actually buy it without me?"

"I'll have to do a bunch more digging," Serena said. "But it looks like he might have."

"I'll see if anyone I know in Trinidad can go check out the property," Violet said.

Violet had Serena print out a copy of the property address, along with the photo of the woman who had used her phone.

Violet and Etta left the laptop with Serena and headed uptown to the FBI office. They wanted to bring in the photo before the office closed.

They asked for the agent whom Violet had spoken to before.

"Here's a photo of the woman who used my phone," Violet said, triumphantly laying a printed image on his desk. Serena had reconstructed the Photoshop file, pulled out the original head shot, and removed the woman's mask.

"Who is she?" the agent asked.

"We don't know," Violet said.

He picked up the picture and scrutinized it. "There are a million women in New York City who look like this."

"We checked all of the files from the One-Eyed King," Etta said. "We can say for sure that she's not an employee."

"Well, that certainly narrows it down," the agent said sarcastically. "By the way, I'm surprised to see that the two of you have teamed up."

"I feel responsible," Etta said. "I pretty much screwed up her life, and I'm just here to help clear her name, so she can go back to Trinidad."

"Clear your name with a laser photo of a Jane Doe?" he asked. "I don't think so. This doesn't prove you're not his mistress. The two of you could have easily cooked this up."

"For what?"

"Maybe he skipped out on both of you. Maybe you're teaming up against the new girl," he said, waving the young woman's photo. "I'm not gonna let you leave town until I find Teddy Hughes or have some kind of conclusive evidence that you weren't involved."

"That could take months," Violet said. "Maybe even years."

"You're a suspect in a major fraud investigation," he said. "He didn't just rob a few strippers, he defrauded some million-dollar investors. For the time being, you live in New York."

Violet stood up with her fists balled. "Members of the damn Bin Laden family left for the Middle East after 9/11, but you won't let me go back to Trinidad?"

"Sir," Etta said to the agent, "what my friend here is trying to say is that we hope this photo will help you locate the woman who used her phone, the woman whose trail may lead you to my husband, okay?" She slid the photo back across the desk toward him. "Anything you can do would be greatly appreciated."

She put an arm around the seething Violet and guided her out the door.

"Take it easy, honey," Etta murmured in Violet's ear.

As they walked out into the lobby, Violet felt Etta's body tense. As they approached security, she saw a young white man in a suit. He and a neat blonde were coming in through the metal detectors.

"Good afternoon, Mrs. Hughes," the man said. He was the same height as Violet. As he came up beside them, Etta in her heels was nearly a head taller than him.

"Oh, now I'm Mrs. Hughes," Etta said. "But you didn't have any respect for the Mrs. title when you were watching my husband gallivant around with that young tramp every day."

"Mrs. Hughes," the man began, "I had no influence over what your husband chose to—"

"I'm not talking about influence," Etta said. "If he was fucking around, he was fucking around. I'm talking about you coming to my house every week for dinner. Eating my food. Complimenting my goddamn chocolate cheesecake. If you were one of his slimy buddies in the street, that's one thing, but you brought your backstabbing ass into my house and pretended you were friends with us as a family. Fuck you, Jared. You're a garbage guy, you know that?"

"Mrs. Hughes—" the blonde began.

"And you?" Etta shot at her. "I wouldn't have even had you in the house for fear that you'd be trying to fuck my husband in the study during the soup course. If I have to lose everything to be rid of the both of you, it might be worth the price." She spat on the ground and strode out of the FBI building.

"Who were those two?" Violet asked, once she'd caught up with Etta on the street.

"Teddy's employees," Etta said. "Jared was Teddy's chief financial officer, and the blonde was his secretary. I forget her name."

"Forget her name as in selective memory?" Violet asked.

"Forget it as in I never bothered to learn it," Etta said.

"Apparently, the FBI has some questions for them, as well," Violet said.

"Exactly," Etta said. "Don't take it personally. They're probably suspects, too. You should just take that photo over to your boyfriend's house and put a spin on it. You found the woman's photo. It's only a matter of time before the FBI tracks her down. You love him, you miss him, you want to start over . . . blah blah blah. Then fuck his brains out and ask for the ring back. At least, that's how I'd do it."

"Not my style," Violet said. "But I think showing Quentin the photo is a great idea."

Violet still had the key to Quentin's apartment. It was 6:45 in the evening by the time she got to his place, but she knew he had racquetball on Thursday nights and would come home to change around 7:30.

She would be waiting for him. With a nice bottle of wine and a negligee she hid in the back of his closet. She didn't exactly plan to fuck his brains out, but she would definitely remind him what he'd been missing.

When she walked in, she saw Quentin's keys in the bowl in the hallway. So much for surprising him.

"Quentin," she called. "It's me . . . Violet."

"What are you doing here?" he asked sharply, coming out into the hallway.

"I have a surprise for you," she said, handing him the photo.

He ignored it. "I thought I had asked for my key back."

"You didn't," Violet said. "You said we were just taking a break."

The bedroom door opened, and Shelby walked in.

"Quentin, I couldn't seem to—" she saw Violet and broke off.

"You couldn't seem to what?" Violet asked, an icy rage filling her body. "Because it looks to me like you really could seem to."

"I'm—I'm sorry, Violet," Shelby said. "It just sort of happened."

Somehow, Violet's stomach managed to be both cold and burning at the same time.

"I thought you were my friend," Violet said. "My best friend. I've been sleeping at your house every night. Unless it all just happened today, you've been lying to my face."

"You two were broken up," Shelby said.

"Broken up?" Violet said. "I told you we were just taking a break. But I now realize that all your encouragement to 'forget about him' wasn't really for my benefit, was it?"

"Violet's been staying with you?" Quentin asked.

"You said you were done with him," Shelby said.

"As in, having an emotional moment with my girlfriend 'I'm done with him'!" Violet yelled. "Not as in 'I'm done with the curling iron, Shelby, now it's your turn'!"

"Violet," Quentin said, "I didn't know—"

"Shut up," Violet spat. "I spent this whole relationship feeling like I had to prove I was good enough for you. I came over here with the photo of the strip club king's mistress to prove that I was faithful, only to find you fucking my best friend. You're the low-class trash, Quentin."

She strode out the front door and threw his apartment key over her shoulder.

Out on the street, Violet hailed a cab. She still had

one of Quentin's credit cards—one he'd given her in case of an emergency—buried deep in her wallet. She decided this was an emergency. She had the driver confirm that it worked, then asked him to drive her downtown to Shelby's. As they drove, she opened the wine and began to drink it. At Shelby's, the cab sat outside with the meter running while she got all of her stuff. Then she asked him to take her to Brooklyn, where she could put some of her things into storage. She wasn't sure where she was going to stay, but she couldn't be running around the city with three suitcases.

As they sat in evening traffic, she finished the bottle. By the time they got to her storage space, she was pretty tipsy, but she rolled the two bigger suitcases into her small unit.

"Where to now, miss?" the driver asked.

"What's the most expensive hotel in Brooklyn?" she asked.

"The Brooklyn Gardens Hotel," he said.

"Perfect," she said through clenched teeth.

On their way over, however, they passed the street that the Caribbean Circus was on.

"Change of plans," Violet said and directed him into the warehouse district, where she would start work in a couple of days.

By the time Violet arrived, the evening show was over. She teetered into the building as most of the performers were filing out.

Violet lingered by the door, feeling suddenly awkward, even in spite of the bravado the buzz had given her. She had decided to duck back into the cab when Nigel stepped out of the dressing room and spotted her.

"Violet, what are you doing here?"

"I was just—just in the neighborhood," she stammered. "I was hoping to catch the tail end of the show before I started—started working here."

"Don't worry," he said. "You'll have lots more chances. Hey, come into the office and chat with me while I get my stuff. Are you hungry? I'm famished after a performance."

He showed her into the small, curtained-off area that was the men's dressing room. Violet expected it to smell like sweaty socks, but it actually smelled like soap and bay rum. He grabbed a Jamaican patty and took a bite.

"So tell me something good that happened today," he said, as he chewed and stuffed his costume into a backpack.

"I went to a . . . sort of health clinic on the Lower East Side," she said. "And I found a photo of the woman who stole my phone."

"Someone stole your phone?"

"Sort of," Violet said. "She more like stole my identity."

"You were hit with identity theft?"

"More like she was impersonating me," Violet tried to explain through the disorientation of the buzz.

"You know you can go to the authorities with that," Nigel said.

"I went to the FBI with the photo, but they didn't believe me," she said.

"You just need to sign an affidavit," Nigel said. "It happened to my aunt."

"It's more complicated than that," Violet said. "She used my phone, and then her man called my phone, and then his jealous wife called my phone, and then the wife came and cussed me out on my job, and that's the real reason I got fired."

"Oh, shit," Nigel said.

"And then my man thought maybe I was lying, but I

thought I was gonna show him I was telling the truth," she said. "I went over there with the picture of the woman who stole someone else's man. Only to find out someone had stolen my man."

"I'm not sure I'm following," Nigel said, looking confused.

"My oldest and best friend was sleeping with Quentin," Violet admitted, bitterly.

"The same one from Harvard?" Nigel asked. "That girl Shelly?"

"Shelby."

"I always thought she seemed a little out for herself," Nigel said.

"What's wrong with me?" Violet said. "Why didn't Quentin believe me? It can't just be that a woman stole my phone. It's gotta be more than that. There's gotta be something about me he doesn't like—doesn't trust. I tried so hard to be what he wanted."

"Oh no," Nigel said. "You can't blame yourself. Quentin is a fool if he doesn't appreciate what he has—had."

"That's right," Violet said. "He was taking me for granted." In her drunken state, it came out "grannit."

She went on. "These rich American boys take everything for granted. Expect everything to be easy. He never really appreciated me for who I was. He needed me to be some little warm vacation island for him to wash up on every night. Somebody he could tell about his mistakes and insecurities at daddy's law firm. But the moment my character came into question, I wasn't good enough to get the benefit of the doubt."

"Violet, you're a beautiful, amazing, powerful West Indian woman," Nigel said. "Don't let yourself internalize his bad decisions. You're made of stronger stuff than that."

"Strong stuff," Violet said. "Is that what I'm made of?" She laid a hand on his shoulder. "Because I know what you're made of. You're made of buss up shut." She put a finger in the tear in his T-shirt as she said "buss up shut," referring to the Trinidadian dish of torn-up roti that looked like a busted-up shirt.

She leaned in to kiss him, but the lunge lurched her stomach. She wobbled to the bathroom and threw up.

After heaving up all the wine—she hadn't eaten since lunch—she flushed the toilet. She stared at the water in the porcelain bowl. *Could she flush herself down?* She couldn't stand the idea of going back out and facing Nigel. Was there a back window she could climb out of? But then she recalled that she was supposed to start work here in a couple of days. She couldn't just escape.

Violet stood up and walked to the sink. Her eyeliner was running. Her eyes always teared up when she vomited. She wiped her eyes, rinsed out her mouth, and straightened out her clothes. This was a disaster. She realized that the cab was still out front with the meter running. With that, she cracked a tiny smile. Not that a big taxi bill would really be hard on a millionaire. But at least it was something.

When she stepped out of the bathroom, she was still drunk, but she had more of her wits about her.

"Nigel, I—" she began.

"Don't worry about it," he said. "You've obviously had a ghastly day. Can I call you a cab?"

"I already have one," she said, and hurried out past him.

In the taxi, the driver asked where she wanted to go. She considered telling him to go to the hotel and having Quentin pay for her to stay there several nights.

That would serve him right. But the thought of facing an empty hotel room made her want to weep. She gave the driver a Manhattan address.

Violet banged on the door of the East Side townhouse. She stared at the cream-colored door. The brass address numbers. When there was no answer, she banged again. She located the bell and leaned on it.

A few minutes later, she heard footsteps.

"What the fuck is going on?" Etta yelled through the door.

"It's Violet," she yelled back. "Let me in."

Etta opened the door. "What are you doing here?" she asked. She had on a red silk kimono and a cheap scarf over her hair.

"I need to stay here tonight," Violet said. "You offered."

"Are you drunk?" Etta asked, opening the door. "Because it's a guest room, not a frat house. If you're gonna stay here, can you come and go at more reasonable hours?"

"So sorry to inconvenience you," Violet said, bitterly. "Since you fucked up my life, I got no job, no man, no apartment, nothing."

"How many times do I have to say I'm sorry?" Etta said, leading Violet across the house. "And what happened to the best friend you were staying with?"

"I found her in my man's bed," Violet said.

"Wha-aat?" Etta asked, as they crossed the living room.

"And both of them making bullshit excuses," Violet added.

"I understand," Etta said, opening the door of the

guest room. "When someone's moving in on your man, you just get a little crazy."

"I know," Violet said, stepping into a large room with a ruffled quilt and puffy pillows. "I was ready to kill them. More her than him. She was my friend. But with Teddy, how are you gonna blame a woman you don't even know?"

"Men are dogs," Etta said. "I expect it from them. I learned to expect backstabbing from women. That's why I don't have female friends."

"How can you dismiss over fifty percent of the population just because a couple of them did wrong by you?"

"Habit, I guess," Etta said, pulling sheets and a pillowcase out of the linen closet. "It's actually kind of nice to have another woman around. It gets lonely up in this house by myself. And I don't have to feel threatened anymore, because I got no man to steal now."

Violet glanced up at the photo of Etta and Teddy Hughes. "I've seen your husband. You were never in any danger from me," Violet said. "No offense."

Etta gave a bitter chuckle. "No offense taken."

Chapter 5

On Violet's first evening of work, she avoided Nigel as much as she could.

There were dozens of performers to make up. She found herself getting lost in the bright shades of lipstick and the glittering eye shadow. The routine of makeup calmed her—the line of a pencil at the edge of a lip, where the hairless plum skin meets tufted brown. The feathery touch of her finger blending accents along cheekbones. The precision of a brushstroke on the fold of skin where the lid of the eye meets the lash, and the whisper-thin edge of a false eyelash as it absorbs the natural one.

After a while, she forgot about Nigel, about Quentin and what best friends of hers he might be screwing, about whether the FBI believed her or not. She was tiptoeing along the curve of an eyebrow, contemplating only the blend of gold to avocado.

And then a sharp voice ruined it.

"Violet? Is that you?"

Lily's voice.

She turned around to see her sister grinning wide. "Violet," Lily asked, "what are you doing here?"

"I work here," Violet said, holding a handful of makeup brushes aloft, a bit like a weapon.

The Caribbean burlesque troupe had come in, and apparently her sister was part of it. Of course she was. Violet looked her sister up and down. Her sister in the mesh shorts with the thong underneath, and the feather bra. Her sister . . . looking like . . . she might as well say it, even to herself. A slut.

These fast women had a lot of nerve calling themselves burlesque dancers. At least stripping was more honest. Trying to call it art. It's not art to shake your batty for a room full of men. A little twitch to each side to make it jiggle is enough for the average idiot to start applauding. Not like carnival, where people were dancing out in public, in broad daylight. And even some of those women were doing way too much. Violet had to work hard not to suck her teeth out loud.

She needed a moment. She turned to walk away, and nearly ran into someone else.

"Violet?" the woman asked.

Violet looked up to see that it was Tyesha, the black girl from the clinic. Perfect. She was walking in with Serena, the petite computer specialist.

Tyesha looked from Lily to Violet. "How do you two know each other?" she asked.

"Violet's my older sister," Lily said. "And I never thought I'd see her in a place like this." This time, Lily looked Violet up and down. "Vi belongs more like at the Metropolitan Opera or someplace like that. But Brooklyn? Something Caribbean? Aren't you full of surprises?"

"I know there's been drama between the two of

you," Tyesha said. "But in Violet's situation, she needs all the help she can get."

"My sister Violet?" Lily said. "Needing help from me? I know it's hot in New York tonight, but somewhere hell is freezing over."

"Seriously, Lily," Tyesha said. "She's got a situation."

"May I talk to my sister for a moment?" Violet asked. "In private?"

"Let's go find our seats," Serena said. "I'm getting cold in here with all this shade." She and Tyesha headed out of the dressing room toward the rows of folding chairs

The moment they were out of earshot, Violet lit into her sister. "You have a lot of nerve talking about me being here, or me needing help, when this whole situation is your fault anyway. I went down to your old job to track you down at that King stripper place. And that's the only reason I was there when this woman . . . basically stole my identity."

"What woman?" Lily asked. "What are you talking about? And how is it my fault? I didn't ask you to go down to my job."

"Mommie asked me," Violet said. "She got worried when you were MIA for nearly two months."

"MIA?" Lily asked. "I wasn't MIA. I been messaging her twice a week. I even sent her the piece we got in the *Village Voice*."

"You been messaging from your cell phone?" Violet asked.

"My cell is disconnected," Lily said. "I been emailing."

"Mom never checks that old Hotmail account," Violet said.

Lily shook her head. "I set up a new account six months ago. She promised she'd check once a week."

"I didn't know anything about it," Violet said.

"She probably just forgot the password," Lily said. "If you talk to her before I do, remind her it's 'VioletAnd-Lily'."

"Sure," Violet said, her voice clipped.

"But after I get paid tonight, I'll probably have enough to get my cell turned back on," Lily said. "See? I'm not MIA. Just broke. Besides, you know Mom over-reacts. Why didn't you send me an email? I know you have my address."

Violet was taken aback. "So you're blaming me now?"

Lily shook her head. "No, Violet," she said pointedly. "Why does it have to be somebody's fault? I didn't pay my phone bill on time. Mom overreacted to the radio silence. And you didn't bother to try emailing. Maybe everybody contributed to the problem. But what I want to know is why you're so ready to believe I'm in some terrible trouble just because I haven't talked to Mom in a few weeks?"

Violet didn't know what to say.

"I'm sorry about this identity theft, and whatever situation Tyesha was talking about," Lily said. "But I've gotta go get ready for the show."

And with that, Lily turned and strutted out toward the knot of dancers, her ass swishing back and forth in the fishnet pum-pum shorts.

Violet wasn't sure why, but her face burned watching Lily wearing such provocative clothing. She felt it was somehow her job to make her sister look decent.

The feeling of humiliation transported her back to another moment with the same ingredients: Lily unfit to be in public, her ass on display. Lily wanton and unapologetic, while Violet's face blazed with shame.

* * *

A few months after Lily had jumped ship in New York, she had finally gotten settled. She had a job, a room in a shared apartment, and a cell phone.

"Let's celebrate," Violet said. "Quentin and I are having dinner tonight with some friends at this new restaurant. Come out with us."

"What kind of food?" Lily asked. "Because I'm not paying fifty dollars for some celery sticks marinated in bourbon and chicken broth."

Violet laughed. "Nothing like that," she said. "It's upscale paleo. Plenty of meat. It's a nice place, so wear a dress, okay?"

For Lily, "a dress" turned out to be more like a coat of bright magenta paint that stretched from her mid-thighs to halfway up her breasts. A tiny pair of straps struggled to keep her ample cleavage from spilling out of the thing. It was January, so Lily also wore a cropped white faux-fur coat and black thigh-high boots.

Violet looked around at the textured driftwood walls and white linen tables. "What in God's name are you wearing?" she hissed.

"You said to wear a dress," Lily hissed back. "This was all I had."

Violet had spent the afternoon trying on several dresses and had settled on a copper-colored wrap dress, knee-length with a cowl neck. She wished she had thought to loan her sister something, but it was too late.

Lily crossed her arms over her chest, self-conscious now. Violet studied the menu.

Violet's boyfriend, Quentin, came back from checking in with the host. He was tall, soft-bodied, and a light brown, with a strong, clean-shaven jaw, and a confident smile. "You must be Lily," he said. "So good to finally meet you. How are you settling in?"

"I'd say fine overall," Lily said, smiling. "But I don't seem to have had time to do as much shopping as I obviously need to do." She cut her eyes at Violet. "But now that I finally have a job, I'm sure that'll get easier. Still it's been a little tough, you know. Getting readjusted to New York."

"You lived here before, right?"

"Yeah," Lily said. "About four years ago."

"I'm surprised I didn't meet you then," Quentin said. "We were just up in Boston."

"But you were so busy with law school," Violet said. "We had plans to see Lily over the winter break."

"Right," Quentin said. "What happened?"

"I left New York that November," Lily said. "My mother—our mother—got sick, and I had to go back home to take care of her."

"It's all coming back to me," Quentin said. "Violet says she's doing okay now, right?"

"Much better," Lily agreed.

The restaurant door opened, and Quentin's two friends came in, a study in contrast. Dale was a young white corporate lawyer in a dark suit. Steven was black and wore a skinny-leg navy suit, a bright red shirt, and a narrow, metallic gold tie.

From the moment Steven was introduced to Lily, he barely spoke another word to the rest of the group.

Quentin and Dale worked together at the corporate law firm started by Quentin's uncle—Ross, Billingsley, and Hoyt—so the two of them mostly talked shop. Meanwhile, Steven and Lily were exchanging the basic info of their lives. Violet already knew that he worked at a gallery and his family was from Nigeria. She certainly could predict everything that Lily was going to say. Violet tuned out from both conversations as she ate her snapper fillet, crusted in seasoned pistachio meal and deep fried in coconut oil.

"This wine is so good," Lily said of the fermented honey drink. She took a generous swallow from a cobalt blue goblet.

"It's just *tej*," Steven said. "You can get this in any Ethiopian restaurant for a third of the price."

"But you know how it is," Lily said. "When immigrants make it, it's only worth a fraction of what you pay if white people make it."

Violet froze mid-bite and glanced at Dale to see if he was offended. The white guy didn't seem to be paying attention.

Violet finished chewing. "Oh, I don't know," she said. "It's supposed to be locally sourced, and the honey is organic, so it justifies the price."

"Come on, Violet," Steven said. "You're an immigrant, too. You're supposed to be on our side."

"You're an immigrant, Violet?" Dale asked, a frown between his green eyes. "I thought you were from New England."

"She went to prep school in New England," Quentin explained. "But she's originally from Trinidad."

"But you wouldn't know it from the way she talks, right?" Lily said. "I think that was the biggest shocker. When Violet would call home and it was this American girl's voice on the phone." Lily screwed up her mouth with what seemed like a herculean effort. "Hyyyyee, Moooommm."

She and Steven laughed.

Violet felt tears sting her eyes.

She remembered that first call home. Her mother hadn't gotten internet service at the house, and she hadn't yet figured out calling cards. She had to borrow her roommate's phone. The girl clattered around the room, gathering her gear for lacrosse. Violet had longed to relax into Trinidadian English but couldn't unmoor her tongue with this blond whirlwind in the background.

"Yaaah, Mooommmm, eyyyeeem fiiiiine." So many days, sitting in class and knowing the answer, but keeping her mouth shut until she could twist it around those flat vowels. Lying in bed at night, listening to podcasts, the news, anything. Her mouth moving as she tried to copy the sounds.

But during that first phone call, the unaccented English she'd worked so hard to perfect felt wrong all of a sudden. Yet her old tongue, the one she'd spoken for fourteen years before she won a scholarship to boarding school, was too private for this American girl to hear.

"I've gotta go to practice," the girl said, holding one hand out for her phone. "But feel free to call again anytime."

Violet didn't call again. She wrote letters, instead. She only called during winter holidays, when she stayed with a friend who lived in Connecticut.

"Are you sure?" she asked her friend's mom. "It's so expensive."

"Go ahead, honey," the mom said. "It's our family's Chanukah present to you."

She would go into the den and close the door. And finally have a long talk with her mother, her voice looping in and out of American and Trinidadian English.

By the summer, her mom had internet at the house. But her mom worked a lot, so Violet rarely had privacy when she caught her mom at home. A lot of evenings, she would Skype with her mom as her roommate studied nearby. Violet drew her American accent tight around herself like a winter coat.

It wouldn't be until college that she had a job and

her own cell phone plan and was able to call more often. By then, her American voice felt normal to her. She couldn't seem to conjure the Trinidadian syntax or the island vowels. More than that, she couldn't quite taste her old voice. Her tongue had lost the muscle memory of having talked any other way.

"What's up, babe?" Quentin asked, putting an arm around her. "You've been so quiet tonight. How was your food?" He gestured down to her plate, which had a few flakes of snapper at the edge and a sprinkle of remaining pistachio crumbs.

"Delicious," she said, as the waitress appeared with the check.

"I got this," Quentin said to the table and pulled out a platinum credit card.

After the bill was settled, Steven asked if anyone wanted to go out for a drink.

"I've got an early meeting," Dale said.

"Sounds fun," Quentin said. "Violet?"

"I'm pretty tired," she said.

Quentin shrugged and put an arm around Violet. "We'll pass."

"Looks like it's just you and me," Lily said, grinning at Steven.

"Let's pretend this is my disappointed face," he said, grinning back.

At the door of the restaurant, everyone said their goodbyes. Violet watched Lily walking away with Steven's arm draped over her shoulder. Lily let out a slightly tipsy laugh, as she swished down the street on her high-heeled boots, her round ass swiveling back and forth in the painted-on dress.

"A drink?" Violet asked, sucking her teeth. "The last thing that girl needs is more alcohol."

At ten the next morning, Violet called Lily on her brand-new cell phone.

"Just checking to make sure that you got home okay," she said.

"Home?" Lily asked, laughing. "I'm still at Steven's."

"You're not serious," Violet said.

"I have a roommate," Lily said. "We couldn't go to my place."

"I can't believe you," Violet fumed. "Getting so drunk that you went home with one of Quentin's friends."

"Seriously?" Lily said. "I would have fucked Steven completely sober. Did you see that rock-solid Nigerian ass? That's the ass of kings and queens in Africa, my sister."

"Steven's a good catch, but he's not gonna take you seriously if you're sleeping with him on the first date."

"Who says I want him to take me seriously?" Lily asked. "I'm just having fun."

"But have you thought through the consequences?" Violet asked.

"What consequences?" Lily asked. "We used a condom. All three times."

"I just mean the consequences of how men see you," Violet said.

"I hope Steven sees me as a woman who's fun to fuck and that we'll do it again soon," Lily said.

"But not just Steven," Violet said. "Men in general."

"This is about your boyfriend, isn't it?" Lily asked.

"First, I show up in a slutty dress. Then I go off and fuck his friend. I'm embarrassing you, aren't I?"

Violet's mouth opened. "Well, to be honest about it," she began, "I think Quentin is going to propose to me soon. I want him to think I'm . . . marriage material."

"And what?" Lily asked. "You're worried he won't buy the milk if the cow's sister gives it away all over town for free?" Lily snorted. "You should be thanking me. I'm the bad cop to your good cop. I make you look like wife material by contrast."

"It's more complicated than that," Violet said. "Quentin's family is . . . they have money. They don't like outsiders."

"So what?" Lily said. "You think you're passing as a black girl from New England? You can change your accent and get your bachelors from Harvard, but you don't have any fucking pedigree. You're just like me—a girl from Trinidad whose mother is a makeup artist and whose dad is married to another woman. The only difference between us is that I'm honest about who I am."

"No," Violet said coldly. "The difference between us is that I aspire to be something better."

"Good luck with that," Lily said, and hung up.

Quentin proposed the following week.

Someone was saying something to her—a man's voice. Violet looked up to see Nigel. He was beckoning her to come out of the dressing room and into the main room.

"Aren't you going to come out and see the show?"

He meant the burlesque show. Lily's show.

"No," she said. "I don't think—I mean, I'm pretty much done here. I was gonna head—" she was going to say "home" but Etta's house barely qualified. "Head out," she finished.

"Can we maybe talk—"

"Another time," she said. She had to get out of there.

She walked out onto the street and made her way to the subway. She caught the train to Manhattan but didn't really want to go back to Etta's. Where could she go?

The train stopped, and she gazed idly out the doors at an ad for a fitness center. Didn't she still have her twenty-four-hour gym membership? Digging through her purse, she found the card. It was still valid. She'd worn sneakers that day. Her T-shirt smudged with makeup and drawstring cotton pants could double as workout gear.

So she went to her gym's location in SoHo and ran on the treadmill until her face burned with something other than shame.

After the show, Lily was jubilant. She had performed in a few burlesque shows before, but they were either predominantly white or mostly black American. There was something so saucy about the fusion between the Caribbean and burlesque.

In the post-show, they were playing a soca classic by the Mighty Sparrow. She walked over to the handsome ringmaster and started dancing up against his body, or as they said in Trinidad, *whinning* on him. He responded, and they danced together for a moment, hips locking in the rhythm.

"You all were great tonight," he said. "What's your name?"

"Lily," she said.

Nigel stepped back. "You're not Violet's sister Lily, are you?"

"So now what?" Lily said. "She talking more shit about me?"

"No, I just—sisters are off limits," he blurted, holding up his open hands as if before a cop.

"You think you have a chance with Violet?" Lily said. "Her highness who's engaged to the black prince of America?"

"They split," Nigel said.

"They what?" Lily asked, incredulous.

"You don't know what's going on?" Nigel asked. "Your sister is in trouble." He explained it all to her. How Violet had lost everything. Her job. Her apartment. Her man. How she was considered a suspect by the FBI. And how she had loaned her phone to a woman outside of a strip club.

"Oh shit," Lily said. "I gotta go talk to somebody."

Fortunately, Lily was tall, six foot six in her heels. She was able to find Tyesha and Serena among the audience members drifting out of the venue.

"You were fabulous," Tyesha said.

"I need to talk to you two about my sister," Lily said. "I had no idea what was going on. Can I help?"

"Definitely," Tyesha said. "The team is meeting tomorrow."

Chapter 6

The following day, Violet and Etta walked into the Maria de la Vega clinic. And when they got to the executive director's office, Tyesha and Marisol were sitting on the couch. A moment later, Serena walked in with a serving tray of coffee.

"Praise God," Etta muttered and poured a decaf with three packets of stevia sweetener.

Violet poured herself a cup of regular and stirred in lots of milk.

"Serena, do you want to start?" Tyesha asked.

"I confirmed that Teddy bought the land in Trinidad several years ago," she began. "Between that and the makeup, it looks like a strong possibility for where he would have gone."

As Serena opened up the laptop, Lily came rushing in.

"Sorry I'm late," she panted.

Violet looked up, startled. She opened her mouth to speak, but nothing came out. Now, on top of everything else, she would have to deal with Lily?

Serena offered a cup of coffee, but Lily declined.

"No thanks," she said with a chuckle. "I've never quite gotten used to coffee."

"Oh, that's right," Tyesha said. "You West Indians like tea. There's some on the side table."

As Lily made herself some English breakfast tea, Violet stared down into her coffee cup with a growing knot in her belly.

Lily brought her tea over to the group, but the chairs were all taken.

"Have a seat, Lily," Marisol said. "That end table next to your sister doubles as a stool."

"That's okay," Violet said. "I'm fine here on the edge of the couch."

She hoisted herself onto the arm of the sofa, with half her ass hanging off.

"So," Tyesha said into the awkward silence, "Serena made an estimate of how much Teddy got away with, and it looks like about ten million."

"Which leads to the big question," Marisol said. "How did he get the funds portable enough to move? It would be hard to skip the country with that much cash, even in hundreds."

Violet furrowed her brow. "What's your interest in this?" Violet asked. It came out sounding kind of rude, so she backpedaled. "Sorry, I mean, thank you so much for helping, but I'm sort of unclear on the clinic's involvement."

"We provide services to the sex worker community," Tyesha said. "Mostly health services, but in a case like this, where there's also a legal problem—even an extralegal problem—we step in to help. We were heavily involved in starting the union. The whole point was to protect the workers from wage theft, and now he has literally stolen the funds and skipped town."

"And is there any movement on Trinidad?" Marisol asked.

"What about Trinidad?" Lily asked.

Tyesha caught her up on the land situation and handed her the copy of the document with the address.

Violet stared at an orchid across the room. "I asked around a little bit," she said. "But our mother lives on the other side of the island from the property."

"I can get one of our cousins to check," Lily said.

"Which cousin?" Violet asked.

"One of our boy cousins has a charter boat," Lily said. "And he's always broke. If you can pay, he can find out."

"Sounds great," Violet said, trying to sound cheerful. She knew this should be good news. But somehow Violet felt like her sister was showing her up.

Later that day, Violet stood outside Caribbean Circus, trying to summon her courage. She had managed to avoid Nigel in the bustle of the evening show with the guest burlesque troupe, but the daytime shows were full of little kids. Even when the place was packed, they could still see each other across the crowded room.

She stood up straight and walked in. She didn't see him in the main room or backstage in the dressing rooms. She thanked God for her good fortune and began to set up her makeup station.

Half an hour later, she was making up a slender South Asian woman from Guyana. Violet had pulled out the fuchsia lipstick, but the dancer had red tones in her skin, so it was too pink. She went for a slightly more orange tone, and it looked great.

"Can you make the foundation extra thick to cover the scar?" she asked, indicating a red patch near her eye.

"I can," Violet said, "but let me try something else." She pulled out her finest brush. "If you don't like it, I can change it."

Lovingly, painstakingly, she transformed the irregularly shaped mark into a bird of paradise flower.

When she had finished, the young woman looked in the mirror. Tears sprang to her eyes.

"It's beautiful!" she said. "Oh, I better not cry and spoil it!" She gave Violet an impromptu kiss on her cheek, leaving a smear of orange-red lipstick.

Violet didn't realize about the lip print until after she had made up all of the dancers. Nigel came in and remarked, "Somebody likes you a lot."

Violet laughed and wiped at the print with a tissue. "Occupational hazard," she said.

Then she reached into her bag and handed him several small pieces of paper. They were sketches she had done for the set design for their next show.

"These are amazing," Nigel said. "Is this your thing? These little square pictures? I still have your set design for *The Wiz* somewhere in a box of stuff from Harvard."

"I guess, yeah, it's sort of my thing," Violet said.

The two of them stood for a moment, not speaking. Suddenly a burst of children's laughter came from the main room.

"Listen," Nigel said, "I don't want things to be awkward between us because of the other night."

"Awkward?" Violet scoffed. "Not at all." She waved a hand as if to brush the thought away.

"I just—" Nigel said. "Violet, I've always had the biggest crush on you. I didn't want to say anything that night because you'd been drinking, but I always regretted not making a move freshman year. And then you've been with Quentin ever since. Until now, I mean."

"Nigel, I—"

"I wasn't going to say anything because I'm your boss, so this is technically sexual harassment, but since you made that move I wouldn't be able to live with myself if I didn't say something now. I'm hoping it's what they say, *en vino hay verdad*—there's truth in wine."

"Nigel, Quentin and I just broke up a couple of days ago," she said.

"Look, I know it's really soon," he said. "Take all the time you want. Just know that I—really care about you."

"It's not just that," Violet said. "I—I still want Quentin back."

Nigel's mouth fell open. "You what?"

"I know," Violet said. "He had sex with Shelby and everything. But it's not like he cheated, because we were broken up—on a break—whatever. And I can't really blame him for thinking the worst. I mean, even the FBI suspects me. I'm not going to give up until I prove my innocence."

Nigel shook his head. "You shouldn't have to prove anything to anyone. He should know who you are and trust that."

Violet took a deep and shaky breath. "He and I have been together—were together—for so many years. We had a whole life planned out together. I'm not gonna give up on my dreams. Quentin only cheated because he thought I cheated. He would never have done that if it wasn't for that woman using my phone."

"So what about all the stuff you said the other night?" He looked directly at her. His gaze was intense, almost like he could see through her.

"I was just—" Violet couldn't meet his eyes. "I was just trying to get back at Quentin. I'm not proud of myself. The wine was talking. It was calling for revenge."

She glanced up at him and could see a sort of switch in his face. He grinned.

"Well," he said with a laugh, "I'm glad we got that cleared up. I'll go back to being your boss who doesn't talk about having feelings for you. But I gotta say, if there's a next time you're drunk and coming to me for revenge sex, I'm not gonna hesitate. Consider yourself warned." He gave her an exaggerated wink and walked out of the dressing room.

Violet slumped down into a chair. Could that have gone worse?

From the stage, she could hear Nigel's deep voice over the loudspeaker. "Ladies and gentlemen . . ."

Later that evening, Violet let herself into the Hughes house with Etta's spare key. She hated staying there. The guest room was nice enough. And Etta had bent over backward to make her feel welcome. But she couldn't stand depending on anyone. And all the unfamiliar surroundings were a constant reminder that her old life had burned down around her.

This time, to avoid going home, she had lingered in Brooklyn. She'd found a roti shop and eaten doubles—she hadn't realized how much she missed the taste of home. Quentin hadn't liked spicy, so they rarely ate Caribbean or even Indian food.

She sat at the counter and piled on the pepper sauce. Feeling the welcome burn on her tongue, tears fell from her eyes. She fanned her mouth and kept eating.

"Well, you certainly like it hot," a young man had slipped into the stool beside her.

"It reminds me of the pepper sauce my mother used to make," she said.

"You Trini?" he asked.

She nodded, wiping her nose from the pepper.

He was, too. They compared basic notes about when they came to New York. They talked and laughed as she drank sorrel to cool her mouth, sucking on the ice cubes when the burn outlasted the drink. There was an easy comfort with him. Just like there had been with Nigel, but now she had fucked that up. On the one hand, he was right, *en vino hay verdad.* Yes, she was attracted to him. Of course she was. Nigel was gorgeous. But she needed to get her life back. To get Quentin back.

"So what do you say?" the young man at the roti shop asked.

Violet blinked.

"Can I get your number?"

She smiled and shook her head. "I—I'm engaged" was what came out of her mouth. Hopefully soon it would be true again.

Other than Quentin, Violet had had only one boyfriend in high school. Dean had started at her prep school during senior year. He was from a liberal, middle-class family in Vermont, and his father had been recruited to chair the school's science department.

Dean had an instant crush on Violet and pursued her from the beginning of the year. Violet found him handsome but hadn't ever imagined herself with a white guy. The girls in her dorm seemed intent on setting her up with one of the black athletes. Violet was amenable, but the athletes seemed intent on ignoring the black girls.

A few boys had made advances, but they were clearly trying to live out some rap video fantasy. Dean was the first white boy who seemed interested in *her.*

His sister, a junior who lived in Violet's dorm, encouraged the match.

"Oh my god," she said in the hall one day. "My brother is dying a slow death of unrequited love. Would you throw him a bone, please?"

"I didn't—" Violet stammered. "But your father teaches here. Wouldn't he feel . . . your father, I mean . . . he wouldn't feel . . . uncomfortable about that?

"Why?" the girl asked. "Because you're black?"

"Well, there aren't a lot of black people where you're from in Vermont, are there?" Violet asked.

"Our parents don't give a damn about that kind of thing," the sister said. "Besides, he's not proposing. He's trying to take you out for pizza."

So Violet went out for pizza. Dean was funny and cute. He was smart and . . . liberal. She liked him. She liked kissing him. He wasn't her first kiss. That was a boy back home in Trinidad.

So Dean became her boyfriend, but she never went much further than kissing, even while girls were doing all kinds of sexual stuff at the school. She kept it strictly over the bra. Dean hadn't approached with a lurid interest in sex, but she wasn't going to be the subject of some white boy locker room talk.

She and Dean had a plan that she would go to Harvard and he would go to Yale. They could meet up on the weekends. But he didn't get in to Yale. She got in to both.

After that, something changed in him. He was cooler. She asked what was wrong, but got a refrain of "nothing."

One night, he went to a party and came by her dorm afterwards.

"I just wanned a goodnight kiss," he slurred. He reeked of beer.

"Are you drunk?" she asked.

"Just one little kiss, babe," he insisted.

"No," she said, and proceeded to close the door on him.

"What?" he yelled through the closed door. "You're too good to kiss me now? Cause you got into all the Ivies you wanted? It's probably just because you're black, you know?"

Maybe it was the beer talking, but he had said it aloud. The very thing so many students seemed to imply when they found out she was going to Harvard. They said, "Really?" And "Violet *Johnson*?" Their disbelief was obvious.

The next day, he said he couldn't remember any of it. But he apologized anyway. He saw how hard she worked. He knew she deserved those admission letters. He believed in her.

Over the summer, he pressed her to have sex before they went off to school.

She refused. They would make out sometimes in the shadows of the trees outside her dorm.

One afternoon, they were sitting on the bleachers out by the football field. He had his arm around her, and they looked out over the vast green landscape of the school.

"Violet, babe," he said, stroking her shoulder. "Don't you want us to have something special to remember each other?"

Below them, the football team trooped in to practice. They all had their backs to Violet and Dean. All straight hair, from blond to dark, except one black guy with a short natural. He was the star player. Never spoke a word to Violet in all four years.

She realized that she didn't want to have anything to remember this place. Least of all, sex with Dean. The sooner she left and forgot it, the better.

"I want to wait," she said.

"Come on," he coaxed. "Sometimes I wonder if you even like me. Why are we a couple if we don't really . . . do anything?"

"I'm just not ready," she said.

"Not ready?" he asked. "That island dance you showed me that one time? The way you moved your ass all around in a circle? You're obviously ready."

Violet's skin blazed hot from her hairline down to her collarbone.

"I should go study," she said. She stood up, shaking off his arm.

"Violet," he said, "we don't have to go all the way. Maybe you could dance for me and give me a hand job or something . . . ?"

Violet couldn't even respond. She just shook her head as she walked away.

He ran to catch up with her. "We're about to be in college," he said. "How long do you expect me to keep being your boyfriend if you treat this relationship like we're still in middle school?"

"If this is such a sacrifice for you, then maybe you shouldn't keep being my boyfriend," she said.

"Violet, I really like you," he said. "But you're acting so high and mighty since your Ivy League affirmative action victory."

His words stopped her in her tracks. He had said it aloud, without a drop of alcohol in his system.

"Come on," he said. "Show me that you're not just smart, that you're also sexy."

He reached out to take her arm. It was a cool afternoon, and she recoiled from his cold fingers.

"Idontwantobeyourgirlfriendanymore," she blurted, backing away from him.

"What?" he asked. "*You* are gonna break up with *me*? After I've been patient all this time?"

She turned and began to walk quickly back toward her dorm. Her arms were crossed over her chest, and her head was down, her face still flaming.

The rest of his words bounced off her back, not because they didn't hurt, but because they were anticlimactic after what he had already said.

"If I didn't know better," he said, "I would say you were acting like a stuck-up bitch."

He said other things, but by then she had walked too far, and the wind blew the words away in the space across the grass between his mouth and her ears.

The last word she heard from him was "bitch."

Later that evening, as she walked into her temporary home, she found Etta sitting in the living room with the white guy they had encountered at the FBI. He was introduced to her as Jared Simons, Teddy Hughes's former money guy.

"You haven't missed anything," Etta told Violet. "We're just getting started."

Jared regarded the two of them with a grim expression. "Last week you wouldn't return my calls. Now suddenly you want a meeting?" he said.

"Sorry," Etta said, "I thought you were in on it. At least, until I saw you at the FBI office."

"Where you told me to fuck myself and called me a garbage guy?"

"I know," Etta said. "But I'm not so crazed now, and I want to apologize."

"And what else?" Jared asked. "I know you must want something. I didn't come for your apology. I came because I want something, too."

"What?" Etta asked.

"Last week I wanted access," Jared said. "I wanted to see some of the records before the FBI seized them. They're incompetent and won't understand them."

"Why do you even care?" Violet asked.

"'Cause I want this asswipe caught," Jared said. "I can't move on with my life until he's brought to justice. I can't work because I've been blacklisted. I didn't get my law degree and MBA only to wait tables. Do you know how much debt I'm in?"

"Tell me about it," Violet said.

"So my only hope is to be the hero," Jared said. "Right now, I'm the money guy for the stripper king who ripped off the strippers and the investors, and might have been involved in the theft. If I solve it, I'm the genius inside man who brought him down. It plays better."

"I'm basically in the same position, professionally," Violet said. "Since the FBI suspects me of involvement, my reputation has been ruined in the circles I've been working in. I can't move on until I get references from people. And I can't get references until I clear my name."

"I thought you wanted to go back to Trinidad," Etta said.

"Only because I can't work here," Violet said.

"Okay," Jared said. "When we find him, we'll let you know and make sure the FBI clears you as well."

"What?" Violet asked. "No way. I'm in this as well. Finding Teddy Hughes and his mistress is my only goal right now."

"So I can see what you get out of it," Jared said. "But what do you bring to the table?"

"I owe her," Etta said. "They set her up, and I fell for it."

"This isn't some personal mission of mercy," he said. "We're trying to find someone who doesn't want to be found. Too many cooks in the kitchen. You bring access," he said to Etta. "I bring financial expertise. We need to just follow the money. I can work with the computerized financial data."

"You have a lot of nerve," Violet said. "You just walk in here and start giving orders. Maybe there are other reasons you're not getting a job, like a lack of social graces. We've already assembled a team, and we've been making plenty of progress without you. One of the other members brings the computer expertise."

"You think I don't know my way around a computer?" he asked.

"Would you know this image was photoshopped just by looking at it?" she asked, pulling out the hard copy of Teddy Hughes's screen saver.

"No," he admitted.

"It's not just about following the money," Violet said. "Our team already has a lead on where he might have gone."

"Okay, so what do you bring to the table?" he asked sarcastically. "Project management?"

"You are such an arrogant asshole, you know that?" Violet asked.

"So I've been told."

"I'm a makeup artist," Violet said.

"What does that have to do with anything?"

"That's what I bring to the table," she said firmly.

He laughed.

"Go ahead and laugh," she said. "But when we're trailing him somewhere in the third world, and we have to get close, you go in there with no makeup and see how far you get, with your lack of a tan. But I can make it so he doesn't even recognize his own wife."

"And I'll get in there and kick his ass," Etta said.

"Except it'll obviously have to be me going in," Violet said. "Because I'm the one he's never seen and the one he won't suspect. They'll be expecting all of you."

"Makeup, huh?" Jared said with a noncommittal shrug. "Okay, makeup. So when can we meet up with this computer expert?"

"She's coming to a breakfast meeting here tomorrow," Etta said.

"See you then," Jared said, standing up. "I hope you'll have coffee."

He walked out the door without a goodbye.

"What an arrogant creep," Violet said.

Etta shook her head. "Just Teddy's type of guy."

But there was something else Violet brought to the team. She had experience with break-ins. In high school, before she met Dean, the alienation was suffocating. Sometimes, especially in winter, she needed a quiet place to be. In warm seasons, she would just go outside and sketch for hours. But in winter, her dorm room became a prison. Her roommate often had loud and obnoxious friends over. The library was full of quiet studying, but when Violet drew, she didn't want people looking over her shoulder, gawking at her drawings. So Violet learned how to break into the art room. The student ID cards were too thick to slip the latch. Credit cards didn't quite work either, because the raised print interfered. Drivers licenses were too thin. But her resident alien card was perfect.

Most winter weekends, she would sneak into the academic building. But instead of heading into the library, she would creep down the corridor to the art room. Glancing up and down the hall to make sure it was empty, she would do her magic with her card and then lose herself in hours of drawing.

She only ran into trouble a few times. One Saturday, a custodian came in to clean. She hid in a supply closet. Another weekend, they had done a project with a chemical adhesive. The fumes were so bad that she had to find another classroom to work in. Besides, the windows were open to ventilate the room, so it was freezing anyway. Fortunately, her card worked on all the classrooms in the building. She decided to draw in the history classroom. She knew it also had a closet to hide in, in case anyone came in.

The biggest problem she encountered was one February weekend when a pair of students came in for a tryst.

It was sunset. Violet planned to pack up soon, but she was finishing her drawing by the last of the natural light. Suddenly, she heard the sound of a key in the lock. Stuffing her notebook into her pocket, she pulled on her coat and hid under one of the room's long tables.

From her hiding place, she could see a girl step into the room with a boy's hands over her eyes.

"Surprise!" he said. "Happy Valentine's Day."

The girl laughed, delighted. "How did you get in here?" she asked.

"With a key I need to return by dinnertime," he said. "Now come here."

The couple began to make out. They were in the center of the room, and Violet was under a table against the window. Violet removed gloves and a dark wool cap from her pocket. She put on the gloves and pulled the cap down low over her face.

The girl had brought a yoga mat, and she laid it out on the floor. When the couple lay down on the floor, Violet slipped out from her hiding place. She carefully crept on top of the table and opened the window. The handle of the old frame made a creaking noise, but fortunately, the pair was making out so ardently, they apparently didn't notice.

However, when Violet pushed the window open, an icy blast of cold air came in.

And as she slid out the window, she heard the girl ask, "Why is it cold all of a sudden?"

Violet glanced up over her shoulder. She saw the dim figure of the boy through the open window. In the evening dusk, with the cap pulled low, there was no way he would be able to identify her. The snow all around her glowed with the reflection of the sun's final rays. It silhouetted her, a lone figure running down along the side of the building, dark from head to toe.

The next morning, Violet woke to the smell of coffee. She wondered, was Etta really brewing up French roast for Jared? How did assholes like that get the whole damn world to do their bidding?

But by the time she got downstairs, she realized that Serena had brought the coffee. She had arrived with compostable tureens of caf and decaf.

"God bless you, child," Etta said and poured herself a cup.

Serena had on a long, coral-colored dress, with a plunging neckline. "I'm going to a wedding," Serena said. "No time to waste getting everyone caffeinated."

"I take my coffee black," Etta said. "But help yourself to milk if you want it. Fridge is through there."

Serena headed into the kitchen.

Violet had had trouble sleeping and selected decaf. As she was stirring sugar into it, there was a knock at the door.

Etta answered it, and Jared walked in with the blond woman they'd seen at the FBI, her mouth twisted into an expression of distaste.

"This is Lee Wellington," he said.

Etta returned the distasteful look. "She was Teddy's secretary."

"Executive assistant," Lee corrected.

"Whatever," Etta said.

Serena walked in from the kitchen with a pint of half and half.

Jared blinked. "You're the computer expert?"

Serena laughed. "And today I'm also a bridesmaid," she said. "Let's get to it."

Half an hour later, they had three laptops open. On one, the executive assistant was downloading Teddy Hughes's calendar from the cloud. She had insisted Teddy had wiped the calendar and that there was no backup, but Serena had worked her magic and recovered it. On another computer, Etta and Violet were looking for real estate information. On the third, Serena and Jared were looking at financials.

"He drained the account," Jared was saying. "But this was the balance before he skipped town."

"Where does this transfer go to?" Serena asked. "Have you identified all of his accounts?"

"I've got statements for six of them," Jared said.

"On the home laptop, I was able to reconstruct data for nine different accounts," Serena said.

Jared's eyes widened. "Nine? That's amazing."

Serena shrugged. "Not if you know where to look." She pulled out a sticky note. "I wrote them all down."

Jared smiled at her. "I don't think I've ever seen a hacker bridesmaid before."

"Jared," Lee interrupted, "I need your help verifying something." She had lost the grimace and offered the finance guy a high-wattage smile.

"Speaking of bridesmaids," Serena said, "I gotta go."

"Let me get those account numbers," Jared said.

Serena looked from Jared to Lee to Etta. "I'm not sure of the chain of command here," she said. "But I work for Etta. No offense, but I just met you."

"No offense taken," he said, taking her hand. "It was great to meet you. I'm impressed."

Serena took her hand back. "I won't be impressed til the workers get their money back and Violet's name is clear," she said. "Keep me updated."

She swept out in a flash of coral.

Both Jared and Lee looked after her.

"What was it you needed me to help with?" Jared asked.

"I forget," Lee said, her mouth back in the scornful twist.

Two hours later, Lee had compiled all of the notes from Teddy's schedule that were outside of his normal activities. Violet, Etta, and Jared were looking over them.

"So what are we looking for?" Etta asked.

"Just use your insider knowledge to identify what these are," Violet said. "We're looking for anything that connects to the Caribbean, that would give us a clue to where he went. Jared, I'm assuming that you'll look for things that have financial implications. Etta, you'll be trying to identify stuff that only a wife would know."

Etta gave a bitter chuckle. "Like 'Lunch with Ernest'?"

"I guess," Lee said. "Who's Ernest?"

Etta shook her head. "There is no Ernest. That's his code for getting waxed."

"Teddy got waxing done?" Lee asked.

"His back and his sack," Etta said.

Jared made a slight involuntary gasp between his teeth that was a sort of hiss.

Violet rolled her eyes. This was all the wrong kind of information.

"What about Peggy?"

"That's a mani-pedi," Etta said.

"A pedi with Peggy?" Lee asked.

"Of course not," Etta said. "The women were Vietnamese, and he just went with whoever was free. He never bothered to ask names. We went together sometimes."

"Okay, who's Val Barber?" Lee asked.

"That one's straightforward," Etta said. "The barber. And Val colored his hair. You don't think he was still a natural brunette, do you? That man would have been totally gray."

"If it comes down to it," Violet said, "we can use that to help track him in the islands."

"Good point," Etta said. "Because I know he's not gonna let his young side chick dye his hair. She's the one he's trying to look young for."

"No offense, but she's a bit more than a side chick now, don't you think?" Lee asked.

"You side chick types are always keeping hope alive," Etta said.

"Hey," Lee started.

"Ladies," Jared said, "can we please focus?"

"Fine," Lee said. "How about this meeting around breakfast time with Rocky?"

Etta's eyes flew wide. "Rocky?" she said, a slight catch in her voice. "He had an appointment with Rocky?"

"Who's Rocky?" Violet asked.

Etta stood up and walked out of the room.

"Where the hell is she going?" Lee asked.

"I think she needs a minute," Violet said.

"Well, I'm not going to sit around while some prima donna—" Lee began.

"Give her a break, Lee," Jared said.

"Oh, come on, Jare," she said, using a nickname he clearly didn't like much. "You used to talk so much shit about her when she would come into the office."

"Yeah, but that was partly because of all the shit Teddy talked about her. I'm not convinced he was painting an accurate picture," Jared said. "Also, my dad dumped my mom for a younger woman. She had put him through school and supported his career for decades. It's a douchebag move."

Lee shook her head. "I know her type. Jealous. Controlling. Suspects every woman within a five-foot range of her man."

"Don't act like you weren't interested when you first started working for him," Jared said.

"My relationship with Teddy Hughes was strictly professional," Lee said.

"Yeah," Jared said with a chuckle, "when you realized his clients were the ones with the bigger money."

"Sorry about that," Etta announced, walking back in. "I went ahead and put a pizza in the oven for us. It's just about lunchtime."

"So can you tell us who Rocky is?" Violet asked gently.

Etta sat back down on the couch, deflated. "Rocky was

our nickname for my engagement ring." She spread the fingers of her left hand, and the large gem sparkled on her third finger. "It was also sort of code for diamonds in general."

"He bought the side chick some diamonds?" Lee asked.

"Which store?" Jared asked.

"Does it matter?" Etta asked.

"Yes," Violet said. "Because maybe it wasn't for her. Maybe he was converting the money to diamonds so he could transport it."

"That's exactly what I was thinking," Jared said.

"Let's cross-reference the credit card receipts with the date and see what we have," Violet suggested.

Fifteen minutes later, they were eating pizza, and Lee found the charge on one of Etta's credit cards.

"Mendel Brothers Jewelers," she said. "Four hundred fifty dollars."

"That's all?" Etta said. "Then it won't last with her. He didn't spend any real money."

"Maybe it was just a down payment," Lee said.

"Either way," Etta said. "So much for the converting to diamonds theory."

"Not really," Jared said. "There's a chain jewelry store near the office. Why didn't he go there? Mendel Brothers was a hike across town, but they would trade in more wholesale stones. He might have gone to do both."

"Or he might have bought something for the mistress as a cover," Violet suggested.

"So the amount he spent on her might not reflect his feelings for her," Lee said.

"Lee," Jared said, "can you please give it a rest?"

Violet took a last bite of pizza. "Argue all you want," she said. "I'm going to see the Mendel brothers."

Jared shook his head. "They won't talk to you," he said.

"But they'll talk to you?" she asked.

"Is it a Jewish thing?" Lee asked. "Are you Jewish?"

"Armenian," Jared said. "But I know someone who used to do a lot of business with them. And he owes me a favor."

That night, when Jimmy, the investor, came into the One-Eyed King, Lily groaned out loud from her perch on the pole. He'd been coming in every night since he and Etta had signed the promissory note, getting drunk and loud. Just as she'd suspected.

In her experience, when men paid for things, they got entitled. Even if it was just a loan. Even after it was paid back, with interest. It was as if the guy had a GIF in his head of the moment when he had put the money in her hand, and it ran on a loop, as if he was forever paying and she was forever indebted.

Up until that point, he'd always come in with a pale and kind of drugged-out friend who was quiet and drank tall glasses of straight rum. A sort of ghostlike yes-man. Jimmy would point to one of the dancers and yell, "Chuco, I know you wanna tap that ass!" The friend—presumably Chuco—stayed silent. Jimmy would pat him on the back with one of his creepy chuckles, as if his friend had agreed. But Chuco seemed to be in it for the drinks.

Tonight, however, the ghost-friend was nowhere in sight, and Jimmy walked in with two guys who were anything but quiet. One was short, and the other one tall; they both had shades on. One wore a trench coat, although the weather was completely clear outside. Lily bet that he had opened up the seam in the pocket and would be jerking off during the show. Asshole.

She kept her eye on the trench coat guy, which was why she was late to realize the other guy was fixated on Hibiscus. He was lurking around the champagne room, and when Hibiscus came out to give a customer a lap dance, he grabbed her ass. Lily was dancing above one of her regulars, but she rushed over to intervene.

Hibiscus's customer was ready to make it about him. "Hey, man—" he started, but Lily cut him off.

"Back off," Lily said. "This is a no-touching club. That includes lap dances. And if you want one, you need to wait your turn." At six feet, Lily was nearly a head taller than Hibiscus. In her high heels, she towered over the guy.

"I just wanted to make sure that ass was real," he said.

"That's right, Hector," Jimmy said with a locker-room laugh. "Sometimes you just gotta check, right?"

The friend in the trench coat laughed along.

"What any of our asses feel like is not your business," Lily said. "Even in a strip club, we can get you thrown out for harassment."

"Harassment?" Hector said. "Listen, bitch, that was me getting friendly. You don't want to know what me harassing looks like."

"Security!" Lily called and pressed an alarm button on the wall.

"Come on now," Jimmy said to Lily. "Don't be like that."

"You mad or something?" Hector asked Lily. "You mad 'cause I don't want you? You ain't got the type of ass I wanna feel; you got the type of ass I wanna kick. Too much coffee and not enough cream."

Lily tilted her head. "Well, you got the type of ass that's about to get thrown out of this club."

A tall, heavyset Dominican woman strode over to them. "What seems to be the problem?"

Hector rolled his eyes. "You can call off your bull-dagger," he said. "We're leaving."

Hector made a big show of pushing past both Lily and the security guard, with Jimmy and the trench coat guy in tow.

Hibiscus gave Lily a grateful look.

Her customer piped up. "If your girl hadn't stopped me, I woulda knocked his ass out. These niggas is so rude, baby. A fine lady like you deserves to be treated right."

"You okay?" Lily asked Hibiscus.

She nodded and took her customer over to a chair for a lap dance.

Lily watched as Jimmy and his two friends strode out. Sure enough, she could see trench coat guy re-arrange his junk through the coat. Nasty.

Tara rushed over to Lily and the guard. "I snapped a picture of that asshole on the way out. We'll put him on the no entry list."

"Tell your girlfriend to start cutting Jimmy checks every time he comes in," Lily said.

"She'll make him sign for them," Tara said.

Lily nodded. "We need to pay him back ASAP," she said.

"Are you okay?" Tara asked. "What he said to you was pretty fucked up."

"Oh that color shit?" Lily asked with a dry chuckle. "I been in this racist-ass business too long to get the least bit bent outta shape by any of that."

Lily shrugged and went back to her customer. But as she shimmied above his chair, she couldn't help but feel that their trouble was just beginning.

Lily hadn't always been immune to the vicious slice of colorism. At nineteen she had been nearly a year in New York and had just started stripping. It still felt luxurious, opulent. The money. The glamour. The attention from men. Of course, she wasn't every man's type, but there were plenty of men who would walk right past the slim blondes and head straight for her stage. She towered over them like some sort of black goddess, collecting their bills as tribute.

She wasn't the Malibu Barbie girl-next-door type who had mass appeal in the US, but she carefully built a niche clientele. She made her money and didn't worry about what other girls were doing.

The first club where she worked was huge and had lots of VIPs. Finance guys. Politicians. Lawyers. Artists. Half the US celebrities were still unknown to her. And what did it matter, anyway? You had to be white or Latina to dance in VIP. Or mixed and really light. Some of the American black women complained about it, but Lily just shrugged it off. Compared to Trinidad, everything here seemed to have white people in the center of it.

Until one night, she recognized the man in the middle of a knot of women in VIP.

Even sitting he was tall. Six foot six. Dark as mahogany. Strapping as fuck. Mirrored shades on his face with a full-lipped scowl. She stopped, faltered. The Jamaican dancehall legend. Bumboozala.

Throughout her teens, he dominated the dancehall

charts throughout the US and the Caribbean. In particular, his YOLO anthem, "Mi do wah mi want," had been her theme song in high school. It brought back the taste of house parties she'd snuck out to, clandestine kisses, and the first time a boy had gone down on her.

And there he was. Just on the other side of the velvet rope. In the club where she worked. He was impossible to miss, in the crush of white and barely-brown women, honey and platinum and strawberry blonde hair.

Because he had on the mirrored shades, she couldn't see the moment when he noticed her, but she did see him stand up, and walk toward her.

Her eyes must have widened. She had on a bikini top with her full breasts spilling out, and a matching thong bottom. She had a line of rhinestones from below her bottom lip to her navel.

She had felt dazzling when she got dressed. But not nearly as dazzled as when Bumboozala stood up and walked over to her. He knocked the rope aside.

"A watta guwaan yasso?" He turned to his handlers and demanded to know where they had been hiding Lily. He removed his shades, walked over, and sidled up close to her. At six feet plus her heels, she stood eye to eye with him. He whispered about sending these skinny, pale girls off the couch so he could have a lap dance with her.

She flushed with delight. He asked her name in that deep, rumbling voice of his. His breath smelled of marijuana and hard liquor.

"Lily," came out of her mouth before she could even stop herself, could offer her stage name: Cleopatra.

He grinned at her and began to walk her into his booth. The other girls didn't like it. With every additional dancer who came in, the tips had to be split one more way.

But before she could step past the rope, a security guard rolled up and blocked her way.

"Sorry, she doesn't work VIP," he said to the artist.

Bumboozala turned his head slowly. "Weh yuh seh?"

"I'm very sorry, sir," the security guard said. "Company policy. She's got a shift on the floor below."

It was true. But Lily knew better. VIPs like Bumboozala could make their own rules. She waited for him to say it. The nearly patented phrase that had dominated the airwaves when she was fifteen. The phrase that she and her friends had said to each other, unsuccessfully mimicking that deep voice: "mi do wah mi want."

Lily's lip had already begun to curl toward the smirk of triumph, when he stepped her past the velvet rope and claimed her, like his queen. The two of them tall and dark against the red couch, the gold wallpaper, the other pale girls.

That was what humiliated her the most. Her hand lifted to him. Expecting him to take it. She hadn't even noticed her arm rising. The split second she forgot her place in the strip club in the US. The moment she fell into the fantasy that this strong man would rescue her, elevate her above all other women. She heard the music in her head. The throbbing bass of his song, and expected the lyrics to fall from his mouth.

Mi do wah mi want.

But he didn't say it. Just shrugged. Put his shades back on. Returned to the couch. Left her standing there. A line of rhinestones from beneath her lower lip to her navel. Her hand extended just enough that she couldn't play it off. Hadn't been thirsty and left high and dry.

Instead, it was the girls on the couch whose lips curved in smug smiles. One less dancer to share with. Their positions unthreatened by this dusky intruder.

Lily didn't dance on the downstairs stage that night. She turned on her six-inch heels and strode away from Bumboozala's booth directly to the dressing room. Back ramrod straight and ass switching with vengeance. She got dressed and walked off the job, tears gumming her false eyelashes in the taxi on the way home.

She never went back to that club. Could never face those smirking girls again. She heard they were hiring at the One-Eyed King.

The following day, Etta, Jared, and Violet were in the back room at Mendel Brothers Jewelers. The proprietor was a Hasidic Jew; he wore a dark suit and hat and a white shirt, and he had perfect graying ringlets on either side of his head.

Jared was sitting across from Mendel. Violet and Etta sat farther back from the desk.

"I know you don't disclose anything about your clients," Jared said. "But you understand that this client has skipped town and is wanted by the police and the FBI."

"Not my concern," Mendel said. "He didn't steal anything from me."

"Of course," Jared said. "But we know he came here shortly before he left town with a large sum of money."

"All he bought here was the bracelet you already know about," Mendel said.

"Are you sure he didn't have another transaction where he converted a large sum of cash into diamonds?"

"I'm sure," Mendel said.

"We have a large unexplained amount of cash that was wired into an account that we think can be traced back to you," Jared said.

Mendel shook his head. "You're bluffing. We deal in

cash only for that kind of thing. Go look for a big cash deposit, and you won't find it. He didn't convert any money to diamonds here. Only a tacky bracelet."

Etta smiled when she heard the word "tacky."

"You would do well to tell us the truth, my friend," Jared said. "You wouldn't want the FBI and police to come asking questions."

"Send them," Mendel said. "There's no crime in selling diamond jewelry to people with no taste."

"We're still combing through his financial records," Jared said. "If we do find a large withdrawal, we'll send the authorities."

Mendel smiled. "Then I have nothing to worry about."

That evening, Serena came by after work. Jared and Lee had just arrived, and they sat around with Violet and Etta, laptops open.

Violet continued with her mission: she was looking through photos on other stripper websites, hoping to find the woman who had used her phone.

Serena walked in and set her large purse on the coffee table. "I looked for big cash withdrawals but couldn't find anything," she said.

"So maybe he did just buy her that bracelet," Jared said.

"The 'tacky' bracelet," Etta said. "Adjectives make all the difference." She was slurring a bit, and pronounced the *j* in adjective a bit like a *sh*.

She had been drinking steadily since they came back from the diamond store around noon. Violet had gone to the gym and worked out, and when she came back much later that afternoon, the brandy bottle was nearly empty.

"I need some dinner," Jared announced.

"I think I need a nap," Etta said.

"There's a great Turkish place around the corner that delivers," Serena said.

"Nobody to bug me in the bed these days," Etta said. "The naps are much better." *Much* sounded like *mush.*

"I love Turkish food," Jared said. "Do they make a good *gözleme*?"

"Really good," Serena said.

Violet came over, and they pulled up the menu on the laptop. Violet had never had Turkish food, so she let Serena order for her. Lee just got a salad.

While they waited for the restaurant delivery, Lee opened a bottle of wine and poured herself a glass.

Forty-five minutes later, when the food arrived, Jared and Serena still had their heads together over one of the laptops. By then, Lee had drained half the bottle of wine.

"Yeah, but where did that five thousand go?" Jared asked Serena.

"You can't just search for all of it," Serena said. "Looks like he broke it down into three different, smaller deposits when he moved it. And did it over a few days."

"Food's here," Lee announced.

"I'll get it in a minute," Jared said, not even looking up.

Lee drained her glass.

Violet looked up from her laptop. "I'm ready for a break," she said. "I swear I'd eat my shoe as a distraction from looking at photographs of strippers right now."

"Strippers," Lee complained. "I broke up with my fiancé because he blew too much money on strip clubs." She opened up several of the containers, looking for her salad. "I learned my lesson."

She poured a glass of wine for Violet.

"So what's the moral of the story? Get a man who isn't into strippers?" Violet asked, taking the wine and opening the takeout containers.

"No," Lee said. "Get a man who has more money. A big spender night at the strip club shouldn't make even the slightest dent in a man's wealth."

Violet looked up from the container of hummus, surprised.

"Don't be naïve," Lee said. "All men are like dogs. Marilyn Monroe's character said it in *Gentlemen Prefer Blondes*: 'It's just as easy to fall in love with a rich man as a poor man.' "

"I don't know," Violet said. "I guess I've never been in love with a poor man."

Now it was Lee's turn to be surprised. "Really?" she said. "I hadn't pegged you as the type."

"I don't know what type I am," Violet said. "I didn't set out to fall in love with an income. It just happened."

"But it's not like you didn't know," Lee said.

"Not at first," Violet said, taking a drink of wine. "I mean, we were in college. We lived in the same dorm. He didn't have a car. Everybody's life looked much more the same on the surface. It took a while to see the differences."

"And when you did?" Lee asked, spearing a cucumber with her fork. "Admit it. It was exciting when you first found out he was rich."

"I—" Violet swirled the wine around in her glass. "I guess in a way it was. But it was also intimidating. Would his family like me? Would they think I was good enough?"

"Of course not," Lee said. "The family never approves. They want someone just like them. That's how those royals all get so pale and inbred."

"Well, his family wasn't pale," Violet said. "He was black."

"Good for you," Lee said, taking another bite of her salad.

"I don't know how good it was," Violet said. "He dumped me when we hit a bump in the road."

"That's the problem with these rich guys," Lee said. "They got no loyalty. Everything comes easy to them. You get old? You make trouble? You have a personal need that inconveniences them? They trade you in."

"You sound like you've been there," Violet said, chewing a mouthful of eggplant.

"I won't lie," Lee said. "I did think about it with Teddy Hughes."

Violet stuck out her tongue in a gesture of disgust.

"You know the worst part about it," Lee confided, refilling their glasses.

"No," Violet said. "Tell me."

"The worst part about it," Lee said, "is that you're so busy chasing the rich old guys that you don't see the up-and-coming guys who are gonna be rich soon enough."

"Not really my situation," Violet said. "I guess my man was the son of the rich guy, so he was always trying to prove himself. He was never really the one with the money. He was always trying to make daddy happy. So, really, we were both trying to be good enough."

"This one guy," Lee said. "He wasn't that old. He was pretty hot and had money. Things were getting serious. I thought he was gonna propose. But then, after Teddy did his little disappearing act, he stopped taking my calls. Like it was my fault or something." She drained her glass. "I was just the damn secretary."

"I know," Violet said. "We're all like Teddy's collateral damage. We just happened to be in the wrong place at the wrong time."

"But I'll tell you what my mistake was," Lee said,

leaning closer to Violet, her voice moist in her ear. "When I first started working for Teddy, Jared asked me out. I said no and kept it strictly professional." Her *strictly* came out as *strigly*.

Violet nodded solemnly and refilled her glass.

"I thought he was too small-time," Lee said. "But now I'm reconsidering. He's the only one who's stood by me." She looked over at Jared, who was sitting closely with Serena, looking at something on the laptop.

"Loyalty," said Violet. "A lost art."

An hour later, Serena and Jared had finally started eating, but Violet and Lee were working their way through a second bottle of wine. They had moved into sharing particular anecdotes.

"Or like when something spills?" Violet said. "And you have to stop yourself from cleaning it, because you remember, oh yeah, I'm supposed to act like I'm used to having a maid."

"Yeah," Lee said. "Your job is to take care of him. He wouldn't want you to waste one single second thinking about anything but his needs."

"And then the maid comes in," Violet went on. "And you wanna chat with her, because you're so fucking bored by day five in this luxury resort, because you don't know anyone and you don't have business to do during the day like he does. And you're having the best conversation that you've had with the maid, and you want to make her your new best friend, but then you remember, oh, she has a job. You can't just be taking up her whole afternoon."

"Right?" Lee said. "What the fuck?"

"Hey, I have a question," Serena said, interrupting their girl talk session.

"Go ahead," Violet said. She tried to look alert, despite feeling tipsy.

"So, other than the strippers who worked for him, where would Teddy Hughes meet women?" Serena asked.

"Please tell us," Violet begged Lee. "I can't keep looking at these stripper photos."

"Were there women couriers who came to the office?" Serena asked. "Was there a woman who delivered food from his favorite restaurant?"

"He always went out to lunch," Jared said.

"Hawkies," Lee said.

"That Midtown restaurant with the nearly naked waitresses?" Violet said, suddenly alert. "Why didn't you tell us?"

"I thought everyone knew that," Lee said.

"He never took me," Jared said. "That asshole."

"Really?" Serena said to Jared in a deadpan. "We get a big clue, and you feel left out 'cause he didn't take you to the titty restaurant?"

"I told you," Lee said. "Men are all dogs."

"Will everybody just shut up?" Violet said, uncharacteristically bold after all the alcohol. "Where is this damn place? I need to try and find this bitch who stole my life."

"I don't think so," Serena said. "You've had a few too many. Why don't you go take a little nap like Etta?"

"Maybe I'll take a nap, too," Lee said. "Jared, let's go take a nap."

Serena raised an eyebrow.

"No thanks, Lee," Jared said. "Let me call you a car."

"You coming with me?" Lee asked.

"Sorry, you live in Queens," Jared said. "I'm gonna go check out Hawkies."

"I don't live far from Lee," Serena said. "We can share a Lyft."

"I thought we might go check out Hawkies together," Jared said.

Serena shook her head. "Not tonight. Text me if you find anything."

As Serena walked the wobbly Lee out the door, the drunk woman called back. "And I'll text you to make sure I got home safe, Jared."

Violet didn't hear if he answered her. She locked the door behind them and made her own way to bed.

If Violet had known from the beginning that Quentin was rich, it probably would have scared her off. But she had begun dating him within a month of her arrival at college. People kept calling him a legacy. This apparently meant that his father and grandfather had gone to the school before him. But none of this really registered with Violet as having to do with money.

Dating him was just one more part of the magic of her Harvard experience. She had a black best friend—Shelby—and a black boyfriend. Other black students complained about the white people, but after the boarding school experience, Harvard was like a black Mecca. She even ran into black people on the street near the campus who had no affiliation with the university. She joined all the black organizations, and the Caribbean Club took them on a long T ride to get Jamaican food in a neighborhood called Mattapan.

Quentin was two years ahead of her, so not only was he a boyfriend, but sort of a mentor as well. He made her feel secure and confident. Unlike with Dean, she never had to wonder if she was some sort of sexual novelty, some sort of category on a list. When they kissed, Quentin was patient. He said he loved her, so nothing they ever did together could be dirty or wrong. Her virginity was a flower. Beautiful. Precious. He would never pressure her.

She was able to get the pill effortlessly at the university's health services office. They were having sex by mid-October.

She didn't realize his family was rich until November.

They were on the train to New York City for Thanksgiving when he slipped into what she called his I-need-to-tell-you-something voice.

"So I should warn you a little about my family," he said.

Violet had never been to New York before. Were they some sort of criminals?

"We have—" he began. "A—sort of—we've got a level of affluence—"

Affluence. Violet knew what the word meant. Quentin was rich? How could that be? Wouldn't it be something she would have noticed? He lived in a dorm like everyone else. His room had the standard single bed.

She had so many questions for him but could tell it wasn't something she could ask about. She hoped he would clarify—maybe say more about it, but he had quickly moved on.

"My dad is going to love you," Quentin said. "He'll probably make some slightly inappropriate comments about how pretty you are and ask how I was able to snag a beauty like you."

"He teases you?" Violet asked.

"You could call it that," Quentin said. "My dad's an asshole, and his goal is humiliation. He was all ready to rub my sister's nose in it when she didn't pass the bar the first time. After all, it took him two tries. But then she passed. He's still mad about it. Served him right. Arrogant fucker. But she's not coming to Thanksgiving this year, so he'll take it out on me."

"Ugh," Violet said. "Sounds terrible."

"I want them to like you," Quentin said. "So don't worry about me. Play along with him a little, okay?"

"Okay," Violet said. "If you say so."

"But not too much," Quentin said. "Or my mother will get jealous. She'll probably be a little jealous anyway. Nobody's good enough for her baby boy."

"But how will I be able to get on the good side of both your parents?" Violet asked.

"I don't know," Quentin said. "But if you figure it out, tell me."

It was a good thing that Quentin had warned her that his family was wealthy and their home was opulent. Otherwise, Violet would have spent the first hour gaping at the four-floor Manhattan apartment that looked like it belonged in a magazine.

Instead, she ignored the marble floors and the crystal chandeliers, the Han dynasty vase, as well as the modern décor. She simply shook his mother's cool hand and said, "So pleased to meet you, Mrs. Ross." It was literally the softest hand she'd ever touched.

The next morning, Violet woke up and checked Jared's Twitter account. She found a late-night tweet:

Went looking for an old friend last night. Phone disconnected/email bounced back. Went by her job. No sign of her in employee photos on wall.

They had agreed not to discuss any details over the usual communication channels. You never knew if the FBI would be monitoring.

"Maybe it's a dead end," Etta said. "Or maybe they just keep their photo wall current. It's still our best lead."

"So should we just go in with her picture and ask if she used to work there?" Violet asked:

"I wouldn't," Etta said. "These places can be funny about giving out info. Guys stalk these girls sometimes."

"I'm obviously not a guy," Violet said.

"Obviously," Etta said. "But you could be a crazy ex-girlfriend. Or some guy could have paid you to get info. You never know."

Etta sprayed nonstick oil into a skillet and poured in some egg whites. "I think one of us should go in posing as a waitress looking for work," she said.

"One of us?" Violet said, sarcastically. "I wonder which one of us you mean."

"I'd go," Etta said. "But they only hire young women. Maybe we could get Lee to go. Or Serena."

"Serena's busy with her real job," Violet said. "And I don't trust Lee. I'll go."

"You want breakfast," Etta asked.

"No thanks," Violet said. "In a place like that, I might throw it up."

A couple of hours later, she stepped off the subway in one of Etta's skimpy dresses.

"Damn, girl," one young man said as she rose above ground.

On the two-block walk to the restaurant, she got a whistle, a hiss, a "Hey, sexy," and a white construction worker yelled, "Nice ass."

Violet rolled her eyes. The last guy was practically a cliché.

And so was the restaurant. The hostesses all had on

red booty shorts and tank tops that showed half their breasts. The red vinyl of the booths matched their outfits.

"Excuse me," Violet said to the perky blond hostess. "I heard one of your girls left and you have an opening?"

"Oh yeah, Chloe left a week ago," the young woman said. "How did you hear about it?"

Chloe? Violet's heart beat faster at the name that might belong to the woman who stole her life. *Chloe.*

"A friend of a friend was telling me," Violet said, trying to appear nonchalant. "Complaining that she left without notice or something. To be honest, I was a little drunk when we were all hanging out. Is the position still open?"

"No, we filled it," the hostess said. "But if you drop off your résumé and photos, we'll call you if there's another opening."

"Thanks," Violet said. "Is there a lot of turnover?"

"Yeah," the hostess shrugged. "But usually they give notice. Chloe just didn't show up one day and then sent a postcard." She indicated a bulletin board in the foyer.

As the hostess greeted a pair of college jock types, Violet made her way out.

She looked at the card on the board. *Keep servin it up hot, bitches! —Chloe.*

Violet took note of the date, and the zip code, 11430. She looked it up on the train ride home and found out it included JFK airport.

"Only thousands of flights a day," Violet said when she got back to the house.

"Yeah, but at least now we know her first name and the day she left," Etta said. "Good work."

"That's assuming it's the right person," Violet said.

"Obviously, we need more information," Etta said. "Maybe Serena can look into it."

Violet texted Serena.

I waited for Chloe at the restaurant, but she never showed. Can you contact her?

Serena texted back.

I'll see what I can find. Let's connect tonight.

That evening, the team met up again at Etta's. Serena came by the house to admit defeat. "I couldn't hack into their payroll records," she said.

"They have that much security?" Violet asked.

Serena laughed. "Hardly. But their personnel system is some kind of dinosaur. Sometimes, when a company has a lot of turnover, they don't bother to computerize. I can only assume they have hard copy files."

"Someone needs to break in there and get her full name and info," Etta said.

"And you should get a photo of her while you're at it," Jared said to Violet.

"Why me?" said Violet. "How come you don't want to be the one to stick your neck out?"

"Other than makeup, this is what you bring to the table, isn't it?" Jared asked. "The ability to recognize the girl?"

"I'll help," Serena said. "I can pick the lock and disable the alarm system."

"I thought you only did cyber crimes," Jared said.

"I'm a woman of many talents," Serena said.

Later that night, Violet learned that restaurants that feature half-naked women stay open very late. She had slept poorly the night before and was somewhat hungover that morning. She had tried to take a nap but was too wired with anxiety, as she prepared to commit a crime. Not just breaking into a classroom to be alone, but an actual crime. Here she was trying to prove she *hadn't* committed a crime, but now she would be committing one to try to document her innocence.

So 3:30 AM found her nervous and exhausted, wired and bitter, jumpy and ashamed. She and Serena had gone to the restaurant near closing time and slipped down the back hallway.

An EMPLOYEES ONLY sign hung on the door past the pair of restrooms. Serena knocked on the office door, but the only sound was the techno music playing in the restaurant.

"Stand lookout for me," Serena said to Violet. "Cough if anyone comes."

Violet walked back up the hallway and peered around the corner into the nearly deserted restaurant. At the office door, Serena was kneeling, using a pair of lock picks.

As Violet stood lookout, she tried to visualize Quentin's face. Him telling her how sorry he was, how he should have trusted her all along.

"Yes!" Serena whispered as the tumbler clicked.

She swung the door open, and the two of them crept across the dark room. Violet opened up the office closet, and it looked rarely used. There was a pile of uniforms, each wrapped in plastic. If you could even call them uniforms. They were made with an amount of fabric that meant they were closer to underwear. There must have been hundreds of them to make a pile large enough for her to hide behind.

"I doubt they'll look in here tonight," Serena whispered. "What do you think?"

Violet just nodded and slid down behind the pile.

Serena stood on a nearby crate and unscrewed the lightbulb a quarter turn, just for good measure.

"Sound the alarm if you get into any trouble," Serena whispered, and Violet nodded, checking her phone. Serena's number was on speed dial.

Then Violet heard rather than saw the closing of the closet door, and for a brief minute the tinny techno of the club was louder as Serena opened and closed the office door.

She sat in silence for the next hour until her phone lit up.

Serena texted:

Looks like they're totally closed up. Lights off. Grate down. Everyone out.

Violet made her way out of her hiding place. Even with the restaurant totally shut down, she didn't want to risk turning on a light, so she used a penlight.

In the office, she found several locked file cabinets. She used the lock picks like Serena had showed her. Eventually, she was able to open each cabinet, and the third one seemed to hold personnel files.

All she had was "Chloe," and the files were by last name. There were hundreds of files.

After half an hour of searching, she managed to find a file section called "current employees," and that narrowed it down to a few dozen. She pulled the corresponding files and looked through all of them. No sign of her. Damn. She had only recently left but was no longer in the active section.

But what about payroll? Even if they'd pulled her file, she'd still be in the payroll system.

Unfortunately, the paychecks only had a first initial.

There were lots of "C" names. She cross-referenced the payroll list with the current employees file, and there were a dozen discrepancies, including a handful of new girls who weren't on the payroll yet and a trio of women who were no longer active, but still had paychecks.

Apparently, they had a lot of turnover. But three names started with the initial "C."

Huang, C.

James, C.

Ranganathan, C.

The woman had been racially ambiguous, so she couldn't rule out names that were European, African, Latina, or even South Asian. She started with Ranganathan. But that wasn't her. Huang? The woman hadn't looked East Asian, but you never knew. Still, she picked James next.

And then there she was: Chloe, the face Violet recalled. The body she had seen poured into the dress. A headshot and a full-body shot. Violet's breath caught. She stared at the pair of photos, air hissing in and out between her teeth. This bitch.

She felt a buzz, as she got a text. Serena wanted to know:

How's it going?

Violet texted back:

Got it.

After photographing every scrap of paper in the file with her cell phone, Violet returned it to the cabinet. She was making her way out of the office in the dark when she heard a distant sound, like the tinkling of a wind chime. A woman's laugh.

More of a giggle, really. It was coming from farther back in the rear of the restaurant. Just beside the back door was some sort of small employee lounge, really just a couch in a back hallway. And on the couch were a woman and man in what looked like a post-coital stupor.

Damn.

Violet retreated and made her way to the front of the restaurant. She might be able to open the door from the inside, but it was covered by a grate with an exterior lock.

Apparently, the back door was her only option. She returned, creeping through the office to the back hall.

The space was dark, except for the ambient glow from a candle the couple had burning.

Violet pressed herself to the wall and slid around the periphery of the hall toward the back door.

"Where does she think you were tonight?" the woman's voice asked.

"At the game with my brother," the man responded. "Then staying over at his house in Queens."

Violet edged her way along the wall behind the couch.

"Damn," the woman said. "What are we going to do after the season ends?"

"I don't know," the man said. "But I better remember to check the final score before I go home."

Finally, Violet had gotten as far as possible without being seen. She was pressed behind a coatrack.

"I got a score for you to check," the woman said and giggled again.

There was nothing to do but break for the door. She leaped toward the rear exit, in full view within the candlelight.

"What the fuck?" the woman yelled.

Violet grabbed the doorknob and yanked. It was locked. She turned the dead bolt above the knob, and the door swung open.

"Hey, wait!" the man yelled, jumping off the couch.

Violet ran out into the alley. She looked over her shoulder at one point and saw the man, standing in the doorway in his boxers. The streetlights illuminated his pale chest, and his torso shone like an irregularly shaped moon in the night.

Back at the Hughes house, Violet and Etta stared at the images on the phone.

A multiracial woman of African heritage stared back at them with a coy, knowing smile.

"Of course, she would have picked you," Etta said. The older woman stood up and refilled her glass of scotch.

Violet handed the phone to Jared, who was sitting across the table.

"She was setting you up," Etta said. "I bet there must have been a hundred people around wherever she used your phone. You probably weren't even the closest. But she picked you because you were his type."

Violet recalled the scene, standing on the street outside the coffee shop near the One-Eyed King. Chloe had definitely zeroed in on her. But at the time, she had assumed Chloe expected another young black woman would be more likely to help.

"Now we need to get into her apartment," Etta said. "If she abandoned it, maybe it's just empty."

"It's only the fifth of the month," Jared said. "The landlord might think the rent is just late."

"We need you to do another break-in," Etta said to Violet.

"Right," Jared said. "Now you're the breaking and entering expert on the team."

* * *

The address in Chloe's file was in Chelsea. The tiny studio was on the ground floor. They walked by a few times and looked in the window. The place was definitely empty. The single room's futon bed was stripped of sheets. The shelves of the kitchenette were practically bare.

Later that night, Violet and Serena came back with a set of lock picks. Serena, who was much faster with the picks, opened the outer door. On the door of the apartment, someone had stuck a three-day eviction notice, dated two days before.

There wasn't much that Violet could see from inside that she couldn't see through the window. The fridge was practically empty; it held only a carton of cheap wine and some condiments. The trash did, however, hold packaging for Hummingbirdwing cosmetics. There was a bag of paper to recycle that looked like junk mail. She took the whole bag. There was a toothbrush in the bathroom. Violet took it. She figured it would have DNA evidence. But it might be someone else's. She fished in the bathtub drain and found a clump of hair. Gross. But also worth collecting. Thank goodness, she had on latex gloves. She put the hair in a Ziploc bag and wiped her gloved hands on a raggedy towel in the bathroom.

A scan of the room yielded absolutely no papers. There were a few old fashion and hair magazines, which she left behind.

She found herself lingering for no particular reason. There was nothing more to find. Nothing to see. But she couldn't seem to tear herself away. This was the house of the woman who had stolen her life. It was as if she expected to find it, a miniature version of her wedding to Quentin inside a snow globe somewhere, herself as a bride and rice falling on them like snow.

She heard a car horn beep three times, Serena's signal that someone was coming.

Violet jammed everything into her backpack and snapped off the penlight. She listened at the front door of the apartment.

She heard the door to the outside open and close, and then the thud of footsteps on the stairs heading up. Once she heard an upstairs door close, she opened the studio door and slid out into the hallway and then into the street.

Serena was parked down at the end of the block, driving a silver two-door compact that apparently belonged to Tyesha from the clinic.

"Find anything good?" Serena asked.

"Just some paper recycling," Violet said. "Plus some DNA evidence. If it comes to that."

"I got all the mail out of her mailbox," Serena said.

"Can I see it?" Violet asked.

"Not out in the street," Serena said. "Mail fraud is a felony."

Violet's pulse was still elevated, and she felt jangled from adrenaline when she walked into Etta's house.

"So?" Etta asked.

"Not much but mail," Violet said, as she put the stack of mail plus the recycling on the coffee table.

Violet pulled out a fresh pair of gloves and started to pick through the bag of recycling. It was mostly junk addressed to "Resident."

Etta pulled the cell phone bill out of the pile of current mail.

Jared took the bank statements and the credit card bill.

Violet sat back on the couch and let her heartbeat slow down.

"No calls to his cell," Etta murmured. "But fortunately, it's a pay-per-call type of phone. Looks like it logs all the calls."

"Low balance in the account," Jared said. "Ten bounced checks and a ton of fees."

"She obviously planned to skip town," Violet said.

After a while they swapped, and Jared got the phone bill, while Etta looked at the financials.

"Hey!" Jared said. "I think I've got something."

Violet and Etta turned toward Jared as he compared the bill to his handheld. "Yes!" he said. "This is the phone booth outside the office."

"Nailed that tramp!" Etta said.

"How do you know the phone number of the booth?" Violet asked.

"I was looking for another job," he said. "Told them to call that number."

"It's not totally conclusive, but it's a start," Violet said. "Plus there are probably other calls to phone booths. The FBI will be able to trace some of these."

"So we have the girl's name, photo, and address," Jared said. "We've got calls from her cell to the pay phone near the office. And we have every reason to believe she's in the tropics."

"Let's take all this to the FBI," Violet said.

"Let's wait til we hear back from your sister's contact about the property," Etta said.

"Oh, right," Violet said without enthusiasm. "My sister."

Since Lily had moved back to New York, the sisters had been on the outs more than they'd been in contact.

About a year ago, Violet and Lily weren't really on speaking terms, thanks to the slutty dress incident and Lily sleeping with Quentin's friend. But one day, Violet got a call from an unfamiliar New York number. By then, Violet was working as the assistant to one of New York's top makeup artists at Facing Manhattan. Violet always had to pick up the phone in case it was someone for her boss.

"Violet Johnson," she said brightly.

"Lily Johnson," her sister said.

Violet didn't know what to say.

"I just called to see if you and Quentin want tickets to a Broadway show that I'm in," Lily said.

"Broadway?" Violet asked. "Really? We saw *Hamilton*, and it was amazing."

"Well, this show probably won't be winning any Tony Awards, but—um—I'd love to see you," Lily said. "I'll send all the info. By the way, congratulations. Mommie told me about your engagement."

"Thanks," Violet said, almost shyly. "Well, I've gotta go. But I look forward to getting that information."

An hour later, she was having dinner with Quentin when she got a text from Lily with a link for a website.

"I heard from my sister," she said. "She invited us to a show . . ." She opened the link. It was for a show called *Lap Dance*, about strippers. In the promotional photo, a blond woman hung upside down from a pole, with her legs splayed apart.

"What show?" Quentin asked.

Lily closed the *Lap Dance* window on her phone. "I dunno . . . some off-off-Broadway thing. And . . . oh damn. It's while we're out on the Vineyard," she said. "Too bad."

In reality, *Lap Dance* played for two months on Broadway. Lily would re-send the invitation every week. Violet kept making excuses.

Finally, her mother called. "Why won't you go see Lily's show? It's about to close."

"Mom, I've just been so busy."

"You girls need to support each other," her mother said. "You sister finally does something really good, and you won't give her two hours of your time? She's giving you tickets worth two hundred dollars. The least you can do is to take time to see her show."

"Mom, it's about strippers," Violet said.

"I know these Americans are ridiculous," she said. "Making everything about sex and the body some big taboo. People have to go to some dark bar to see women dance. Thank goodness you grew up here where people understand the body is natural and parade down the street in carnival half naked. Nobody raises an eyebrow."

But it was a big deal to Violet. At nearly fifteen, when her breasts and hips finally fully sprouted, she was in boarding school in New England, where nobody paraded down any street half naked. There was only a Fourth of July parade, with white girls in sparkling miniskirts twirling batons. Meanwhile, the scholarship student from the Caribbean who didn't have money to fly home stayed in the dorms and did summer school.

On the closing weekend of *Lap Dance*, Violet had planned to go to the matinee by herself. But she got food poisoning. During her final chance to see her sister on Broadway, she was vomiting into the toilet.

She made her apologies to Lily and their mother.

* * *

Violet saw Lily again later that summer, this time on the news. Lily stood at a podium at some health center, reading a prepared statement that had something to do with a strip club union.

"Yesterday afternoon, at approximately two PM, I was walking down Avenue D to meet the organizers from the other One-Eyed King franchises in the boroughs, and a dark SUV was following them. Then the man in the passenger seat leaned out and shot at them. No one was injured, and the gunman fled. But this illustrates the kind of intimidation that sex workers are up against."

The video cut to a reporter from the *Daily Clarion.* "But how do you know?" the reporter asked loudly.

The camera cut back to Lily and several women walking away from the podium. In the background, Violet heard another male voice. "They said no questions. Show some respect."

"How do you know this was a retaliation for union efforts?" the *Daily Clarion* guy insisted. "I mean, couldn't it have been one of their boyfriends or something?"

The camera was back on Lily, as she slowly turned around. "Listen, mother [BLEEP]. You wouldn't be asking that same question to someone from the teacher's union. But if somebody shoots at some sex workers, they must be to blame? [BLEEP] you!"

Violet turned off the TV. That was it, she had decided at the time. Lily was definitely not invited to the wedding.

Lily was dancing at the One-Eyed King that night, when Jimmy came back into the club with his ghostly friend.

Tara met him at the door with a check for three thousand dollars and had him sign for it. Then he swaggered to the bar, where he ordered top-shelf drinks.

He was about four shots of high-end tequila in when he asked Giselle for a lap dance.

Lily caught her friend's eye-roll, but Giselle turned to Jimmy and smiled, telling him she'd meet him in the champagne room right after her number on stage.

Ten minutes later, Lily had a lap dance customer when Giselle led Jimmy to a nearby chair in the room. Lily kept glancing over to make sure Giselle was okay.

"Don't get distracted," her customer said.

She smiled down at him. He was one of her favorites. Young, hot, and he tipped well.

"Sorry, baby," she said. "Just looking out for one of my friends. Maybe we could do a two-girl dance for you one of these days."

He grinned up at her. "Nope," he said. "I just want you."

Lily laughed and glided above him, brushing the tip of his nose with her breast. She was just turning over to shake her ass in his face when she heard Giselle.

"Hey!" she said sharply. "Let go of me."

Jimmy had both hands on her waist and was holding her pelvis against his. "Come on, Gigi. If a lap dance costs fifty dollars, I should at least get some grinding action for thirty K. Maybe I could slip that thong aside and get in there."

Lily stepped away from her client, giving his hand a squeeze.

"You heard her," she said to Jimmy. "Let her go." Lily pressed the alarm button.

Jimmy loosened his grip a bit, and Giselle wriggled away.

"What the fuck?" he said. "I gave you bitches a lot of money."

"Bullshit," Lily said. "You invested in a business. You haven't pre-paid for lap dances, and you certainly haven't paid enough for full-service sex work. At the rate we're going, we'll have your investment back by next week. You're drunk, and you need to leave."

"Come on, man," Lily's client said. "You're fucking it up for the rest of us."

"Shut up," Jimmy said. "I ain't leaving. I practically own this place."

Here we go, Lily thought, as the security guard rolled up—a tall, white girl with a face full of piercings.

"I don't care how many dog-face chicks you bring to try to throw me out," Jimmy said. "I paid my money, and I'm all up in this bitch for the rest of the night."

"You wanna be an owner?" Lily said. "We'll treat you like an owner. This is a union shop. We can all go on strike, and this place would go broke."

The security guard smirked at him. "Then you'd never see your money," she said.

"See, we don't care," Lily went on. "You got no keys. You got no name on the lease. All you have is a promissory note that says you'll get paid back in the next thirty days from earnings at the One-Eyed King franchise. Read the fine print. If we strike, you won't get shit."

Jimmy narrowed his eyes. You could see him thinking it over.

"Or," Lily said, "you could keep your agreement and follow the rules. Up to you."

"I'll think about it," Jimmy said, as he stood up. "Right now, I wanna look over my investments. I think I'll check out the club in the Bronx."

He strode over to his ghostly friend, and the two of them walked out.

"I'm gonna warn security at the Bronx club," the tall woman with the piercings said.

Lily nodded and went back to her customer.

Later that night, Lily and Giselle were counting tips.

Giselle shook her head. "I think I should just blow him and get him to calm the fuck down," she said.

"No way," Lily said.

"It's my fault he's here in the first place," Giselle said.

"Guys like him?" Lily said. "Power only makes them act crazier. Let's just make money and pay him off as soon as possible."

"Goddamn investors," Giselle said. "First the Ukrainian mob and now this motherfucker."

The two of them logged their earnings and upped the percentage of their tips for the club.

The following day, the team was sitting around at Etta's. Violet sat as far as she could from Lily, who was leaning forward on the couch, between Serena and Jared, her cell in her hand.

"Clive, can you hear me?" Lily asked. "I'm putting you on speaker."

She pressed the button and the phone crackled to life.

"Hello, all," Clive said.

"I'm here with my sister, Violet, and some of our friends."

"Violet!" Clive said. "I've only seen pictures. Hope you're well."

"I'm fine, thanks," Violet said automatically. Then suddenly she flushed. She wasn't okay. Who was this cousin? She wanted to be anywhere but there, yet she needed her sister and this cousin-stranger Clive.

"I don't know if there's anyone staying on that property," Clive said. There was lots of static in the background. "Locals report a couple of unknown cars going down along that road lately. They couldn't tell who was in the car, though."

"Are there any buildings?" Serena asked.

"It's hard to tell because the acreage is fenced off as private property. The land is mostly hills, so they could have built something inside and no one would see a thing. One neighbor did say that his uncle worked on the property several years ago. They set up plumbing and electricity but didn't build anything."

"Okay," Lily said. "You told the neighbors to contact you if they saw anything, right?"

"Neighbors is stretching it," Clive said. "The closest house is a mile away. And there's no cell reception in the area. Not to mention that a lot of the country folks who live out there wouldn't be able to afford a mobile anyway."

"Won't they have to go out for supplies at some point?"

"In theory," Clive said. "But some people get lots of supplies shipped in. They send hired folks to pick it up. No one gets in their business."

"Damn," Lily said. "If he is there, he's gotten it pretty well locked down."

"I won't be able to get back to check it out for about two weeks," Clive said. "I have a big fishing charter tomorrow. But I can go back after that and see if the neighbors have any word. Also, if you give me photos of them, I can show them around to the folks who live closest."

"That's why you're my favorite cousin, Clive," Lily said. "You're not just pretty, but you got brains, too."

He laughed. "I'll let you know something as soon as I hear it," he said.

"Perfect," said Lily. "And please, let me know if the money doesn't come through to your account."

"Be careful," Clive said. "Whoever this guy is, he's got barbed wire on top of the fence."

"But there's certainly not any tourist activity there, right?" Etta asked.

"Definitely not," Clive said.

"Okay," Lily said. "Talk to you soon."

They signed off.

"I wish he had better news," Lily said.

"It's not all bad news," Etta said. "At least I know some other bitch isn't living the life I planned, retiring on a boutique resort in Trinidad."

"You mean Tobago," Lily corrected her.

"What?"

"It's Trinidad and Tobago," Lily said. "Mostly people say Trinidad, but the tourist stuff is all in Tobago."

"No, the property is in Trinidad," Etta said. "I saw photos. It's beachfront in Arima."

"Arima?" Lily asked. "Arima is in the center of the island. There's no beach there. I don't know what you saw pictures of, but it's not Arima."

Etta opened the email program on her phone. "I'm sure he said Arima . . ."

"And they're not into a lot of tourist development," Lily said. "If your husband bought land for a boutique hotel, it would be on Tobago, not Trinidad. Didn't Violet tell you?"

The group turned to Violet, who didn't know what to say.

"It doesn't matter," Etta said. "I'm gonna go find

those photos to see what the hell Teddy sent me pictures of."

Violet stood and looked at her watch. "I'm late for work," she announced and walked out.

In fact, Violet was early for work. Nearly an hour early. She stood outside the Caribbean Circus building, hoping to kill time, but then Nigel came down the street, waving with a wide grin.

"Are you that eager to get to work today?" he asked, as he opened the door.

"In some ways, yes," she said.

As he got closer, he scrutinized her face. "What's wrong?" he asked.

Violet opened her mouth. "I—let's go inside."

It seemed easier to tell him when her hands were busy. She brought out the various jars and packages of makeup. Then, with the colors flashing before her, she could stand to recall the scene with Lily and the team.

"I can't believe I didn't know that," she said. "About my own country." She arranged her brushes and sponges.

"You left when you were what? Thirteen? Fourteen?" Nigel asked. "You can't be expected to have all the information."

She laughed suddenly. "So I'm not a Caribbean Oreo?"

"What?" he asked.

"Brown on the outside, white on the inside," Violet said.

Nigel walked over to her. "Of course not," he said. "Being Caribbean isn't at all about knowing your geography. It's about who you are. You were born a West Indian girl and grew up to be a West Indian woman. He reached for her bangle. It's about these strong fists on your wrist. And even without this, you'd still be Caribbean. It's who you are."

For a moment, they leaned toward each other. His lips looked so soft and inviting.

Abruptly, the outside door banged open and shut. Violet jerked back. Nigel looked startled, then composed his face.

"And if you weren't West Indian, you certainly wouldn't be white." He looked her up and down, even craned his neck to the side and looked at her ass. "Nothing white going on with you, sis."

"So rude," she said, laughing.

He shrugged and retreated, just as a pair of dancers came in to get their faces made up.

After the show had started, he came backstage and opened the door that adjoined another room. It had a makeshift partition from the main warehouse floor. Against the far wall were stacks of boxes and tall pieces from old sets. An undersea panorama. A mountain landscape. An expansive night sky. Just inside the door were large pieces of plywood and buckets of paint.

"So this is the other part of your job," he said. "Set design."

"I already did the designs," she said.

"Of course," he said. "That's how I knew which colors to buy. But now you need to paint the backdrop."

Violet blinked. The canvas was giant. Over ten feet tall and probably thirty feet wide.

"It's so big," she said.

Nigel laughed. "Isn't it great?" he said, wheeling over a ladder. "I've got paints, brushes, rollers. Is there anything else you need?"

Violet looked from the small scrap of square paper to the giant canvas. "No," she said. "I guess I have everything."

"Have you ever painted a set before?"

Violet shook her head.

"Would you like a tip?"

"Yes, please," Violet breathed in relief.

"Draw a black and white outline, and we can project it onto the canvas. Then you trace it and can color things in."

"I never would have thought of that," Violet said.

"That's why I get paid the big bucks," Nigel said and laughed. Violet laughed, too, knowing he lived in a small room above the circus.

An hour later, Violet found herself standing on the ladder, going over the outline of her sketch with charcoal. The scale felt enormous, like what she imagined looking into the Grand Canyon must be like. Even the physical aspect of it was strange. She was accustomed to the muscle memory of drawing being made up of tiny movements with an instrument she held tightly between her fingers. Now she was swooping her arm wide with rollers filled with green paint. Yet many of the images were the same. Palm fronds. Banana leaves. Birds of paradise.

Three hours later, she stepped off the ladder. She had only filled the upper corner of all the outlined images, but the work had been satisfying.

In college, she had marveled at seeing her design in such a large scale for *The Wiz,* but that skyline was an American city. This was her original muse, the tangle of nature from back home.

* * *

Serena and Lily spent the afternoon over at Etta's. Serena managed to hack into Teddy's phone records for the last two years.

"Look for a 787 area code," Lily suggested. That code covered the Caribbean.

In a phone log that was eighteen months old, Serena finally came across a number that belonged to a Caribbean building and contracting company.

When Violet got home, Etta was calling the company on the phone. As Serena and Lily got Violet up to speed, Etta was explaining to the company that she was Teddy's wife, and she wanted to throw him a surprise party. She needed to find out more about the status of the project to see if it would be done in time. But when they asked her to confirm the phone number he used for the account, it didn't match. They wouldn't give her any information.

"Okay," Etta said, brightly. "But don't tell him I called. I don't want to spoil the surprise."

She listened for a moment. "Thanks, sweetie."

Then she hung up. "Son of a bitch," she said.

"Leave his mother out of it," Lily said.

"Let me try something," Violet said. She pulled up her cell phone and called the company back.

"Yes, I'm looking to remodel my house," she said. "Do you work in Trinidad?"

"Sorry," came the reply.

"How about Tobago?" she asked.

"Unfortunately, we only work in Saint Kitts and Nevis."

"You don't work on any of the other islands?" Violet's mouth opened in surprise.

"Our apologies," the man said.

Violet hung up. "We've been looking on the wrong island."

"Where are those photos he sent?" Serena asked. "I had assumed they were just something he pulled off the internet."

"But what if they were real photos from a different location?" Violet asked.

"Maybe I can find some location info," Serena said. "Digital photos all have that data embedded now."

Etta began flipping through photos on her laptop.

Half an hour later, Serena had found what she was looking for.

"Saint Kitts," she said. "Maybe on the northern coast."

"So let's take all this to the FBI," Jared said. "It's enough to give them probable cause to search his property in the islands. Then they can go in, guns blazing."

"The FBI?" Lily said. "I don't trust them not to fuck up an operation in the Caribbean."

"They can't even operate internationally," Serena said. "At least not legally. It would be the CIA."

"Even worse," Lily said.

"Fine," Jared said. "Let's get your cousin to go by and take some pictures."

"I can't ask Clive to trespass on some American guy's property and spy on him," Lily said.

"I wasn't thinking of your cousin to do the spying," Jared said. "I was thinking of your sister."

"Me?" Violet said. "That's crazy. The FBI won't even let me travel."

"By plane," Jared said. "But why don't you ask your cousin to come in his boat and pick you up."

"Smuggle her out of the country?" Lily asked.

"That's too much of a risk," Violet said. "Besides, if

he was gonna come get me here, I'd say take me back to Trinidad."

"So you can be a fugitive?" Jared said. "In a country with an extradition treaty?"

"How do you know about Trinidad's extradition treaties?" Lily asked.

"I've been tracking extradition laws every place we thought Teddy might be," he said.

"You need to do this, Violet," Etta said. "This is about getting your life back."

"Or about getting caught and put in jail," Serena said.

"Look," Etta said, "I'd go, but I'm obviously an American. And either of them would recognize me right away. Jared and Serena are both white and would stick out like the marshmallow in a s'more."

"I could go," Lily said. "To Saint Kitts, I mean. To spy."

"What is this?" Violet asked sarcastically. "*The Hunger Games*? Except this time the younger sister offers herself as tribute? No, Lily. This isn't your fight; it's mine. I'll go."

"Don't act like you don't need your sister," Etta said. "She's the one who has your cousin's contact information so you could even get out of the country."

"I can solve that problem," Lily said. She wrote Clive's number on a scrap of paper. "There," she said. "If all you needed from me was our cousin's number, you got it. If you need something else, call me. If not, good luck."

Lily handed the phone number to Violet and swished out the door.

That night, Jimmy didn't come in to the One-Eyed King. Lily spent the entire night with her radar up for him. She scanned the room from the stage. She scoped out the champagne room when she was in there with customers. She kept expecting him to walk in, but he never did. Maybe her strike threat had worked.

When her shift ended at 2:00 AM, Lily was in a great mood. She was toweling the sweat off her skin in the dressing room when Tara came in.

"You leaving, too?" Lily asked.

"Wanna get a drink?" Tara asked. "I feel like we have something to celebrate tonight."

"Yes," Lily said. "That dick Jimmy is on his way out of our lives."

"My girlfriend and I are meeting some friends at a club uptown," Tara said.

"Sounds great," Lily said.

"It's a girls' club," Tara added.

Lily grinned. "I like girls."

Lily was sweating again from dancing at the club with Tara. They played a great mix of Latin House, drum 'n' bass, and world beat. The DJ mixed from James Brown into Fela Kuti and back. Lily felt the bass reverberate through her body and pounded out all the stress through dance.

When the song ended, her heart was hammering, and she was breathing heavily. She walked off the dance floor to get them some drinks.

The bar was crowded, and she had to wait to get her order in. As she waited, a Latinx butch leaned over. "Hey, don't I recognize you from somewhere?"

"Come on now," Lily said with an eye-roll. "That is the world's oldest line."

"It's not a line," the woman said. "Do you organize domestic workers?"

Lily laughed. "You could say that," she said. "I'm with the stripper's union at the One-Eyed King."

"Yes!" the woman said. "I recognize you from the press conference. You cussed out that reporter."

"I see you are familiar with my work," Lily said, with a smug smile.

"If you dance half as good as you cuss, I'd love to see your work at the One-Eyed King," she said with a friendly leer. "Do you all have a ladies' night?"

"No, but we're halfway to becoming a cooperative," Lily said. "I'll suggest that."

"Yes, *mami,*" the woman said. "I'd like to see those beautiful legs wrapped around a pole."

"Keep talking like that, and they might end up wrapped around something else," Lily grinned.

The woman laughed. "Can we start with a dance?"

"Absolutely," Lily said.

The DJ played a bass-heavy dance-hall reggae song, and the woman took Lily's hand and walked her onto the dance floor. The two women began to wind toward each other, along to the encouraging growls of the emcee. They pressed their hips together, and Lily looked in her face and smiled. She liked this woman's boldness as much as she liked her own.

Lily did a slow turn around, preparing to revolve 360 degrees. But the woman caught her at 180 and pulled her hips backward toward her.

Lily chuckled. She was at least eight inches taller in her heels, but the woman didn't mind. She took hold of both of Lily's hips and ran her hands down from her waist to her mid thighs.

An hour later, they were still on the dance floor,

drunk with the music and the buzz of sexual energy between them.

Tara and her girlfriend yelled a good night over the music.

Lily waved goodbye and turned back to her partner. The woman put a firm hand on her waist and held her other hand for a fast merengue, their thighs pressing together as she alternately pulled her close and spun her.

"What's your name?" the woman asked, when they went back to the bar for a drink.

"Lily," she said. "And you?"

"Jimena," she said. "But you can call me Jay."

"Okay, Jay," Lily said. "You wanna get out of here?"

Jay grinned. "What did you have in mind?"

The moment the pair made it through the door of Jay's apartment, their mouths found each other. Insistent tongues, tasting the salt from their lips curled in a new partner dance, pressing, then twirling, then pressing again.

Jay stripped off Lily's clothes, peeling down the tank top and unhooking the bra. She had her stripped to the waist and laid back on the bed before Lily could even get one shoe off.

She kicked off the pumps and unbuttoned Jay's shirt. Underneath, she had on an athletic bra with elastic that flattened her considerable breasts.

Lily undid the front hooks of the bra but left the shirt on. She began to stroke Jay's nipples, and they hardened under her touch.

Jay hiked up Lily's skirt and pulled off her panties.

Lily scooted back toward the headboard, and Jay

reached for the iPod on the night table. She pressed a few buttons, and then music was playing. A throbbing Latin house jam.

And then Jay began another dance. Her hands sliding down the insides of Lily's thighs and parting her lips. Her tongue sliding up and down along her clitoris, thrusting into her and out again.

The music was continuous, song after song. Jay was enjoying the feel and taste of Lily, the clench and hiss of her pleasure. As Lily teetered on the verge of orgasm, Jay was merciless, licking harder than before.

Lily moaned with the pleasure of the orgasm, and after it subsided, she put a hand on Jay's head and attempted, with weak legs, to get up from under that insistent tongue.

But Jay wouldn't stop. Not until Lily came again, even harder this time.

After the last shudder subsided, Lily laughed out loud. "You're treacherous, woman," she said.

She sat up on the bed and stumbled to the bathroom. Her first attempt led to a closet. But her second attempt was a success. She emptied her bladder and washed her hands.

When she returned to the bedroom, she kissed Jay hard and slid a hand down her pants, the other hand insistently stroking her breast.

Jay was taken by surprise, tipping back onto the bed. Lily grinned, kissed her hard and kept stroking, until Jay came hard, Lily's tongue in her mouth, thumb on her nipple, fingers inside her, pressing and stroking in rhythm to the music

A few days later, a new subset of the team was assembled in Tyesha's office at the Maria de la Vega clinic.

Marisol, Serena, Etta, and Violet. It was Saturday, and the place was quiet. Afternoon sun slanted in through the office windows.

Etta had unearthed a set of plans that Teddy had paid for years ago. There was a four-story boutique hotel, but also a smaller house for the owner to live in.

Violet hadn't wanted to wait for Clive, so she had gotten Etta to pay for a private detective to go look at the property in Saint Kitts. There was a recently built house, and an older white man and a younger brown woman were rumored to be living there.

Etta rolled the large pieces of paper out onto Tyesha's desk.

The first three pages were for the hotel, and they discarded them.

The final page was of a three-bedroom house with three bathrooms. They compared the exterior silhouette with the various photographs the private investigator had taken of the place from different angles.

"That's the upstairs lookout deck," Tyesha said. Visible in both the blueprint and on the house itself was a deck on top of the roof, from which, presumably, one could see the ocean.

"The plans look like they're a reasonable match," Violet said.

"They could have revised them since, but the outside shape is consistent," Serena said.

They unrolled the house blueprint and taped it to the desk. Violet began to try to visualize the spaces. She would enter into a large living room. It opened into a dining room and a kitchen. There were a master bedroom and a den toward the back of the house, and a second story with two additional bedrooms that connected to another bath. An exterior staircase on the side of the second story led to the deck.

Marisol leaned over the blueprints and began to run her finger along the wall lines. She started at the front door and worked her way around the edges of the house. Her light brown finger slid along the white paper, between the blue lines, as if they were a lane or a maze. She worked her way through the living room, the kitchen, a few of the bedrooms, and into the den.

"Here!" she said, her finger stopped on a short stretch of wall between the den and the bathroom of the master bedroom, right behind the toilet.

"What?" Etta said. "I don't see anything."

"It's thicker here," Marisol said.

Violet blinked. She could see that the chunk of wall there was a bit thicker than the others.

"You think he's got a safe there?" Serena asked.

"Nothing else would make sense," Marisol said.

"Right," Violet agreed. "You wouldn't want an extra deep cabinet behind a toilet."

"And you couldn't insulate sounds between the rooms by making it thicker in only part of the wall," Serena agreed.

"But that would be a perfect place for a safe," Marisol said. "Corner of the den. Just put a picture over it."

"We gotta get that money back for the workers," Serena said. "But who's gonna go hit the safe?"

"Let's get a crew of four," Marisol said. "Serena, you do tech support from a distance. I'll call a couple of other team members for backup on the ground."

"That won't work," Violet said. "The island's too small. And anyone who's not black will be too noticeable. I should go. But I don't know how to crack a safe."

"You can learn," Tyesha said.

"It's not that simple," Marisol said.

"I was with her when she did two break-ins here," Serena said. "She was a natural."

"This is a really big job," Marisol said. "I just think—"

"But who else would go?" Tyesha asked. "The only black folks on the team are me, Etta, Violet, and Lily."

"It can't be you," Marisol said. "As executive director, you need to be here in New York, nurturing your plausible deniability."

"And it can't be Etta," Serena said. "Because she can't be trusted not to do something stupid the moment she sees Teddy or Chloe."

"Then Lily needs to go, too," Marisol said.

Violet shook her head. "Lily and I don't get along."

Serena nodded. "You always taught us that the most important part of a team is trust," she said to Marisol. "They don't have it."

Tyesha shook her head. "You're always like this, Marisol." She turned to Serena. "She was like this when we talked about bringing you onto the team. Always protecting everyone."

"I think she can do this," Serena said. "You can teach her how to crack the safe. I can stand by for backup on the phone and with any other tech support she needs. I've mapped it out. Her cousin Clive can be docked at Christophe Harbour. It's on the far end of the island from the Hughes house, but Saint Kitts is so small that nothing is really far away."

"I think it's too dangerous," Marisol said.

"Stop talking about me like I'm not even here," Violet snapped. "I'm doing this. At this point, I basically have nothing to lose. No job. No man. No prospects. I'm a prisoner in New York. I know I might get caught—"

"Caught?" Marisol scoffed. "You might get killed."

"I can't live like this anymore," Violet said. "Watching everything I've accomplished slip further away each day. These people stole my damn life, and I'm going to do whatever it takes to get it back."

Violet was shaking with the intensity of her declaration. She felt pressure behind her eyes, but she was determined not to cry.

For a moment, no one spoke.

Then Tyesha took a slow breath. "She's the only one on the team that can go," she said quietly to Marisol. "And you're the only one who can teach her to crack the safe."

Marisol pursed her lips as she picked up her phone to make a call.

"For the record, I think this is crazy," she said. "But it's not like it's the first crazy thing we've ever done."

Two hours later, a pair of young women walked into the office. One was tall and blond, the other petite and Asian. The tall blonde was muscular and had short, spiky hair. She wheeled a hand truck that held a large canvas sack. It was generally rectangular but had irregular bulges pressing against the white canvas.

The team had removed the blueprints, and the desk was cluttered with the remains of a takeout lunch.

The pair of newcomers smiled at the assembled crew.

The Asian girl looked from the blueprints to the grim expressions on Violet and Etta's faces.

"Are we making introductions?" she asked. Her shoulder-length black hair was pulled back into a loop bun.

"Probably not," Marisol said.

"Okay," the tall blonde said, easing the large canvas bag onto the floor. It looked heavy. "We're just the delivery chicks."

"Hope you have as much fun with these as I did," the Asian girl said, and they walked out, wheeling the empty hand truck.

When the door closed behind them, Marisol walked over and dragged the sack next to the desk. She motioned to Serena, and one by one, they brought out large, flat objects, each one in several layers of bubble wrap. As the two women hauled them up onto the desk, Violet could tell by the tension in their muscles that each one must be heavy.

Marisol arranged them in two rows of three on the desktop, and Serena began to remove the bubble wrap.

Violet blinked in surprise. A few moments later, she was staring at the dials of six different combination safes.

Like the façade of a western town, the six safes were really just faces. They had been sawed or lasered off the safes in question, if there had ever been safes attached.

Chapter 7

After leaving the Maria de la Vega clinic, Tyesha and Lily shared a Lyft heading downtown. Tyesha was going home to Brooklyn, but it was easy to drop Lily off at the One-Eyed King.

"Yes, girl," Tyesha was saying. "Woof just got back from Atlanta tonight. Your girl is 'bout to, what? Get. Some."

"That reminds me," Lily said. "I might call this new girl I met the other night."

"What new girl?" Tyesha asked.

"I gotta get to work," Lily said. "I'll call you later with all the details."

As they pulled up in front of the strip club, Tyesha was grinning in anticipation of a night with her man and catching up on all the juicy details of Lily's sex life. The Lyft driver pulled up in front of the club.

But the grin on Tyesha's face abruptly dropped when saw Jimmy and his pale friend striding up to the club's entrance.

She grabbed Lily's arm. "Hold up. You see that guy?

Not the pale one, the big Latino guy? He's really dangerous."

"Tell me about it," Lily said.

They kept their voices low, but the driver appeared to be listening to the 80s anthem rock he was playing.

"You should tell the folks at the door not to let Jimmy in," Tyesha insisted.

"We don't have a choice," Lily said. "He's our investor."

"Oh shit!" Tyesha said, totally shook. "Jimmy Rios is the investor? He's more than just basic bad news. His brother was a vicious pimp. He—oh fuck. Lily, you can't owe anything to a guy like that."

"That's what I've been telling you," Lily said.

"I think I know someone who can help," Tyesha said.

"That's how we got into this mess in the first place," Lily complained. "Giselle said, 'I know a guy.'"

"Yeah, well I know a woman," Tyesha said.

"I'd definitely rather owe a woman than this badjohn," Lily said. "We're doing everything we can to pay him faster."

"I'll see if I can get some funds for you tonight," Tyesha said.

"We still owe him twenty thousand," Lily said.

"Fuck!" Tyesha said. "Twenty thousand? I'll let you know. But be careful around him."

"I will," Lily said, and opened the car door.

As Lily stepped out of the Lyft, Tyesha turned to the driver. "I'm changing the second destination. We're going back to the Lower East Side."

She texted her boyfriend that she was going to be late.

* * *

When Lily got into the club, Jimmy was buying a round of drinks for three friends, including the ghostly guy.

She put on a bikini top and booty shorts, then had a string of clients who kept her tied up in the champagne room. Lily didn't see Jimmy again til a few hours later, after he had clearly had lots of alcohol.

"You see this?" he said, pulling a paper out of his pocket. "This is a promissory motherfucking note. Says these bitches owe me thirty thousand dollars. That's right. I can afford to loan out thirty motherfucking thousand."

"I thought Hector was the only guy in the Bronx loaning out money like that," one of the guys said.

"Hector?" Jimmy scoffed. "Hector's a little bitch. Thinks he owns the Bronx. Thinks he owns me. He don't own me. That little bitch. I do what the fuck I want. I brought Hector in here the other night. I hosted his ass. I'm the host up in here, not that little bitch." He reached out and grabbed Giselle's arm. "I'm the host, and I say, free lap dances for all my friends."

Giselle looked from him to his trio of buddies. "Jimmy, we can't do that," she said in a discreet murmur.

"Put it on my tab," Jimmy said.

"That's not part of our agreement," Lily said. "And you best believe all this is gonna be deducted from our bill. We don't get paid, we don't get to pay you."

"Oh well," Jimmy said, grinning, "I guess it'll take you a little longer to pay than expected. Meanwhile, I'll be around."

Lily and Giselle led the trio into the champagne room. Tara was finishing up with a customer, and they explained what was going on.

"How do we even document the free lap dances?" Tara asked.

"I don't know," Lily said. "Let's take a photo of each one, and"—she reached into her boot for her phone—"and . . . I don't know. Print them out with invoices to attach to his check."

"I can't fucking believe I got us into this," Giselle said.

"We're halfway done paying up," Tara said. "My girl is cutting a check for five grand right now."

"Don't give it to him yet," Lily said. "I got a friend trying to get the money to buy him out all at once."

"Dear God, let it be so," Tara muttered, as she proceeded to give a listless lap dance to one of Jimmy's friends.

"I hope your people can come through," Lily said into Tyesha's voice mail. "He's treating the club like a private party every night. Either his friends are creepy and abusive, or they're trying to get free lap dances. We've raised another five thousand. If you could come up with fifteen, we could get him the fuck out of here. Anything you can do would be great."

Later that night, Tyesha texted back:

We can't get $ til the bank opens, but we should have it first thing Monday.

Before Lily went to sleep she texted back:

Bless u.

Chapter 8

It was Sunday night, and Violet hadn't slept for over thirty-six hours. She was still at the Maria de la Vega clinic working on the combination safes.

She wandered, bleary-eyed, out of Tyesha's office to the outer office, where Serena had her desk. She went to the coffee maker in the corner and made a fresh pot of Americano. She also found a couple of small cubes of cheese. She had no idea how old they were, but they smelled okay. She ate them both.

Violet had been figuring out how to open the safes, and each one was increasingly difficult. Marisol taught her how—both with and without latex gloves—to turn the dial with an achingly delicate precision, and how to listen through the echoing tunnel of a stethoscope for the slightest clicks.

Violet was a natural. She had always been a good listener. Hadn't she learned how to substitute the bland, unaccented American speech for her own Trinidadian lilt? Hadn't she learned how to listen for the contextual and nonverbal cues to explain the idiomatic expressions and jokes of everyone around her in the US? Hadn't she strained to hear the inflections of Quentin's speech to understand the most nuanced tones of what did and did not please him? The barely audible low sigh in the back of his throat when he didn't like her dress. The slightly higher pitch of his voice when he was excited about something. From the moment she had set foot on the continent of North America, she had been listening for the combination that would allow her entry. The clicks of a safe were simply the latest code to crack.

Marisol had gone home to her boyfriend on Saturday evening, but she came back Sunday afternoon. Violet seemed to be making good progress, so she had left again to get dinner.

When Marisol came back around 10:30, Violet was totally frazzled. She had figured out how to open five of the six safes. But the last one, a Superlative, felt nearly impossible.

"Maybe we should call it a night," Marisol said.

Violet felt guilty for keeping Marisol. A handsome Latino man had come to drop her off after dinner. From the way the two of them kissed goodbye, Violet could tell Marisol would rather be with him than her.

"Do you need to go?" Violet asked.

"Not at all," Marisol said. "I'm committed to making sure we get the strippers' pension money back. But you look exhausted. This is not easy to do, and it's worse when you're really tired."

"But tomorrow is Monday," Violet said. "Tyesha is going to need her office back in the morning. I've gotta get this last safe."

"Okay," Marisol said. "Then you need to eat something." She pulled out a bag of leftovers from dinner.

"Eat this," she said.

She pulled out a full serving of *mofongo*, a pile of mashed plantains with shrimp and tomato sauce.

Violet dug in. "Oh my god," she said. "This is the best food I've ever eaten."

"First meal of the day, huh?" Marisol asked.

"Do cheese and a candy bar count?" Violet asked.

"Not really," Marisol said, dumping out Violet's coffee cup and bringing her a glass of water.

After eating, Violet felt infinitely better. But after half an hour working on the Superlative, she was stressing again.

"Let's take a break," Marisol said. "You're getting too tense."

"Maybe you were right," Violet said. "Maybe I can't do this."

"No, Serena was right," Marisol said. "You're a natural. But I think you've done this before. What was it? Shoplifting? You break into the liquor cabinet at home when you were a teenager?"

"Prep school," Violet said. "I used to break into the art room."

Marisol raised an eyebrow. "Okay," she said. "Then imagine you're back at school."

"I thought you wanted me less tense," Violet said. "Thinking about high school won't help."

Marisol laughed. "I understand," she said. "Same here."

"You're the first person I've ever told," Violet said. "About breaking into the art room, I mean."

"I see it as a good sign," Marisol said. "I think maybe you can do this. So first of all, loosen your body. Shake it out."

Violet shook her hands as she stepped back from the safe face. Marisol had propped it up on a pair of banker's boxes on an end table. It was about the height a safe would be.

Marisol stood and faced her, hands on both of Violet's shoulders. Violet looked into the woman's face, realizing she was older than she'd originally thought—at least forty. Her hair showed no trace of gray, and her skin was supple and sandy brown. She had smile indentations and crow's feet beside her eyes. She even had tiny lines around her mouth as if maybe she used to smoke.

"What's a peaceful image from when you were little?" Marisol asked. "Mine was the beach."

Violet shook her head. "Mine would be the hammock at my grandmother's house."

"Good!" Marisol said. "The safe is like a hammock. It rocks back and forth."

Marisol stood across from Violet and held her by the shoulders. "Close your eyes," Marisol instructed.

Gently, Marisol began to sway the two of them back and forth. With each sway, Violet could feel herself relaxing. "Breathe," Marisol said, and Violet inhaled deeply, and she could tell her body was becoming less tight.

Marisol peeled the latex gloves off Violet's hands. She gently placed the stethoscope in her ears and the other end in one of her hands.

"Keep your eyes closed," Marisol said, as she drew both of Violet's hands up to the safe, one on the dial and the other next to it, pressing the scope to the steel.

"Don't look," Marisol crooned. "Just listen."

The pads of Violet's fingers worked with an incremental precision—the speed painstakingly slow, but consistent. She just kept turning the dial to the right. She let the exterior sounds drift. Traffic noise on the street five stories below. An emergency vehicle shrieking down the adjacent avenue. She simply kept the dial moving, unhurried, relaxed, as if she were in a hammock.

And then she heard it. The whispered click of a gear, like a catch in the back of your throat between an inhale and an exhale. Her eyes flew open.

"You heard it?" Marisol asked.

Violet couldn't speak, just nodded, and gently began to swing the dial back in the other direction, her ears tuned to the right pitch. Now, she knew what she was listening for. Five minutes later, she felt an unparalleled rush when the safe finally swung open.

The next day, Violet woke up late and came downstairs at Etta's house only to find Etta, Serena, and Lily. Her sister was stretched out on the couch with her shoes off, typing on her phone.

"What are you doing here?" Violet asked her sister.

"Serena called me," Lily said.

"For what?" Violet asked. "We're all set."

"No, we're not," Etta said. "We haven't gotten in touch with Clive."

"I thought you all were working on that," Violet said. "While I was learning to—while Marisol was helping me."

"We've called over a dozen times," Serena said.

"I thought maybe it was because Serena's number was unfamiliar," Lily said. "So I even tried calling and left a couple of messages."

"It goes straight to voice mail every time," Serena said. "And now the voice mail is full."

"Besides," Lily said, "I have a better idea than him coming up to smuggle you out of the US." She sat up on the couch and reached into a pocket on her painted-on jeans. "Why don't you just use my passport?"

Violet's mouth opened to protest, but it was actually a good idea.

"I'm finally legal and all with my green card," Lily said. "We look enough alike. With extra high heels, you could be my height."

"You could fly directly into Saint Kitts and be done in a couple of days," Serena said.

"I don't know," Violet said, resisting the idea. "And what about Clive? Is he okay?" It felt absurd, worrying about this cousin she hadn't ever met. But she hated to accept Lily's help, as though that made things somehow even between them.

Lily stood up. "You don't have to decide now," she said, laying the Trinidadian passport down on the coffee table with a gentle *thwap*.

Violet recognized the familiar crest and crown with the pair of tropical birds on the passport's cover. Peeking out of it was Lily's Permanent Resident Card.

"I'll leave these," Lily said. "And if you don't use them, Serena can get them back to me."

And then, for the second time, she swished out the door of Etta's house.

Serena and Etta both turned to Violet, expectantly.

Violet looked from one to the other.

"Well, then," she said, scooping the dark blue booklet off the table, "I better go give notice at work."

"And should I be booking you a flight to Saint Kitts?" Etta asked.

"No, you should be booking it for Lily Claudette Johnson," Violet said, reciting her sister's full name, without even opening the small blue booklet.

* * *

At the Caribbean Circus, Violet had come in early to finish up the backdrop. She brought headphones and painted while she listened to old-school calypso. Engrossed in the painting and music, she lost track of time. A few hours before showtime, she heard Nigel's voice in the room next door.

After she shaded the last leaf on the canvas, she walked quietly into the dressing room to begin the process of making up the performers. Only after she was nearly packed up did she approach Nigel.

"I have some bad news," she said.

His eyes flew open in alarm. "Is everything okay?"

She shook her head. "Nothing really bad," she said. "I just need to let you know that I won't be coming back to work after today. Sorry I wasn't able to give you more notice."

"That's the least of it," he said. "What's up? Did you get another job?"

Violet shook her head. "I'm headed on a . . . a trip."

"A trip?" Nigel asked. "I thought—" He lowered his voice. "I thought you were told to stay in the area by the FBI."

Violet groaned. What else had she told him that night when she was drunk? "It's a long story, but—I'm going to the Caribbean for a little while. A short trip. Hopefully, by the time I get back, all this will be cleared up."

"Where the hell are you going, Violet?"

"How is that even your business?"

"You're looking for the guy, aren't you?" Nigel asked. "The stripper king—what's his name? Do you know where he is?"

Violet shushed him and looked around. "No, we don't know."

"But you suspect," Nigel said. "Don't you? Is it Jamaica? If it is, you've gotta take me with you. I could help out. Most of my family is still there. Except my sisters. One's in Barbados, and another one's in Saint Kitts."

Violet hadn't meant for her face to react, but it had.

"You're going to Saint Kitts?" he asked. "You gotta let me go with you. I been looking for a reason to visit my sister."

"Absolutely not," Violet said. "I'm just here to give my notice. Not get you mixed up in—" She shook her head. "Look, forget it, Nigel. Take care of yourself."

Later that night, Lily's buzzer rang insistently.

She wasn't expecting anyone. Was it Jay showing up unexpectedly? That was kind of hot. But also a little stalkerish. She didn't know how she felt about that.

"Who is it?" she asked.

"Nigel," the voice said, and she trotted down the stairs to meet him.

"What are you doing here?" she asked.

"Your sister is going to Saint Kitts," he said.

"Maybe she is," Lily said. "It's not my business if she wants to take a vacation."

"Don't play dumb with me, Lily," Nigel said. "This has something to do with that strip club king. He could be dangerous. I can help. My sister lives in Saint Kitts."

"Help Violet?" Lily said with a bark of laughter. "She'll barely let me do anything for her. Violet certainly won't accept your help."

"Is she really going alone?" Nigel asked.

"Probably," Lily said.

"Does she know anyone else on the island?" Nigel asked.

"I don't think so," Lily said.

"Then just give me her flight details," Nigel said.

"Are you seriously trying to fly all the way down to Saint Kitts to try to help a woman who doesn't want your help?"

"Yes," Nigel said, his face set.

"You got it bad for her," Lily said, her face softening.

"Since freshman year in college," Nigel said.

"You know she's still holding out hope to get back together with His Majesty," Lily said, using her nickname for Quentin.

"I don't care," Nigel said. "He dumped her and slept with her best friend. If ever I had a chance, it would be now."

"Shelby hooked up with Quentin?" Lily asked, incredulous.

"While Violet was still living with her," Nigel said.

"That two-faced—" Lily shook her head and pulled out her phone. "I don't know her flight details, but I know who will." Lily dialed Serena's number.

Violet's flight was delayed. She hadn't checked in ahead of time, so she got to JFK three hours early. She cursed her mistake. How was she this far off her game? She used to be so conscientious with each little detail. She had handled everything when she traveled with Quentin.

Her luggage was only a carry-on. She got her boarding pass and stood in line to go through security. As she got closer to the front of the line, she looked at the various TSA agents. Two were white guys who looked bored. One was a middle-aged black woman with a frown. The black woman peered at everyone's documents for an extended period of time through a pair of half-moon glasses.

Not her, she murmured to herself, as she got closer to the front of the line. One of the white guys was helping a family—a single mom, two small children, and a baby. It was taking the woman a minute to get all the boarding passes. And now she couldn't find her ID.

"Honeybun," she asked her oldest wearily, "where did you put Mommy's phone?"

"Next?" the other white guy said to the woman in front of her. She had a dog in a carry-on. She accidentally banged the carrier against the agent's desk, and the dog began to bark loudly.

"He's a service animal," the woman explained.

"He can't bark like that during the flight," the TSA agent explained.

Violet stood at the front of the line.

The black woman looked irritated with her customer. "Your ID doesn't match your reservation," she said.

"It's just my middle name," the man said, scrambling to pull out his driver's license and a social security card.

Please, not her, Violet prayed. Bored white guys thought all black people looked alike. That woman had a sharp eye and a bad attitude.

Violet looked at the single mom, praying that she would get through quickly. The woman was pulling her ID out of a pocket in her cell phone case.

"Next?"

Violet looked up to see that the black woman was calling her.

She pasted on a smile and walked forward with her sister's passport and boarding card in her hand.

"Good evening," she said with forced cheerfulness.

The woman wrote on the boarding card, then looked from the passport to her face.

"You're from Trinidad?" she asked. The frown line deepened between her brows. "You don't sound like it."

"Originally," Violet said. "I've been here for quite a while."

The woman looked from the photo of Lily to Violet's face.

"And you're much darker in this picture," she said.

"When I'm back home, I get a lot more sun," she said. "Here I'm inside working all the time. This is so pale for me." She laughed, and it sounded brittle in her mouth.

The woman scrutinized the document again. "And you're how tall?" she asked.

"Six feet," Violet said with what she hoped sounded like authority. She had on her tallest heels and a maxi dress to cover them. She stood as straight as she could.

The woman looked again from the photo to Violet's face. Then she shrugged. "Have a good flight," she said and waved for the next passenger to come up.

Violet moved into the metal detector line. She waited til the last minute, when she was as far from the woman as possible to remove her shoes and put them on the security belt along with her carry-on bag, phone, and jacket.

She had just gone through the body scanner, and her bags were coming out of the metal detector.

"Please come with me, miss," the TSA agent said. He was a tall Latino guy with a goatee.

Violet's heart began to bang in her throat. It wasn't all good. The woman hadn't really believed her. Maybe the woman had called her supervisor. She would be found out. The FBI would come. She would be arrested, a fugitive attempting to escape. Then they would really think she was guilty.

At the desk, the man dug through her jacket. From one pocket, he pulled out a tiny, purple Swiss Army knife.

"My nail file," Violet breathed, her throat constricted.

He looked at her sharply. "I'm going to have to confiscate this, ma'am."

"Of course," Violet said.

"We'll need to search the rest of your belongings," he said.

Violet nodded. She still had her tall shoes under her arm. She felt conspicuous in her bare feet. At five foot six, she obviously wasn't the woman on the passport.

The agent opened her carry-on suitcase and rummaged through. A pair of sneakers. A few pieces of clothing. He pulled up a large, clear plastic item.

"What is this, ma'am?"

"It's for weight loss," she said.

He frowned at her. "You're trying to lose weight?"

"For my aunt," she said, hoping her voice sounded steady. "They can't get those kinds of things outside the states."

He held it up to the light. It was a sort of hollowed-out cylinder. A zipper would close it around her body.

She looked at him more closely. He had a bit of an accent. He was clearly not white. She took a chance. "You know how it is. When you go home, you have to get all the stuff from the US your family can't get. Some of the things they're better off without."

He laughed. "Tell me about it." With a swift movement, he closed her suitcase. "Have a safe flight."

And then, before he or the woman at the desk could change their minds, she was jamming her feet into her shoes and striding off toward her gate.

Later that night, Jimmy was back in the club with his pale friend. It was just more of the same. Lap dances on his "tab."

Lily was onstage, but her eyes kept darting to the front door. She was eager for Tyesha to come by the club, as she had promised, to bring a check from the Maria de la Vega clinic. They had a new promissory note printed out for Etta to sign, owing the clinic instead of Jimmy.

She twisted and twerked her body around the pole, her face wearing an autopilot sexy grin. As her song was nearly over, she tried to remember to make eye contact to get more tips.

It was nearly midnight when Tyesha finally showed up.

"A crisis at work," she said. "Where's Jimmy? Let's get this over with."

"He's in the champagne room getting a lap dance," Lily said.

The other Trinidadian dancer, Hibiscus, was leaning backward over Jimmy, rocking her ass back and forth just above his crotch.

The two women retreated to the far side of the room and waited for the song to finish.

In all the loud music and patron noise of the club, it was hard to hear any individual voice, but a single tenor growl began to rise above the din.

"Jimmy! Where's that motherfucker at?"

The voice came closer, and when three guys came into the champagne room, Lily recognized one of them. He was the abusive guy from earlier that week. The one who had called her a bitch.

"Hector," Jimmy said, with an unwelcome hand on Hibiscus's hip. "Come get some of this."

"Oh, you gonna be friendly to my face now?" Hector asked.

"What do you mean?" Jimmy asked.

"You was in here last night saying I was a little bitch?" Hector asked. "That I don't run the Bronx?"

"Nah, nah," Jimmy said. "I was just saying I hosted you here earlier this week. And I'm glad to host you again. Have a free lap dance. On me."

"Don't think you can put some hoe's ass in my face and distract me from the fact that you was up here talking shit about me," Hector said. "Did you call me a little bitch or not?"

"Of course not," Jimmy said. "I musta been talking about these sexy bitches up in here. Come on man, let me hook you up with a lap dance."

Up until that point, the two men had been loud, but business as usual was able to go on around them. Three different girls had lap dance customers, and the throbbing bass of an early Thug Woofer song urged everybody to "clack that ass, cackalack that ass."

But everything changed when Hector pulled out a gun. Hibiscus froze. Giselle gasped. Lily and Tyesha flattened themselves against the far wall. The dancers in the room caught the motion in their peripheral vision and looked over.

They saw Hector with the handgun pointed at Jimmy and his pale friend. The girls giving lap dances stopped abruptly and either ducked behind chairs or backed out of the room if they were near the door. The other customers slowly surfaced themselves from their sexually aroused states to take in what was going on.

Hector swung the gun so it was pointing directly at Jerry's pale friend. "Tell the truth, Chuco!" he demanded.

"Was Jimmy calling me a little bitch up in this motherfucker? They said you was here."

"I don't—" Chuco began.

"You mean to tell me you're willing to take a bullet for his ass," Hector said. "When you know he was taking his own life in his hands, calling me a bitch in front of guys from my neighborhood."

Chuco looked from Hector to Jimmy and back. More specifically, he looked at Hector's gun.

"Yeah," Chuco said quietly, his voice barely audible above the rap music. "He called you a little bitch. More than once. Everybody heard him."

"Chuco," Jimmy said. "What the fuck, man?"

Chuco shrugged slightly, as Hector turned the gun on Jimmy.

"Hector," Jimmy said, "it's loud as fuck in here. Anybody could get it wrong. I told you, I said it was sexy bitches up in here. Sexy bitches."

"You think you a killer like ya big brotha?" Hector asked. "Well, you ain't. You just a cheap imitation."

The first bullet hit Jimmy in the chest. The shot itself was loud, but Hibiscus screamed, a piercing sound that cut through the loud bass of the music.

The second shot hit him in the neck, and by then both customers and dancers were rushing out of the champagne room. Patrons and workers in the main room also realized that something was wrong, and they joined the panic. Guys jumped up off couches and chairs. Dancers unwrapped themselves from poles and clambered down off stages. They all joined the rush to the front door.

Lily felt a sharp elbow as Chuco, Jimmy's pale friend, pushed past them.

She looked back through the door of the champagne room and saw Hector standing over the body of the fallen Jimmy. He stuck the gun back in his waistband and strode toward the back exit of the rapidly emptying club.

The moment the thugs were out of the room, Tyesha grabbed Lily's arm and pulled her out into the main part of the club.

Lily yanked her arm back from Tyesha. "Wait," she said, and turned back to the champagne room.

"Lily, are you fucking crazy?" she asked, reaching for her friend's shoulder, but Lily shook off her hand and slipped past her.

Jimmy lay on the floor of the champagne room, the blood pooling below him on the linoleum. Lily tried not to look at his upper body, the wet stain on his chest, and the hole blasted through his thick neck. She knelt at his waist, looking toward his big feet in the sneakers. The club's dress code didn't allow athletic gear, but Jimmy had never followed any of the rules.

In the main room, everything was surreal. Panicked patrons and dancers were bottlenecked at the front door, trying to get out. Meanwhile, Hector strode leisurely down the back hallway. The rear door was an emergency exit, and when he hit the push bar, the alarm shrieked into the melee. He and his crew strolled out into the alley, as if they had nowhere to be anytime soon.

In the champagne room, Lily felt a wave of nausea. She closed her eyes and reached into Jimmy's pocket. The fabric against his skin was warm and almost humid. The pockets were deep, and her hand was practically covered to the wrist before she felt the hard edge of folded paper.

Gingerly, she slid out the slightly damp paper. She

half-unfolded it, to confirm it was the promissory note. Relieved, she tucked it into her bra and rushed to catch up with Tyesha.

"Have you lost your mind?" Tyesha asked. "We need to get out of here."

Lily nodded, brushing her hand against her thigh, over and over again.

Out on the street, Lily and Tyesha joined the cluster of dancers that had gathered.

"Is everyone okay?" Tara asked. "Did all the girls get out?"

"I think this is everyone," Giselle said. "Is the shooter still in there?"

"We saw the whole thing," Tyesha said. "He just wanted Jimmy. He went out the back."

"Who's gonna deal with the cops?" Tara asked.

"I can't take the chance," Hibiscus said.

"Before anyone leaves," Lily said, "if the cops ask, we had paid him what we owed."

"I can't be talking to no cops," Hibiscus said and pulled a phone out of a tiny pocket in her Catholic schoolgirl micro miniskirt. She turned toward the bright avenue block, trooping down the street on Lucite stiletto sandals.

"What about the promissory note?" Tara asked.

"I got it," Lily said and proceeded to throw up into the gutter.

Later that night, Lily, like the other dancers, would tell the authorities the truth about nearly everything. Yes, she knew the victim, Jimmy Rios. No, she didn't have last names for the guy named Hector, who shot him, or the guy named Chuco, who was ostensibly involved. Yes, she had also heard they were all from the Bronx. Yes, Jimmy Rios had been an investor in the club. He had given them a very short-term loan, and they had paid him back with interest.

The police found it hard to believe that he had loaned them such a large sum of money for less than a week. But Tara was bold.

"Is someone saying that we didn't pay?" she demanded. "I got a paper trail for all the checks he cashed."

The officer looked at his paperwork.

"Several of the victim's friends reported that Rios said the club owed him money," the cop said.

"What?" Lily asked. "The police are just acting on gossip these days? You're gonna take the word of the man who got himself killed tonight for talking shit?"

"We're just following all possible leads," the cop said.

Later that night, Lily and Tyesha turned the gas up to high on the front burner of Tyesha's stove.

"Are there any more copies of this?" Tyesha asked glancing at the promissory note.

"Etta Hughes has the only other copy," Lily said.

Tyesha nodded. They held three pieces of paper over the gas flames: the promissory note and two checks made out to Jimmy Rios. One from the One-Eyed King and the other from the Maria de la Vega health clinic. Jimmy's $20K ignited in a burst of flames. They had records, in case the cops ever investigated. But with the evidence they were burning that night, it was unlikely the cops would ever put it together.

When the fire got too close to her fingers, Tyesha

put the burning papers in a cast-iron frying pan, and the two women watched them blacken and curl to ashes.

Lily couldn't stop wiping her hand on one of Tyesha's dish towels. In reality, her skin was dry. But she couldn't seem to wipe off the feeling of damp from reaching into a dead man's pocket.

Chapter 9

The moment Violet arrived in Saint Kitts, she could feel some part of herself breathe differently. The air tasted almost like home in Trinidad. New York had been hot and humid, but it didn't have the same tang of sea salt in the air. New York's flora was mostly in the patterns on women's clothes. But the Caribbean was dripping in green from the moment she stepped out onto the curb in front of Robert L. Bradshaw International Airport.

In New York, every inch of the city was built up to the very edge of JFK. But in Saint Kitts, she landed in green space with mountains, bisected by a strip of highway. Houses—mostly low-slung and painted bright colors—were clustered on the flat expanses, but even between them, she could see more green. Unlike the city where she'd lived for the last several years, this land was alive.

She had taken the red-eye. She'd left New York at midnight and had a layover in Florida. She'd slept on the plane and dozed in the airport. By the time she got out of customs, it was only eight in the morning. The customs line was short coming into Saint Kitts; it would only be long on the return trip. She strode quickly through the small airport. She stepped out through the glass doors, wheeling her carry-on and searching for a taxi.

A yellow cab pulled up to the curb; the driver had a Caribbean Airlines baseball cap pulled down over his face.

"Where to, miss?" he asked in what sounded like a Jamaican accent. A shame. She had hoped to strike up a conversation with one of the locals on the way, to get familiar with the lilt of Saint Kitts.

She gave him the address, and he headed out onto the main road. In Saint Kitts, as throughout the British West Indies, they drove on the left side of the road.

They headed away from Christophe Harbour, where, presumably, Clive would be docked, waiting to help if they needed him.

She sat in the backseat, studying the photos she'd taken of Teddy Hughes's floor plan on her phone. She glanced up as they moved into and through the capital city of Basseterre and onto the road that led to the other end of the island.

When the taxi hit a long, more rural stretch, the driver began to slow down. He put on his turn indicator as if he planned to pull to the side of the road.

Violet looked up from her tablet where she was studying the floor plans. She should have been paying better attention. Was he going to rob her? She reached into her handbag for—for what? Her phone was inaccessible somewhere in the bottom of her bag. And the TSA had confiscated her pocketknife.

"Why are we stopping?" she demanded in her fiercest voice.

She stared at the back of the driver's head, his hair

in a neat fade above his dark brown neck, as he maneuvered the car to a stop.

"Violet—" Nigel began, as he turned in the driver's seat.

"Are you fucking kidding me?" Violet yelled. "You practically gave me a goddamn heart attack. What the hell are you doing here? Trying to kill me?"

"Trying to keep you alive," Nigel said. "You just gonna get in a car with some strange man without looking him over, looking in his eyes? You obviously been going around too many places with your rich American boyfriend, where you didn't have to look out for yourself."

"Fiancé," she corrected, and then caught herself. "At least he used to be."

"You're way out of your league with this," Nigel said.

"No, I'm not," Violet said. "I've done a number of successful break-ins."

"Slipping the latch on the art room at prep school doesn't count," Nigel said.

"How did you know about that?" Violet asked.

"You told me in college," Nigel said.

Violet blinked. She didn't remember. "Well, I just did two successful break-ins back in Manhattan."

"The point isn't for you to prove your robbery bona fides," Nigel said. "The point is that you need to stop acting like you're out here all alone. You're not still a West Indian scholarship girl in a US prep school. You have friends. Family. You need to let people help you."

"Don't act like you're not here with an ulterior motive," she spat. "What? Did you think I was some damsel in distress? That I'd be so grateful for your help that my panties would fall off?"

Nigel blinked. "I'd be lying if I said that the idea never occurred to me," he said. "But mostly I spent the plane ride making peace with the idea that I might help you do whatever you came here to do . . . and you'd still go back to Quentin."

"I told you that's what I want," she said.

"I know," he said. "And I can live with that. But if I didn't come to help, and anything happened to you? I couldn't live with that. That's why I'm here. As a friend. Because friends don't let friends go on half-baked missions in the Caribbean by themselves."

"Did Lily tell you where to find me?" Violet asked.

"Technically, Serena did," Quentin said. "But Lily cares about you. That's why she gave me Serena's number."

"And where the hell did you get a taxi?" Violet asked.

"It's not a taxi," Nigel said. "It's a yellow rental car. I brought a couple of props from the circus."

"You're crazy, you know that?" Violet said.

"Crazy enough to drive the getaway car for you?" Nigel said.

Violet looked around. She was on a rural road in a country where she knew no one and had only a slow internet connection and a set of blueprints to help her make her way around. Maybe Nigel helping her wasn't the worst idea in the world.

"Yes," Violet said. "Crazy enough for that."

Her heart was still banging in her chest, as she thought back to Marisol's words. She knew she wasn't getting the whole story about what that woman did. She was obviously some kind of master criminal. Maybe Marisol had been right the first time—that Violet wasn't really up to the task of this heist. At least not alone. But now she had Nigel. Plus Serena via phone and Clive with a boat. That would have to be enough.

* * *

An hour later, the two of them pulled up at the foot of the road that led up to what Violet presumed was Teddy Hughes's house. The land was a bit wild and overgrown. The path had been paved at one time, but it was now rutted and filled with potholes.

There was no unobtrusive place to sit in a bright yellow car and wait. Fortunately, however, the back windows were tinted, so the pair sat in the back, peering out at the empty road. Every ten to fifteen minutes, a car went by on the road, but otherwise, the only sounds were the wind and a far-off pair or trio of roosters that seemed to be having a loud argument, repeating themselves over and over.

After fifteen minutes of waiting, the car became like a sauna. Nigel opened the sunroof, and that helped a little. He cracked both the front windows. Then the back windows.

The two of them sat there in silence, soaked in sweat, and waited.

At nearly noon, a woman came walking up the road from the northwest. She was middle-aged and wore a faded floral dress. In her hand was a caddy full of cleaning supplies.

"You were right," Nigel whispered. "They do have a cleaning lady."

"I knew it," Violet said. "The mistress isn't gonna clean anything. And Teddy's used to having everything spotless." Violet recalled watching Etta scrub their house whenever she was anxious.

There were no other visible houses, but Violet didn't want to presume. She waited until the woman began to climb the private road to the house and then stepped out of the cab.

"Good afternoon," Violet said, wiping her forehead.

The sound of her own voice shocked her. Without trying to, her Trinidadian lilt had just come out.

"You lost?" the woman asked. "The tourist hotel is down the road."

"No," Violet said smiling. "I believe I was looking for you."

"What do you want with me?" she asked, suspiciously. The woman's Saint Kitts accent was simultaneously familiar and different to Violet's Trini ear.

"You've been doing the cleaning for these Americans, right?" Violet asked.

"You have a villa you need cleaned?" she asked. "I'm busy today and tomorrow, but I can fit you in the day after."

"How much you charge?"

The woman quoted an amount in local currency that was the equivalent of three dollars, US. "I just clean," she said. "No cooking."

"I'll give you five times that much if you'll let me take your place today," Violet said.

"I don't think so," the woman said. "I don't want any trouble."

"I'll give you a hundred American dollars," Violet offered.

"You foreigners coming here," she said. "I don't know you. I don't know what you have in mind. You go to clean in my place, whatever trouble you bring coming back to my door. For all I know, you want to murder these people."

Violet shook her head. "Nothing like that," she said. "He stole something from some friends of mine. I need to get it back."

"Just as I said," the woman arched an eyebrow. "When they find it missing, they gonna come looking for me.

You be long gone with whatever it is, and I got some rich angry Americans trying to find me. No thank you."

"What would make it worth the trouble?" Violet asked.

"Well," the woman began, "I would have to leave and go visit my sister for a while."

"How about two hundred dollars, US?" Violet asked.

"Five hundred," the woman insisted.

"I only have two hundred and fifty," Violet said, recalling her mother haggling at the open-air market on weekends.

"Four hundred," the woman pushed back.

"I don't have it."

"Then no, thank you," the woman said and stepped forward, as if to walk past her.

"Wait!" Violet said. She reached into her wallet and took out a knot of twenties. It was all she had. She hadn't wanted to spend it all here, but this woman was her only way in.

Violet counted out the bills. "Three hundred," she offered, opening the wallet to show it was really empty now. "Please, miss."

The woman looked her over. "Okay," she said. "But only because they so rude they deserve what they gonna get from you."

Violet handed over the bills.

"Tell them you've come in place of Katherine," the woman said. "They can pay me at the end of the week." Then the woman handed her the tote of cleaning supplies. "Nobody asks questions when they don't have to pay any money til later."

She pocketed the cash and turned around, walking back up the road in the direction she had come from.

In the taxi, Violet asked Nigel to turn on the engine and blast the air-conditioning. She couldn't apply her makeup when she was sweating so much. After the car had cooled, she blotted her face with a towel and used contour shading to change the shape of her cheeks, eyes, and nose a bit. Then she put on a wig with long bangs and a loose-fitting dress. Under the dress, she put on the inflatable plastic corset that the TSA agent had flagged. As she went in, it would be filled with air. When she came out, it would be filled with whatever she found in the safe.

"How do I look?" she asked Nigel, putting on a pair of thick-rimmed glasses.

"Ready to clean some American tourist's house," he said.

"Good," she said and closed the door behind her.

He put the car in gear, and Violet watched it disappear behind a nearby crumbling shed. They'd agreed that he would wait where the cab couldn't be seen.

On her way up the drive, Violet kept looping the single line in her head. "I've come in place of Katherine. You can pay her at the end of the week."

In her mind, she tried to copy the Saint Kitts accent. Teddy wouldn't notice, but the woman might. No telling if she was West Indian or not.

Halfway up the drive, the house came into view. It was just like the photos, with the deck on top. There was a dark SUV in the driveway.

The sun beat down on her face. The wig made her scalp incredibly hot. The plastic corset was slick with sweat where it wrapped her torso. She tilted her head down a bit and continued to practice.

"What are you doing here?" a woman's voice asked. "You crazy? Up here talking to yourself?"

Violet looked up to see the woman from in front of the One-Eyed King. She was standing on the porch, smoking a cigarette. Again with too much eye makeup and the lipstick too loud. The woman who had stolen her life. The woman who had set her up and was prepared to live off the money that other women stripped for. With another woman's man. Violet swallowed her rage like bile.

"I've come in place of Katherine," Violet said, her throat tight. "You can pay her at the end of the week."

"Fine, then," the woman said. "Come on in. My husband and I were just going into town. This climate is murder on my hair."

Violet nodded deferentially and hustled into the house. Husband? she thought. Shameless. Laying claim to a married man like that.

The house was done in wicker furniture and pastel shades. It was devoid of personality, like a hotel.

When Violet walked in, Teddy looked up from his newspaper.

She repeated her line. "I've come in place of Katherine. You can pay her at the end of the week."

"A nice change of scenery," he said, looking her up and down.

Violet was startled. She had thought that the thick padding would be enough to make her body shapeless and desexualized. But his leer was unmistakable.

"Where should I get started?" she asked.

"The bedroom?" Teddy asked, eyebrows raised.

"Honey," Chloe wafted in, "let's go to town for some lunch."

"Where should I get started, ma'am?" Violet asked.

"Don't ever call me ma'am," Chloe said. "And start with the kitchen."

"Yes . . . miss," Violet said. She walked through the living room into the dining room and through to the kitchen. Her caddy had plenty of supplies, and the rest were under the sink. For twenty minutes, she actually cleaned, washing dishes, scrubbing the tile, and mopping the floor.

After the pair left, she went straight to the den. She pulled back the picture on the proper spot from the blueprint. All she saw was plain, white wall. No sign of a safe.

She walked around to the other side of the wall, behind the toilet. No painting. Nothing but white wall. Could the safe be under the plaster? She knocked on the wall, and it sounded hollow. No safe.

Dammit.

She retraced her steps to the living room and began to look behind all the paintings. Nothing. Nothing in the dining room. She skipped the kitchen for the time being. The paintings were small, and it seemed like an unlikely place.

She moved to the downstairs master bedroom. There was a triptych of female nudes in neon. She recognized the images from the One-Eyed King. Of course.

She slid each one aside on the wall. Behind the third one was the safe.

She bent over to get the stethoscope from her caddy and heard a voice behind her.

"Perfect," Teddy Hughes said. "Stay just like that."

Violet snapped up and looked at him, advancing toward her.

"I thought you'd like my suggestion to do some cleaning in the bedroom," he said. "I have something I need cleaned. Something very personal."

"No—no, sir," Violet stammered. "You misunderstand me."

"I like a big girl," he said.

"I've come in place of Katherine," Violet said, her

voice disconnected from her body. "You can pay her at the end of the week."

"Katherine was a little old for me," he said. "But you're not."

"I've come only to clean the house, sir," Violet said. "Not anything personal."

But still he advanced toward her and pulled her roughly toward him.

Violet swung the caddy at his head, and it knocked him back on the bed. She scrambled past him and out through the house to the front door. She flew through it, slamming it behind her.

The driveway to the road was exposed, so she ran off to the side to make her way down through the overgrown greenery.

As she rushed along, she saw a flash of yellow as a cab came up the drive. At first, she thought it might be Nigel, but then she saw Chloe through the back window.

At the foot of the driveway, she turned and ran to the fallen shed. Behind it, Nigel's yellow vehicle sat looking abandoned. She ran to it and banged on the window.

Nigel had dozed off in the driver's seat. His torso was covered in sweat, making the thin T-shirt stick to his skin. The translucent white fabric outlined every ridge and ripple of his chest, shoulders, back, and abdominal muscles. Even in her frantic state, one part of Violet couldn't help but notice.

Nigel opened the car door, and Violet jumped in.

He started the taxi and took off down the road.

"Did you get away clean?" he asked.

Violet opened her mouth and burst into tears, her body slumping down against the inflatable plastic. In between sobs, she gasped for air. Between the pressure of the seat back and her slouching torso, the apparatus encircled her like a vise.

On that same day in New York, Serena dropped by the co-working space where Jared and Lee had been working. It was in Manhattan, near one of her favorite Greek delis. She had come from meeting a friend for lunch, the only person from high school she was still in touch with. In high school, Serena's name was Samouel, but everyone called her Sam. It was androgynous enough, but when she started living as a girl, she chose the name Serena. Most of her friends were from the clinic or from the years just before that. She had been living on the street after she ran away from home at seventeen.

The friend from lunch, Danielle, was also a Greek immigrant. They were the same age, but Danielle had arrived a few years earlier, and she had taken Sam under her wing. Danielle was the one person Sam, age fourteen, told that she thought she was gay. They were sitting on a swing set in the park by their apartment, and she had pulled aside her friend's silky brown hair and whispered it in her ear in Greek.

Danielle had laughed. "I know that," she had whispered back.

By spring of freshman year, the two of them were walking home from tryouts for the school play when she had told Danielle, "I think maybe I'm not gay. I think maybe I'm a girl."

Danielle had blinked in surprise. Then she grinned. "Of course you are."

They had lost touch after Serena ran away but had reconnected recently. Now Danielle lived in New Jersey with her husband and three small kids. They talked on the phone a couple days a week. But on the rare occasions when Danielle had business in the city, they always met for lunch. In addition to just loving Danielle, it always felt good to see someone who knew her from those years. Especially now that she was settled in herself in a new way.

The co-working space had been converted from a retail store, and they had fitted it out with long work tables and office chairs, as well as meeting rooms you could rent. They had also built little soundproof booths for privacy when people took sensitive phone calls.

Serena looked around until she spied Lee and walked over to her.

Lee had on a snug-fitting navy dress with a surplice neckline that showed her cleavage. Serena had on a Maria de la Vega T-shirt and a maxi skirt.

"This place is great," Serena said.

"It should be," Lee said. "It costs enough to be a member."

"How do you afford it?" Serena asked.

"I know the manager," Lee said. "He gives us a deal."

"Good for you," Serena said. "Is Jared around?"

"He was here earlier," Lee said. "I'm not sure where he went."

"I have some news. Etta remembered that Teddy had had drinks with an old friend a short time before he left," Serena said. "The guy might be a bond trader."

"I can let Jared know," Lee said.

Serena looked at the dark leather case on the opposite chair.

"Well, that's his bag, right?" Serena said. "He can't be far. I'll wait."

"It might have been a job interview or something," Lee said. "He might be gone for hours."

"Without his bag?" Serena asked.

"I'm just saying I can't guarantee that he'll be back in a timely manner," Lee said.

Serena grinned. "Girl, I'm the same way," she said. "I find myself doing secretary duty when I'm off the clock. Sometimes people will call for my housemate on the landline and I'll say. 'Was she expecting your call?' " Serena cracked up.

Lee turned and faced Serena, her eyes cold, her mouth unsmiling. "You need to stop embarrassing yourself," Lee said, an edge of contempt in her voice.

The laughter died in Serena's throat.

"Throwing yourself at him," Lee went on. "Jared would never be interested in your kind of . . . woman." She emphasized the second syllable of the last word, so that the word "man" was clearly articulated. "I know he feels that way—not about you, he's never said anything about you in particular—but about how he's never really comfortable around your type. I thought you would want to know."

Maybe on another day, if Serena hadn't had lunch with the friend from high school, it wouldn't have stung so much. But she remembered being a high school freshman. Fresh? Man? Feeling estranged from everything. The new country, the impossible English language, the secrecy of being undocumented. And her body, how it had begun to betray her as it grew into something she felt she was never meant to be. She had always been petite, light, picked on, teased, even beaten up for being too much like a girl. Called a girl, like it was an insult. She had always felt like a girl.

Her parents were so religious. She had known for years that she was going to hell for her feelings about boys. Her parents talked about how maybe she would marry Danielle. Or when they went back to Greece, she could marry one of the pretty girls she spent time with as a child. But that was never going to happen. They were girls who understood without words that Serena—Samouel then—was like a sister to them. Serena dressed them up and did their makeup and styled their hair and imagined it was her own.

But then her uncle had gotten her father an under-the-table job in New York, and they moved to the US for high school.

And then something awful was happening to her body. She smelled different. Her voice was changing. She felt like she was suffocating. She loathed herself inside that trap, despairing that she would ever get to be herself. She had made her first suicide attempt.

Usually Serena had her armor on. She had survived past her life expectancy as a transgender immigrant woman. Usually, she was bulletproof: head high, jaw tight, ready with *I wish a motherfucker would* hovering just behind her teeth. But seeing Danielle had her open. No shield up.

The contempt in Lee's eyes sliced like a blade, bringing all the shame and self-hatred back.

Throwing yourself at him.

Your type.

Wo-MAN.

Never.

Tears sprang to Serena's eyes. She had that old, familiar feeling of suffocating. Her throat tightened; she needed air. She turned and fled from the industrial building. She didn't even notice Jared walking toward her, his open face smiling. He was just another blur she passed on the way out. She burst onto Eighth Avenue, gasping as if she'd come up from underwater.

* * *

Nigel drove a ways down the road, while Violet sobbed silently into a handkerchief. When he had gotten maybe a quarter mile from the Hughes house, he stopped the car.

"Are you okay?" he asked. "What happened?"

"I didn't get it," Violet said, drying her eyes. "Hughes came back before I could open the safe."

"Did he try something with you?" Nigel asked.

How did he know?

Violet waved it off. "Of course. He tries it with every woman under the age of forty . . . or fifty. He's no threat."

"Did the girlfriend see you?" he asked.

"I don't think so," Violet said.

"What do we do now?" Nigel asked.

Violet shrugged. "I guess we wait for another opportunity."

"Should we go back and stake the place out again?"

"Sounds good," Violet said. "Katherine told me she didn't cook. And there was nothing but alcohol in that fridge. So I figure they've gotta go out to get dinner at some point."

They returned to the spot behind the crumbling shack and waited.

"You ever visit your sister here in Saint Kitts?" Violet asked Nigel.

"No, but I've been meaning to," he said. "Thanks for motivating me."

She laughed.

"Seriously, though," he said, "I'll surprise her with a visit before I leave."

"How about you?" he asked. "You travel in the Caribbean much? I mean other than going home?"

She had. Quentin had taken her to various luxury destinations. But she couldn't bring herself to talk about Quentin. Not when she was prepared to benefit from Nigel's incredible generosity. How could she then turn around and go back to the man who had rejected her?

"Not really," she said. "And I haven't been home, either. How about you?"

"The Caribbean Circus did a few carnivals," he said. "Back when we had money."

"The circus had money?" Violet asked, surprised.

"We did a big collaboration one year," he said. "We got a bunch of grant funding to work with this designer out of England. He worked in only shades of blue. And this woman choreographer, who did a sort of Caribbean/modern dance fusion."

"Sounds very avant-garde," Violet said, laughing.

"It was a little out there," he agreed. "They wanted to tour the US and Europe. I agreed, but only if we did the Caribbean, too."

"Wow," Violet said. "That must have been a big grant."

"Just ten performers," Nigel said. "We took a tour bus in the US and Europe."

"And what about the Caribbean?"

"We had a charter boat."

"How did you do it, Nigel?" Violet asked, suddenly serious. "How did you just defy everything your parents expected, everything you were supposed to do, and just do whatever the hell you wanted?"

"I don't know," he said. "I just—I tried other things, and they didn't make me happy. I was working in advertising, and we got this client who was working with Cirque des Étoiles. And I would sit in the meetings, looking at the images, and I realized I wanted to climb into them. And they had this show called 'Safari,' with all these white people dressed up as African animals. And a few black performers. And I wondered, why can't we have a Caribbean Circus? All the color of carnival, with our music, and a tropical set?"

"So you just did it?" Violet asked.

"I sold it with a tourist angle at first," Nigel said. "Come enjoy the tropics of the Caribbean, right here in New York."

Violet laughed. "Did you use the word *exotic*?"

"I will not be admitting that here today," Nigel said. "But I was coming out of advertising, so yes, there is that distinct possibility. Also, I may have done some cheesy poolside shows in Atlantic City. But I dare you to find any photos on the internet."

"But you did it," she said. "You just said fuck it, and you did you. I tried for finance. I sort of compromised with wanting a makeup company. I really wanted to paint, but I was never that brave."

"It's not just about brave," Nigel said. "I had people to back me up. My mother in Jamaica didn't like it, but my aunt in Brooklyn could understand. She saw I was dying in that corporate job. She even helped me get a bunch of contracts with the New York City public schools. That's our bread and butter. But you were here all by yourself. You had nobody. And at that prep school? You were lucky to get out with your soul intact."

"I should have gone to art school," she said. "My high school drawing teacher suggested it, but—but she seemed crazy. I would have felt like I was letting everyone down."

"I never could have done circus arts for college," Nigel said. "I couldn't even do it after college, only after

I'd saved six months' worth of living expenses from corporate America. And I promised everyone I'd find another job if it didn't work out."

"That was smart," Violet said.

Nigel shrugged. "From the time I got to this country, I was primed for the dream. The good job with the good money. It's supposed to make you so happy and fulfilled. Then you get there, and it doesn't satisfy you like it's supposed to. But until you achieve it, you think you'll be happy once you've 'arrived.' "

Arrived. She'd thought about that in connection to being married to Quentin. She had that sense that her life was incomplete. That she was unfulfilled. She expected that it would be solved by marrying Quentin and raising a family. But what if it wouldn't? Becoming permanently connected to Quentin seemed to be the gateway to the good life. Together they'd have a family. That was her dream, wasn't it? But what if some part of her would still be trapped in a stack of 4-inch x 4-inch notebooks in her storage space? What if marrying Quentin would lead her to realize that she had manifested somebody else's dream?

"Are you hungry?" Nigel asked.

Violet snapped out of her reverie. She realized she hadn't eaten since having a snack on the way out of the airport. "Yes," she said, "I'm famished."

Nigel opened his backpack, and there were over a dozen energy bars in shiny wrappers.

"Was there a Saint Nigel?" she asked.

He laughed. "I don't think so."

She tore open a wrapper and bit off half a bar. With a full mouth, she said, "There is now."

* * *

"Violet."

Nigel was whispering urgently to her. She had fallen asleep. All she remembered was the gorgeous sunset over the trees and dozing off. Now the sky blazed with deep fuchsia and gold. It had ignited the greenery, the flaming colors reflecting off some of the shining leaves.

"Violet," he hissed and shook her shoulder.

She roused herself. She had slumped down onto Nigel and had her head in his lap. She could feel his rock-hard thighs against her ear, her neck.

She sat up quickly. Her cheek was suddenly cool where it had rested against him.

Blinking, her eyes adjusted to the dusk. There were no streetlights along the road, but she could discern the outlines of things. The crumbling shack. A cluster of trees in front of the house.

"I think they're starting the car," he whispered.

And then she heard it, too. The rumble of an engine in a deeper tone than the ubiquitous whine and buzz of insects.

Violet reached into her bag and pulled out a pair of binoculars.

A few moments later, the SUV eased down the driveway and headed back toward town. Because the road was so rutted, the vehicle had to move slowly. With the help of the magnification, Violet was able to see two heads in the front seat, even in the gathering dusk of the sunset.

As soon as the vehicle disappeared, Violet suited back up into the corset, but without the wig. She left Nigel in the makeshift taxi and stepped out into the night.

* * *

The moon was waning, and it hung bright and heavy in the sky. She used its light to find her way as she crept up the drive to the Hughes house. She was alert for any alarms they might have set.

When she got to the front door, she was grateful that there was no one around to see her in latex gloves fumbling with the lock picks. The porch had a long shade roof that blocked the moonglow. She didn't want to risk a light. It took nearly ten minutes to open both locks, but finally she was in.

She waited to hear if there was an alarm, but she heard nothing beyond the rural night sounds outside and the hum of the refrigerator inside.

Moonlight filtered in through the large windows, illuminating her path to move around the house. She tiptoed up to the bedroom and opened the door.

The moonlight shone on the silvery bedspread on the four-poster king bed that dominated the space.

Violet crossed the room and removed the painting. She pulled her tools from her pocket. The first was a headlamp that she had covered with tape so it emitted only a tiny beam of light. She put it around her head and snapped it on. The second tool was a stethoscope, which she pressed up against the door of the safe.

Teddy had installed one of the brands she had worked on. They were mid-level difficult.

Breathe. She recalled Marisol's words.

She tuned in to the quiet sounds of the night. The cicadas in the bush outside. A distant car going by on the road. Something flying past. Maybe a bat.

The tropical sounds soothed her, brought her into her body. She began to turn the dial to the right, listening for the click—that sound memory she had brought from New York—to sing a familiar note in her ear.

She turned three times and breathed. And then she heard it. She smiled in the dark and turned the dial to the left. No sound. *Damn.* She had gotten overconfident. Had moved too fast. She spun the dial a few times to reset it, taking off her stethoscope and shaking her head to clear it. Then she started again with the first number in the combination, which she now knew.

This time, when she turned to the left, she did it just as she'd been taught. An achingly precise drag of the dial, maintaining a consistent slow velocity. And she was rewarded for her patience. A gentle click in her ear.

Violet's heart leaped. She was almost there. She could visualize herself walking back into New York, victorious.

Focus. She turned the dial back to the right. She was so focused, so busy blocking out any sound other than the safe's that she didn't pay any attention to a motor sound below. The opening and closing of a car door. Nigel was keeping watch. Her only job was to open the safe. And then she heard the final click, and she swung the door open.

There it was. Stacks of paper staring at her. She had expected cash, but it was bigger. Bonds.

After she'd taken them out, she felt around in the back of the safe. She found a pair of passports. They had fake names but pictures of Teddy and Chloe. She took those as well.

She pulled up her shirt and stuffed the passports and the bonds into the plastic around her middle. The process was awkward, as the plastic stuck to her skin, which was sticky with sweat. There were lots of bonds, and she had to rotate the plastic around like a carousel to stuff them all in. By the time she was done, she had a thick layer of paper around her entire body.

She carefully closed the door of the safe and replaced the picture.

She took off the stethoscope and headlamp and listened to the sounds around her. The house was quiet. Outside, the cicadas continued their night song.

She slipped out of the bedroom door and down the hall to the back door.

Just as she opened it to leave, she felt the crush of a body against her back, a sudden press of hard metal at her throat.

Panic seized her. She expected Teddy, enraged at her earlier rebuff, but it was Chloe's voice in her ear:

"Bitches who fuck with what's mine get their throats slit. You hear me, you little backwoods island slut?" Chloe's voice hissed in her ear, moist and vicious. "I saw you before, all pressed up against my man with your trashy little roadside ass. You thought it was your juicy little secret, but I have a nannycam."

"No," Violet gasped. She wanted to say that he had come onto her, that she had rejected him, but would that be any better? Instead, she said, "Please . . ."

"Are you waiting for him to come back? You thought you were gonna meet him here and finish what you started?"

How could she be to blame for that? But some people always blamed the woman, no matter the circumstances.

Violet found her voice. "This is all been a terrible misunderstanding," she said.

"Oh, I understand," Chloe said. "He likes you to struggle a little bit, hit him maybe, but then come back to him, begging for it. I've played that game with him before."

"No, I didn't—"

"I saw you," Chloe said. "I saw you running from the house when I came home. What? You think you're gonna take my man? Gonna fuck my man and run away? Well, you're not, you trashy little island bitch."

There was a sound at the front of the house. The cross-breeze from the open back door pulled the front door open, and it banged against the back of the sofa. Apparently, Chloe hadn't closed it completely.

In the second that Chloe was distracted, Violet pushed her arm away and twisted free.

She was halfway out the back door when Chloe brought the blade down on her lower back, just above her hip. The power of the blow knocked Violet to her knees, but the blade lodged in the bonds, the tip of the knife barely scratching her skin.

"Skanks get shanked," Chloe shrilled in her ear, and the two women struggled for a moment, Violet trying to escape and Chloe trying to retrieve the knife.

Chloe finally pushed Violet all the way forward and pulled out the knife.

Violet scrambled to her feet, awkward with the bonds around her torso.

Chloe raised the blade in triumph, expecting it to be red, dripping. But the moon's bluish glow revealed only the silver of steel.

Violet was crawling away, trying to get herself upright, but Chloe descended on her in a frenzy of rage. She stabbed Violet in the stomach, but the blade lodged again in the bonds. She swung it down several times, stabbing as hard as she could. Many blows hit the bonds, as it was the largest target. Chloe swung the blade hard, burying it into Violet's torso, but the bonds caught it each time, leaving only shallow cuts on her skin. Except in one spot, on Violet's side, where Chloe managed to slice between stacks of bonds. She buried the knife deep in the muscle. Chloe pulled it back out and raised it with both hands. But in her rage-blindness, she missed Violet entirely, lodging the blade hard in the dense dirt.

Violet stumbled back, a searing pain in her side.

She summoned the strength to crab-walk back from Chloe, who had finally managed to pull the knife from the ground.

Violet looked from the dirt and blood-covered knife to the deranged face of the woman before her, advancing with the knife raised for a final blow.

Before she could bring it down, Violet grabbed a rock from the ground and swung it at Chloe's head. Chloe fell back, as a cut above her eye sent blood gushing.

Violet staggered to her feet and ran out into the night.

"You're not gonna get away, bitch," Chloe rasped, pulling herself to her feet and staggering after her.

Violet attempted to run toward the broken-down shack and Nigel, but somehow she had gotten turned around. She found herself running along a river, the moon peeking at her through the trees.

She could feel the blood, warm and sticky, oozing from the wound beneath the bonds. She pressed on it the best she could. Behind her, Chloe ranted. Violet couldn't make out the words, just the ragged tune and cadence of rage. The moonlight allowed Violet to see where she was going, but it also gave Chloe a clear view of her.

Violet stepped through a cluster of trees, sheltering her from Chloe's sight.

On the other side was an old woman, drinking a beer on the steps of her screened-in back porch.

"Please, miss," Violet said. "Please help. There's an insane woman trying to kill me."

"Take this craziness from my house, you hear?" the woman said, retreating into the covered porch.

"Please, miss," Violet hissed. "She stabbed me. Can I just hide in your house for ten minutes?"

"Get away from here," the woman said. She turned as if to go into the house, through the much more solid back door.

"I'll make it worth your while," Violet promised. Then she remembered that she'd given all her cash to Katherine.

"Why would I let some crazy stabbed-up foreign lady in my house?" the old woman asked, opening the inner back door. "I don't know what you did or who chasin' you."

Violet reached for her bangle. "Here. It's gold." Violet held it up in front of the screen door. "I'll give it to you if you'll just hide me from this lunatic."

The woman opened the screen door. In the moonlight, she inspected the bangle. "Not in the house," she said. "Under the porch."

Violet handed over the bracelet, and the woman showed her the little opening beneath the porch. Violet had barely crawled underneath as Chloe broke through the trees.

Violet's pursuer had parted her hair on the side and pulled some of it down over her forehead. It covered the cut where the rock had split the skin. If it had been daylight, the blood would have been clearly visible. But in the diffuse moonlight, the dark red seeping into Chloe's hair looked like a dull shadow.

"Excuse me, ma'am," she said, in a perfectly calm and rational tone. "Have you seen a woman go by? She stole something from me."

"A few minutes ago," the woman said, through the screen door. "Someone came out of those same trees and ran that way." The woman pointed down along the path by the river.

"Thank you," Chloe said and began to walk in the direction the woman had indicated.

Violet watched Chloe's dark shape retreat in the moonlight. She heard the woman go back through the porch and inside the house.

After Chloe seemed to be a safe distance away, she crawled out from under the porch. Her shirt and pants were soaked with blood. She felt weak. She tried to stand but couldn't. She had planned to knock on the woman's door for help, but she could only kneel beside the steps and knock on the bottom of the door. No one came to answer.

Violet reached into the pocket of her dress and pulled out her cell phone.

She dialed Nigel's number.

"The SUV hasn't come back yet," he said.

"Nigel," Violet croaked, "she stabbed me."

"What?" he asked. "Who stabbed you?"

"Chloe," she wheezed.

She could feel her body getting faint. She sank back down onto the ground.

"Where are you?" Nigel asked, his voice tight with panic.

"At some woman's house," Violet mumbled. "I don't know. There was a river." With her last bit of physical strength, she dragged herself back under the porch.

"How can I get to you?"

"Call Serena," Violet said, as the phone fell to the ground. And she passed out, her hand clasped around the spot where the bangle had been, as if covering a second wound.

* * *

Violet's mother had given her the bangle when she was seven years old. Her own mother wore several silver bangles but had no gold jewelry of her own. Lily had a pair of gold hoop earrings, but they were tiny.

In prep school, a girl in her history class had remarked on it. "I like your bracelet," she said, looking at the simple gold line across Violet's brown forearm. But then the girl had rotated Violet's wrist around to see the bracelet's clasp and had instead found a pair of fists, one on each end.

She abruptly dropped Violet's wrist. "How come your bracelet has hands on it?" she asked. "That's so weird."

Violet didn't know why her bracelet had hands on it. The bangle was practically part of her body. She didn't ever take it off. Her skin didn't even register the sensation when the metal tapped against her wrist bone when she raised her hand in class. Why did her bracelet have hands on it? Why did she have only three pieces of jewelry to her name? One bracelet, one gold necklace, and one pair of gold hoop earrings? Especially when all the other girls seemed to have boxes stuffed with jewelry of all different sorts. And they were always shopping for more.

Hands? Weird? She didn't know the why of any of it. That day, she had thought of maybe taking off the bangle. But it was the most expensive, most precious thing she owned. What if it got lost? Or stolen? Out of necessity, Violet kept it on but was careful to turn the fists onto the inside of her wrist, where they were less conspicuous. And she began to raise her other hand in class.

In college, she met other black folks. Other Caribbean folks. She relaxed about the bangle. But the first time Quentin's mother came to Boston, she tried on five different outfits. She borrowed a fancier necklace from Shelby. She contemplated leaving the bangle at home. But it was the most expensive thing she owned. Naïvely, she thought wearing gold would make her seem more prosperous, more worthy to be the girlfriend of the son of an American millionaire.

"Violet, are you there?" Nigel asked. "Violet?!"

Nigel was frantic. He called Serena and it just rang.

He texted:

Violet stabbed! 911!

Then he added:

It's Nigel.

Serena called back thirty seconds later.

"Where is she?" Serena asked. "Do you need the location of the nearest hospital?"

"I don't know where she is," he said. "She didn't know. She said to call you."

"I'll pull up the GPS on her cell to get her exact location," Serena said.

Within three minutes, Serena had managed to get both of their phones on her screen.

"Head north," she said.

"Which way is north?" Nigel asked.

"Just start walking," she said.

Nigel climbed out of the cab and walked toward the Hughes house.

"Go to your left," Serena said.

Nigel followed her directions. Slowly, he made his way out behind the house and heard running water.

"The river," he said. "Violet talked about a river."

He walked along the bank until he got to a grove of trees. Beyond it was a small house.

"She should be right there," Serena said.

"I don't see her," he said.

"Let me call her phone," Serena offered.

Nigel couldn't hear anything, but he did see a faint glow in the darkness. It seemed to be coming from beneath the porch.

He ran to the house and found the glowing cell phone beside the form of Violet on the ground.

When he first saw her, he was afraid she was dead. He stifled a cry and checked for a pulse. She was alive, but her heartbeat was weak.

When he went to pick her up, he felt the blood that he couldn't see.

"Nigel?" Serena asked. "Are you still there?"

"Yes," Nigel said. "But she's bleeding a lot."

"The nearest hospital is in Basseterre," Serena said.

"The nearest doctor is my sister," Nigel said and lifted Violet from under the porch. She was dead weight in his arms.

"Hold on, love," he said and ran along the bank of the river back to the taxi.

Forty-five minutes later, he pulled up at his sister Janine's house, having said every prayer he knew. He had called ahead, so Janine came running to the car.

In the back, Violet lay in a pool of blood.

"Jesus," Janine said. "Bring her in. Hurry."

Nigel carried her through the front door and lay her down on the cool tile of the living room floor. Janine unceremoniously ripped off Violet's dress, only to find the strange plastic tube with the bonds around her body. Blood was everywhere. On her clothes, on the bonds, on the plastic.

"She's lost a lot of blood," Janine said. She used a strong anti-bacterial solution to clean the wounds on

Violet's chest. They were all relatively shallow, and she closed them with surgical tape. The stab wound in Violet's side was deeper, and she cleaned it thoroughly before she sewed it up.

"What was she stabbed with?"

"No idea," Nigel said.

Janine nodded and gave Violet a tetanus shot. Just in case.

"She'll probably be okay," Janine said. "But she should really go to hospital."

Nigel shook his head. "We need to get her out of here," he said.

"She owes her life to those papers she was wearing around her waist. What the hell are they?"

Nigel shook his head. "You don't want to know."

Chapter 10

Violet stands at the altar in a gorgeous Dilani Mara dress. Her hair is stunning, and her makeup is flawless. She feels vindicated, unassailable. Quentin's mother, Mrs. Ross, sits in the front pew of the upscale church with the proper expression of the gracious hostess, but deep down Violet knows that she—the immigrant girl, the stone that the builder refused—has won.

Violet blinks, and her view of the guests is suddenly hazy. She realizes it's because she has on a thick veil.

The minister begins to conduct the ceremony. She turns to the groom and regards him through the tulle. His face somehow manages to be blurry as well as warm and loving.

The minister asks her questions: *love, honor, cherish? In sickness and in health? Til death do you part?* And to each she responds, *I do.*

She lifts her left hand, and instead of a ring, he slips a tiny bangle onto her third finger, a miniature replica of the gold one she gave away.

She's confused. Where's the diamond? Where's the plain gold band she and Quentin had picked out?

A strong male hand lifts her veil, and it's Nigel leaning in to kiss her. Violet recoils in shock. She looks down at her dress, and she's somehow wearing the plastic cylinder of bonds on the outside of the Dilani Mara dress. The corset of bonds is hot and suffocating, and the currency is marred with stab wounds. Her flesh is torn as well, as she bleeds a river of red into the couture fabric of the white dress.

In the background, Glenda Ross begins to laugh. The minister is telling everyone it's time to kiss the bride.

Glenda is laughing. No. Not Glenda. The Ross family is gone. Chloe. Chloe is laughing, walking down the aisle in a skintight wedding dress with a bouquet of knives.

Violet awoke into another dream. Her childhood home in Trinidad. Her old bedroom that she shared with Lily. She was in her single bed, looking across at Lily's matching bed, the mattress sunken in the middle. But the room was no longer hers. It still had the morning sun, the red-flowered curtains, the sky-blue walls. But now it had only Lily's stuff. Possessions of a grown Lily. A few old dresses hanging in the open closet.

Where were Violet's things? Her teddy bear and her childhood Catholic school uniform? She waited for something to happen. Blood? Chloe? The FBI riding in to rescue her?

Morning sunlight streamed in. The sounds of cars on the street outside. The sound of a neighbor calling across the driveway.

"How's your daughter doing today, Mrs. Johnson?" the neighbor called. Mrs. Johnson was her mother. Never actually married, but she had taken to the name.

"Still resting." It was her mother's voice. Sounding

so near. It had been years since she'd heard her mother's voice so near. Only on phones and in dreams.

"She's only been home from hospital for a couple of days," her mother was saying. "They tell me she'll be fine, but she needs rest."

And then familiar sounds: the closing of the house's front door and the shuffle of her mother's feet in house shoes coming into her room. She had come in so many nights after work, saying, "Girls, did you get all your homework done?" or "Girls, come clear up these dinner dishes" or "Violet, where has your sister gotten to? You know it's your job to keep her in line."

But this time the footsteps shuffled in and stood quietly.

Violet visualized the footwear before she even opened her eyes. Chinese slippers with a beaded flower across the light mesh. Her mother bought them for mere change at the Chinese store. Whatever color they had in her size. Eight.

As she opened her eyes, she realized this pair was a dull gray that had once been silver. At that point, it hit her that she wasn't dreaming. She was really in her childhood home in Trinidad.

"Mommie?" the childhood name for her mother just slipped out. Violet hadn't called her that in years. But it came out like a croak. Her voice felt like sandpaper grating against her throat.

Her mother nodded and moved toward the bed, a smile cracking the mask of worry that had been there only a moment ago.

"You're awake," her mother said. "Oh, praise God. My baby is awake."

Her mother knelt at the bedside and gave Violet a

drink of water. The cool liquid felt heavenly against her dry throat. She took a second gulp and held it in her mouth, which also felt dry and sour.

"How long have I been—" Violet didn't know what to say. Asleep? Knocked out? In a coma? What had she been?

"Unconscious?" her mother asked. "A few days, love."

Violet flexed her toes, clenched and unclenched her hands, experimentally. She lifted her head.

"I need to pee," she rasped.

"Hold on," her mother cautioned, and only then did Violet see the bag of fluid that was dripping into her arm, rigged up on a floor lamp.

"What the hell is that?" Violet wondered if maybe this *was* a dream. Her mother was drugging her?

"Just fluids to keep you hydrated," her mother said.

"Well, it's working," Violet said, feeling a strong pressure in her bladder. She went to sit up, and then she felt it. A searing pain in her side.

Suddenly, it all came back to her in an instant of recall: the Hughes house in Saint Kitts. The safe. The bonds. Chloe and the knife. The deranged woman stabbing her over and over. Finally getting away.

"Mommie, I'm sorry I lost my bangle," she said and began to lose consciousness.

The last thing she heard was her mother's gentle words, "It's okay, love. You're not in trouble."

She felt shadows. Sometimes it was her mom. Sometimes it felt like someone else. She had dreams of hearing voices from her childhood. Her mother. Lily. Other voices. Neighbors? Friends? It was a blur. The only consistent thing was that no one sounded American.

* * *

When she woke again, it was evening. Looking around, she realized she was still in her childhood bedroom. She didn't have to pee anymore. This time she moved gingerly. She slid her free hand under the covers and felt around. She realized she wasn't in her childhood single bed, but rather in a hospital bed, with a bedpan.

She lay there for a while, recalling the earlier pain and afraid to move.

She heard the shuffle of her mother's slippers.

"Don't try to move yet, sweetheart," her mother cautioned. "You need to take it slow."

She gave Violet another sip of water to moisten her mouth and throat. "I called the doctor yesterday after you passed out. She said you're healing fine but need to rest another day before you try to get up. You don't want to burst your stitches."

"It was yesterday that I woke up?" Violet croaked. "How did I get here? Home to Trinidad?"

"Your cousin Clive brought you," she said. "By boat."

Violet had a vague recollection of the swaying feeling of being in a boat. And some kind of contrast between that and the bumping feeling of being in a car. But they were stored in a memory that held only physical sensation. No visuals. No sound. No smells or tastes.

She closed her eyes again.

"Everything's going to be fine," her mother said. "Your body just needs rest."

The thought sounded good. Violet's eyes began to close. It was like being a kid again. Her mother soothing her to take a nap. To sleep.

"That's right," her mother said. "Just rest. You've been through so much. The injury. The blood transfusion. You just need to rest . . ."

* * *

The next time Violet woke, something was different. She felt more herself. Her body felt strong, alive. She was determined to get up today. She carefully reached for the cup of water with her good arm. It was awkward, because she had to reach across her body. She fumbled but got it. She was lying flat on her back, so when she took a few sips, she spilled water onto the bed. But she had hydrated her voice enough that she could speak.

"Mommie," she called, her voice stronger, sounding a bit more like herself. "Come in."

Her mother appeared in the doorway.

"Listen to you," she said. "Giving commands and all."

Violet tried to smile, but her lips felt chapped.

"Here," her mother said. "Let me help you."

Her mother smoothed on some lip balm. "You ready to get up?"

Violet nodded.

"You need to take it slow. And don't use your own muscles to sit up. Let us help you."

"Us?" Violet asked. "Who's us."

"Me and the young man who came here with you," her mother said.

"What young man?" Violet asked.

"Nigel," her mother said. "The Jamaican."

Violet's head swam. Nigel was here? She couldn't process it.

"How do you think you got here?" her mother asked. "He's been sleeping on the living room floor for over a week. I'll call him in."

Violet couldn't find her voice to say no, to stop her mother.

"Nigel," her mother called. "Guess who's awake."

When Nigel walked in, it was as if Violet was really

seeing him for the first time. His large brown eyes were liquid with concern. His smile was wide and warm. She remembered the college freshman he'd been, how she'd felt immediately connected to him because he reminded her of home. And now he was here, actually in her home.

She stopped worrying about feeling ashamed. He had helped her. Had come all this way. She didn't need to worry about what she looked like. What—God forbid—she smelled like. Or that her ass was halfway out of her clothes so she could piss in some chamber pot connected to the bed. Nigel was family. More than family. They were a team. They had done something impossible together. Her body had paid the price, but they had been a team.

"The doctor says you have to completely relax and not use that side muscle at first when you get up," her mother said.

So Violet relaxed and let Nigel do the work. He lifted her up to a sitting position. And she recalled those arms. They were part of the sense memory that had held rippling waves and bumping car rides. The other form of transport had been his arms.

From sitting, his arms helped her stand. From standing, she leaned on him to walk. She refused to have him lift her off the toilet. So she had her mother put up the seat and give her some privacy. Violet peed standing up.

Lily had convinced her to do it as a kid and they'd gotten in trouble for peeing all over the seat.

She laughed, as she unrolled the toilet paper and wiped. "Mommie," she called. "Do you remember when me and Lily made a mess and—"

"Did somebody call my name?"

Violet was stunned to hear Lily's voice.

She staggered out of the bathroom. "What are you doing here?"

"What am I doing here?" Lily asked, sarcastically. "I don't know, Violet. I just decided I wanted a vacation in the sunny Caribbean."

"Do you know I almost died?" Violet asked.

"Are you fucking serious right now?" Lily asked.

"Violet," her mother said gently, "Lily gave you the blood transfusion that saved your life."

"Well, I don't want it," Violet said, wishing she could give the blood back. "I don't want anything from her!"

"Please, Violet—" her mother began.

"What is wrong with you?" Lily asked Violet. "You'll let Mr. Yardie Hunk here help you, but you won't accept help from your own sister?"

"Because you're the whole fucking reason I was in this situation in the first place," Violet raged. She felt a stab of pain in her side, but she went on. "If you hadn't been working at that strip club, I never would have been there for Chloe to use my phone."

"Girls, please don't fight," their mother said. "Violet's just starting to—"

"I never asked you to go by my old job," Lily said. "We already established that. But most of all, I'm certainly not responsible for your no-loyalty best American friend fucking your no-loyalty American boyfriend."

"Fiancé," Violet shouted.

"You run after these Americans, kissing their asses. The fiancé, his mother, the friend, the boss. They don't care about you. Look how they all treated you. If anything, you should be thanking me. For showing you what a group of disloyal, shallow, fair-weather friends you had. You're welcome. For that and the two pints of blood," Lily spat, and stormed out of the house.

"Lily, wait," their mother said, jumping up from her seat.

"Fine!" Violet said "Go running after her messy-ass, like you always do."

Suddenly, Violet felt dizzy.

She collapsed back against the wall.

In an instant, Nigel was beside her, an arm around her shoulder.

"Are you okay?" he asked.

She slumped against him.

"Let's get you back to bed," he said, and walked her toward the bedroom.

When Lily and their mom came back in, Violet was in a deep sleep.

When Violet woke up the next day, Lily was sitting across the room from her, reading a book.

"You're awake," Lily said. "I'll let Mommie know."

"Wait," Violet said. "I just . . . I wanted to thank you. For the blood, I mean. And for coming down here to help me. And the passport. I really do appreciate it. And I'm sorry I had an attitude yesterday."

"Okay," Lily said. "I'll go get Mom."

"I'm trying to apologize," Violet said. "You aren't even going to accept my apology?"

"I find it a little hard to accept," Lily said, "when it's clear that you blame me for this whole problem."

"Fine," Violet said. "Let's drop it."

"I have just one question," Lily said. "If I was working someplace respectable—like a bank—and a woman borrowed your phone and started this mess, then would you still think it was my fault?"

"You're ignoring the whole point," Violet said. "She wasn't the bank president's mistress. She was the strip club king's mistress. I'd be less likely to be targeted by someone like her if I was outside a bank."

"What?" Lily said. "You believe that people who work in banks don't go to strip clubs? Who do you think is in the club? Bankers. Stockbrokers. Men who work in firms like Quentin's."

Violet's mouth fell open. "Oh my god, did Quentin come into that club? Is that what you're trying to tell me?"

"What?" Lily asked.

"Did he or didn't he?" Violet insisted.

"Are you serious right now?" Lily asked. "Your best friend fucks your man, and you're ready to forgive him. But if he went to a strip club?"

"You still haven't answered my question," Violet said.

"I have no idea if he went into the club," Lily said. "I never saw him. But that's why I can't accept your apology or your thanks. Because it's all dripping in your whorephobia."

"My what?"

"Your whorephobia," Lily said. "You bashing me because I'm a sex worker. It's like kicking me while I'm down. Isn't it bad enough that I'm already the ugly one?"

"What are you talking about?" Violet asked. "That's ridiculous."

"Give me a fucking break," Lily said. "Mommie tried so hard to act like people weren't color-struck here. Oh, it's Trinidad. We're all mixed. Bullshit. I was black as tar, and you were golden brown. You think everybody treated us the same? Think again."

"Don't believe the prejudice of a few ignorant people," Violet said.

"That's exactly what Mommie always said. Like I was just going to encounter one or two people who thought that." Lily's tone was bitter. "Like it wasn't most of the boys I went to school with who ranked girls by shape and color. My body and particularly my ass was good, but my hair and skin were bad."

Lily paced up and down the narrow bedroom. "Like the girls didn't say things like, 'You need to tone down your attitude, Lily, you already have two strikes against you'—namely, my black skin and my African features."

Lily poked a framed photo on the wall. "Even in grade school, the teachers always cast me as a boy in the school play. Of course, I was tall, but I wanted to play the princess, not the king."

Lily took her index finger away from the glass of the photo, and her fingertip was covered in dust. In the photo, Lily was standing in the back row of several children with a bright smile and a paper crown on her head.

"But, right," she continued sarcastically, "everybody was saying some shit, and I was supposed to ignore it, not let it bother me, when the only person who ever said that you and I were equally beautiful was our mother." Lily pointed to the photo of Violet and Lily in a heart-shaped frame. "And, at the time, it looked like she was just trying to make me feel better."

"How can you say that?" Violet asked, openmouthed. "Mommie loved us both."

"Maybe she did," Lily said. "But it wasn't enough. Yeah, we're all mixed, but there's a right mix to be. Only two African things are a blessing on a woman: lips and ass." Lily kissed her finger and slapped her behind.

"You better get that Indian hair and that light skin and those fine facial features. Don't act like I'm crazy," she said, and Violet realized she was frowning. "Like I've got some kind of complex. Like it's not all around us. You've seen those creams in the Pennywise store."

Violet didn't know what to say. She had seen the different brands of skin-bleaching creams, and the smiling, white- and light-skinned East Indian and East Asian–looking models. The brands had names like "Skin Success" and "So White."

Violet had always dismissed them as ridiculous. But if she thought about it, she had known that people thought she was the pretty one. It wasn't news, just something they never spoke about. Something she had tried to ignore. Because they—their mother insisted—were above such petty things. But maybe it was easier to be above something that favored you. By pretending it didn't exist, it was just one more thing that she got to be better than. The other thing being her sister's complexion.

The front door opened, and Mrs. Johnson and Nigel came in with bags of groceries.

"I told Lily to come get me when you got up," her mother said. "Nigel was helping me in the yard. Where's Lily?"

"She went out," Violet said, eyes averted.

"Is everything okay?" her mother said.

"We got into a fight," Violet said, looking down at her fingernails.

"I told you to be nicer to her," her mother admonished and turned from the room.

"So you're just gonna go running after her again?" Violet said. "Every time she runs out of the house in a huff?"

Nigel advanced toward the front door. "I could go and make sure she's okay, Mrs. Johnson," he said.

"Thank you, Nigel," she said. "You'll probably find her down at the end of the block."

As soon as he had left, Violet's mom turned around, tears in her eyes.

"You can't judge your sister so harshly," she said.

"Why are there totally different standards for the two of us?" Violet demanded. "Even when I was a child, I was never allowed to run off in a huff and have you chase me down. I don't think so. Lily's a grown woman, but she gets to act like a brat?"

"It's different for Lily," her mother said.

"You're damn right it's different," Violet said. "I was up in that boarding school slaving away with all those white people, and you would tell me 'study hard,' and 'get good grades,' but meanwhile she's waltzing around doing God knows what and bringing shame on the family."

"Don't be so dramatic," her mother said.

"Dramatic?" Violet asked. "Did you know Lily was a stripper, Mommie? A stripper. That's how this whole mess started. I haven't wanted to tell you, but at this point I can't keep the secret anymore. So she can call me whorephobic or whatever she wants."

"I know," her mother said. "I'm perfectly aware of how Lily's been earning her money."

Violet's mouth fell open.

"You knew?" Violet asked. "You knew the whole time? You approve?"

"I don't know if I approve," she said. "I just understand. She's doing what she has to in order to survive."

"What about working a respectable job?" Violet asked.

"And how she supposed to get that respectable job?" her mother asked. "With no papers and no university degree?"

"She should have worked hard and gone to college," Violet suggested.

"And how was she supposed to pay for college?" her mother asked.

"She could get a scholarship," Violet said. "Like I did."

Her mother opened her mouth to say something, but then closed it. "I better put those vegetables away."

Violet frowned. "What, Mommie? What were you going to say?"

Her mother took a deep breath. "I was going to say, no. Lily couldn't get a scholarship."

"What do you mean?" Violet asked. "She couldn't work hard? Last I checked that was called laziness."

"I mean," her mother said. "She couldn't get the same scholarship you got."

"Why not?" Violet demanded. "Why are the rules different for Lily?"

"Because it—it wasn't really a scholarship," her mother said, dropping her eyes.

"What are you talking about?" Violet said. "It was. It was the Beryl McBurnie Memorial Scholarship for Excellence in Young Women of Trinidad. I won it."

"That is the story," her mother said. "That is what we told everyone. What we told you. It was easy to explain it that way." The older woman dropped her eyes. "But it wasn't exactly a scholarship."

"Well, what the hell was it?" Violet asked, confused. "A fairy godmother?"

"Your father," her mother said.

"My father?" Violet asked, stunned.

They never spoke about her father. He was a distant, brittle memory, a handsome charming stranger with a British accent. She had met him only once as a child. She had been little, and Lily just a baby. She had hidden behind her mother's skirt, watching as the father stranger met his second daughter for the first time. He had lifted baby Lily out of the crib. He had admired how much she, like Violet, favored him, with their matching slanting brown eyes and high cheekbones. He had given the baby a pair of gold earrings. Lily's ears hadn't even been pierced yet.

Violet never thought about that day, preferring to think of him as dead. Not in England. Uninterested. But there it was. Their only meeting. Although now she realized for the first time that she must have seen him before. Perhaps when he was on the island to conceive Lily. Or perhaps when she herself was a baby. Because he must have been the source of her bangle, as well. No way her mother could have afforded it.

Her mother shook her head. "Your father sent money when you were little. And he promised to pay to educate both of you," she said, her voice a low murmur. "When it came time for you to go to high school, he wanted to pay for you. But he—by then he had gotten married. They had a baby on the way. His wife was worried about money. So he founded the Beryl McBurnie Memorial Scholarship for Excellence in Young Women of Trinidad fund. And he paid for you that way. So his—his wife wouldn't know."

"His wife was pregnant?" Violet asked. "I have another sibling?"

"Two," her mother said. "He had two boys. I asked for a picture, but he never sent it. But I kept sending him pictures of Lily. So he would make good on his promise. Your sister wanted so much to be just like you. To go to that same school in America. You were three years apart, so her first year would have been your senior year. You would teach her all the ropes and everything. She studied so hard. She came in at the top of her class. But by then, your father—he had a new girlfriend. She was expensive. He didn't keep his promise to educate Lily also. I had to beg him to finish paying for your school."

Violet blinked. She couldn't take it all in.

"Why didn't you ever tell me?" Violet asked.

"I couldn't tell you over the phone," her mother said. "And Lily was so angry after that. She ran away. She started hanging out with the wrong people. I had my hands full just trying to keep her out of trouble. And then you went on to Harvard, and I was so proud of you."

"Why didn't you say something at my graduation?"

"What on earth was I going to say?" her mother asked. "'Happy graduation! And by the way, sweetie, your father secretly paid for your boarding school. But he started dating an expensive white girl, so he couldn't pay for your sister. Enjoy your special day!'?" her mother shook her head bitterly.

"I couldn't spoil your graduation," she said. "Certainly not with Glenda Ross and Quentin Ross, and those rich and proper Americans. I needed to show them that we were good people. So I just kept my mouth shut. But it's been the thing that came between you and Lily this whole time."

Violet felt like she'd been hit in the stomach. She felt nauseous and unsteady. Still, she said, "Lily deserves to know."

Her mother began to cry. "All this time," she said, "I felt like I could only choose one of you. I knew it would break your heart to know, and it was breaking her heart not to know."

Violet moved over to her mom and put her arms around her.

Her mother waved her away. "I can't put this on you," she said. "Your body is healing."

But Violet didn't pull away.

Her mother cried with her body rigid, tears streaming down her cheeks.

"We need to tell Lily," Violet said, starting to cry as well. "She was right. Finding out those Americans were fake was a favor. The truth can finally come out."

It took Nigel a while to find Lily. She had stormed off down the street and sat down beneath a tree at the end of the block. She had a small journal in her pocket and began to write:

Too big, too black, too stupid to be like my sister.

"I told you not to listen to that kind of low-class talk," Mommie says. She acts like it's just so simple to ignore. Every day, they would taunt me. I started to talk back. One day soon, I would be going to the US. I would leave them all behind. Just like my sister.

They would see. And then there was no scholarship for me. And then I had to face them. Now not only too tall and too black, but now also too stupid to go to the US like my pretty sister.

So yeah, I started skipping school. I started looking over my shoulder when boys tried to sweet-talk me. It sounded good. Not the ones who said I was pretty for a black girl, but the ones who thought I was extra sweet. Didn't matter that they only wanted to taste. I learned to enjoy the taste, too. And don't talk to me about the blacker the berry. I'm not a goddamned piece of fruit.

"What are you writing?" Nigel asked, once he caught up with her.

"Nothing," Lily said, closing the 4 x 4-inch notebook.

"Oh come on," he said. "Something for your slam poetry. I heard you won a slam at the Nuyorican."

"Slam?" Lily asked. "I can say with one hundred percent certainty that I would never read this on stage."

She stood up and leaned on the tree. Slipping her notebook into her back pocket, she dusted off her shorts, and they headed back to the house. Hanging from her back pocket was a blue handkerchief, slightly sodden with tears.

That same afternoon in New York, Jared had gotten an email that the statement archives for several of Teddy Hughes's accounts were available. They had been cleaned out, but he was able to see all the activity for the last several years. It was tedious work, and he had been at it all day.

By 6:00 PM, his vision was blurring, and he was fatigued.

"Are you gonna take a dinner break?" Lee asked. "Maybe knock off for the night? There's that great new paleo place that opened down the street," she said. "Meat for you and salads for me."

"I might send out for some pizza," he said. "I just want to get through one more quarter tonight."

"Come on," Lee said. "All this is gonna be over soon. And when it is, you'll bounce right back. You'll be a hero. Get your picture taken with a bunch of grateful strippers." She put a hand on his arm. "You know, I'm the type of girl who wouldn't mind that kind of thing. If you and I were dating, I mean."

"But we're not dating," Jared said, taking her hand off his arm.

"But maybe we could be," she said. "I still remember when we first met and you asked me out. I was a fool to turn you down. I just—I mean I found you attractive, but I thought it wasn't really right to date someone who worked in the same office."

Jared just looked at her, blinking.

"So," she shrugged coyly, "does the offer for a date still stand or what?"

Jared inhaled. "No," he said, with a sigh. "It doesn't. I'm—kind of seeing someone else. Working on it, anyway."

Lee's face fell. "Is it Serena?"

"Not that it's any of your business," Jared said, "but yes."

"It can't be that serious yet," she said. "You should keep your options open. We should at least go out a couple times. Let you see what you're missing."

"That's exactly the problem," Jared said. "You're always looking for what you're missing because you're the type who wants whatever you can't have. Right now, that's me, and now that I'm interested in someone else, it makes me look appealing. But I've watched you for years. You always want the biggest fish. If we got our lives back and made a go of it together, you'd be with me for a while, but then you'd dump me for someone richer. Let's just keep it professional."

"Did you know that she's a tranny?"

"Excuse me?" Jared asked.

"A transgender," she said.

"Who's a transgender?" Jared asked, confused.

"Serena," Lee said. "She used to be a man."

"I—no—" Jared stammered. "She seemed—" He recalled her jawline, her smooth cheek, her narrow hips, her perky breasts. Transgender?

Lee shrugged again, but this time with an eye-roll. "So if it doesn't work out with mister sister there, maybe you'll want to call me."

"No, Lee," Jared said. "I definitely won't want to call

you. I didn't realize Serena was trans-whatever. But she's more than just beautiful—she's smart and funny, and overall a good person. Which is something I've never been able to say about you."

"So much for my mercy date offer," Lee called over her shoulder as she strutted out, shaking her own narrow ass extra hard. Jared didn't even notice.

Fifteen minutes later, Jared's phone buzzed. It was Etta, with news that Violet had recovered some bonds. Nigel had sent photos. She was forwarding them, and could Jared make an initial appraisal? And did it void bonds if they were damaged? Bloodstained, to be specific.

When Lily walked back into the house, Violet was quiet. She sat back on the hospital bed, propped up against several pillows. It was a high-end model, incredibly expensive, but rented for her by Etta.

"Nigel said you wanted to talk to me," Lily said flatly. She didn't make eye contact.

Violet cleared her throat. "First of all, I just want to thank you for coming all this way for me," she began.

"Don't worry," Lily said. "I know you didn't ask me to come. So I'm not gonna hold it against you or anything. I just wouldn't have been able to forgive myself if you'd died. But obviously you're okay, so I'll head back to the states as soon as I can get a flight out."

Violet shook her head. "Lily, I'm sorry," she said. "I'm sorry for all the ways I've been—I mean I didn't realize how difficult things had been for you—"

"You know how you didn't want my help?" Lily asked. "Well, I certainly don't want your pity."

"It's not pity," Violet said. "I just didn't have the whole picture."

"What?" Lily said. "Now that you've been down here and awake for five hours, you see how underprivileged I was all these years?" Lily crossed her arms and stared out the window. "I don't get it. What changed?"

"I thought Mommie was gonna be here for this talk," Violet said, irritated. "Mom," she called across the house.

Their mother walked in and stood in the doorway.

"Can you tell her, Mommie?" Violet asked. "Tell her what you told me."

Mrs. Johnson looked from one to the other of her daughters. "I'm long overdue in telling you this. But we live so far apart, and there never seemed to be a good time. But I want you to know that I always wanted the best for you. For both of you . . ."

"Can you just get to the point, Mom?" Lily asked.

"There—there never was a scholarship," she began. And the whole story came out.

"You told me the scholarship ran out of money," Lily said. "But I always thought it was something I did wrong." Tears sprang into her eyes.

Violet picked up her good arm and reached out to her sister. Lily came over to her and took Violet's hand, kneeling beside the bed and sobbing into the crisp hospital sheet.

Their mother came and knelt beside Lily, putting her arms around both of them.

"I'm so sorry, Lily," Violet said as she stroked her hair.

After the crying had passed, the three of them sat together peacefully, hearing cars go by out on the road.

Finally, Violet spoke. "All these years, I thought I was better than you because I got ahead with education, but you got ahead using . . . I mean by becoming . . ."

"By using my ass and being a sex worker?" Lily asked with a laugh. She dried her eyes on the bedsheet.

"I judged you, and I'm sorry," Violet said. "And I wasn't just wrong about you. I was wrong about myself. I always thought I had made my own way. And it was a lie the whole time."

"Nobody makes it out there on their own," their mother said. "That's why I been telling you girls to stick together."

By dinnertime, eyes were all dried, and Mrs. Johnson had made curry goat with callaloo, chickpeas, and squash.

"Are you serious?" Nigel asked Violet. "You never saw *Lap Dance* when it was on Broadway?"

"I know," Violet said. "I can't believe I was such a jerk about it."

"More like a snob," Lily said.

"I wasn't a snob," Violet said.

"Oh, please," Lily said. "If I had been in some Shakespeare shit, you would have had front-row seats."

Nigel laughed and nearly spit out his chana masala.

"Okay," Violet said. "That's probably fair."

"Did you even see me do the burlesque that night when you were already in the building?" Lily demanded.

"No," Violet said, with a sheepish chuckle. "But those pum-pum shorts. Mom, she had on fishnet shorts and a thong. I was like, lord, that's just—just—so much ass right there."

Now it was Lily's turn to laugh.

"It was burlesque," Lily insisted. "Nigel, those shorts were totally appropriate for burlesque, right?"

"Lily," Nigel said, "when it comes to your ass, I have

no comment, and I will never have any comment. Not a single word."

"How about the word 'context'?" Lily said. "You could tell my sister, it was appropriate for the context."

"'Context' is a word," Nigel said. "And I already explained I'm not having one single word drop outta this mouth about your posterior, woman."

"Okay, so let's say—hypothetically—that a woman, who might or might not have a big ass, was performing in a burlesque show," Lily said. "Now, if this hypothetical woman had on a thong and fishnet pum-pum shorts, would that or would that not be appropriate to the context?"

"Hypothetically, yes."

"See!" Lily said and jumped up from the table, shaking her ass in Violet's face.

Violet squealed in mock horror and covered her head. Lily proceeded to wind her ass against Violet's shoulder, singing "Vin-di-CA-tion! Vin-di-CA-tion!" in a soca dance style.

Everybody was laughing. Nigel nearly choked, and their mother was wiping tears from her eyes.

"Have mercy!" Violet shrieked.

"You're both my witnesses," Lily said and looked from her mother to Nigel and back.

When the laughter died down, Violet said. "But, seriously, I really regret missing your shows. Is your burlesque troupe performing again soon?"

Lily shook her head. "We don't have any dates on the calendar right now."

Violet swallowed. "I could come see you at the—the One-Eyed King, if you like."

Now it was Lily's turn to laugh. "Oh, God," she howled. "Violet look like she ready to throw herself into a volcano or something. Humaaaan saacrifiiiiiiice!"

Violet laughed, too. "But I'm declaring my undying sisterly love for you. Ready to walk into a man cave of iniquity. For you, Lily Johnson!" Violet stood up and pounded facetiously in her chest. "That's how much I love you!"

Lily laughed. "Well, I can spare you the indignity," she said. "I've also been doing slam poetry. At the Nuyorican Poets Café. Fully clothed."

"Lord be praised," Violet said, flinging a hand in the air. "But let the record show I was ready to take that journey to the underworld."

Lily smiled. "Duly noted."

The next morning, as Lily waited for her taxi to the airport, she went back into their bedroom. She cut her eyes toward the living room, where Nigel was sitting on the couch reading the paper. "The double standard is still in effect," Lily said quietly to Violet. "Mommie would never let me have a Yardie hunk with the hots for me sleeping under her roof."

"It's not like that," Violet said.

"My Yardie would be sleeping in the yard," Lily said. "And I'd have enough sense to climb out the window and get some of dat."

"Lily, you wild, lascivious woman," Violet joked.

"I certainly hope so," Lily said. "Listen, you take good care of yourself, you hear?"

"I'll try," Violet said.

"Or, better yet," Lily said, "let Nigel take care of you. He's staying on, isn't he?"

"He offered," Violet said. "And Mommie said yes. I told her only for a few days. Til I'm stronger."

"Stronger?" Lily said. "If it was me, I'd practically be fainting all over the house." She mock-swooned and fell over the back of a chair with her ass in the air. "Oh, Nigel," she said in a falsetto. "I neeeeed you riiiight noooowww."

"Shut up!" Violet said. She playfully smacked her sister, but she couldn't keep from laughing.

Nigel walked into the room. "What's so funny?"

"Nothing," they both said at the same time.

When the cab pulled up to their house, Mrs. Johnson waved at the driver.

"Don't drive too fast, Mr. Bhattacharya," she said, as she pulled Lily into a tight hug.

He smiled at her. "I promise," he said as he opened the door for Lily.

She gave Nigel a fist bump, then hugged her sister.

As Lily climbed into the taxi, she said to Violet, "I guess I'm not sick of you just yet." She closed the door and spoke through the open window. "Maybe we'll cross paths in New York sometime."

"Sounds good," Violet said. "I'll have my people call your people."

Lily laughed and blew a kiss as the cab drove off. The leather satchel on the backseat beside her was filled with bloody bonds. Lily was taking them back to New York on her own passport.

Lily was carrying the cash equivalent of seven million dollars. Yet the cavalier way she tossed it onto the taxi seat made Violet feel confident instead of concerned. For the first time when her sister walked away, she didn't worry. She just felt like a part of herself was going missing.

When Lily arrived at JFK, she was escorted off the plane by two FBI agents. They took her directly to a back room, where they opened her carry-on suitcase. It contained exactly what she had said it would contain, over seven million dollars in slightly damaged bonds.

From there, Lily was taken to FBI headquarters in Manhattan. They showed her into a conference room with Etta and Jared. The three of them offered Chloe's name and address, the JFK postcard, and the location of the Hughes villa, as well as surveillance photos of both of them that the investigator had taken.

"Nice work," one of the agents said. "We'll follow up on all of this. That'll be it for now."

"What about my sister, Violet?" Lily asked. "Can she get her passport back?"

"If we find what we're looking for," the agent said, "then definitely. But until this checks out, she's still our number-one suspect."

Lily opened her mouth to protest, but Etta grabbed her arm and squeezed tightly.

"Thank you for your time," Etta said brightly, and their crew left the building.

Two days after Lily left, Violet could get up and down from the bed by herself. She even coughed once and felt a sharp but brief stitch where her wound was, instead of a searing pain. She could walk without help, and she and Nigel were walking through her neighborhood. Her mother lived in Tunapuna, a small town far inland from the coast.

The two of them strolled away from her house, crossing the street to the main road.

"So I see that my services will no longer be needed," Nigel said.

Violet laughed. "Lily referred to you as my Yardie Hunk."

Nigel laughed, too. "Yes, ma'am. Yardie Hunk, Incorporated. We aim to please."

He made a little bow, and Violet couldn't help but notice the thick muscles in his back and shoulders.

"So I guess my work is done here," he said. "You've gotten a chance to take advantage of our free introductory offer. So if you like what you experienced, you should look us up in New York. I'd really like for you to try the deluxe package."

They reached the roadside stand where he'd catch a bus to the capital.

The two of them went to hug goodbye. His skin was warm, and his body firm. In the press of his chest, she didn't want to pull away.

Over his shoulder, she could see the bus driver take a last drag off his cigarette and toss it into the road.

"Come on if you're coming," the driver said.

Nigel gently pulled away from Violet. "See you back in Brooklyn," he said and followed the driver onto the bus.

He had just stepped onto the bottom step, and the driver was about to close the bus door.

"Nigel, wait!" Violet said, grabbing his hand. "Don't leave."

"I gotta go," the driver grumbled, reaching for the lever that closed the door. "The next bus is in an hour."

Nigel jumped off the step, and the driver shut the door. The bus took off down the road and left the two of them standing at the stop.

"Violet, what are you saying?" he asked.

"I'm—I'm saying that I don't want you to leave yet," she said. "Can you change your plane ticket for one more day? I haven't even been able to show you around."

"Okay," Nigel said, with a smile. "One more day."

He hoisted up the backpack that held his clothes. He had one other pair of pants, two T-shirts, and a small assortment of underwear. He also had a toothbrush and a small bottle of soap that he used as both body wash and laundry detergent.

"So," he asked, "where does our sightseeing tour start?"

"The spot where I spent most of my time as a kid," Violet said.

She was still a slow walker as they made their way across town. Forty minutes later, they arrived at her Catholic primary school.

Nigel took in the pastel-painted plaster buildings, the chain-link fence, and the barbed wire on top.

"This place reminds me of Kingston," he said.

"But this is such a small town," Violet said. "Isn't Kingston the capital of Jamaica?"

"Yeah," he said, "but Jamaica isn't as developed as Trinidad."

The two of them strolled along the outside perimeter of the school, beside the athletic field.

"I wish you could see the town where I grew up," Nigel said. "So small. Only cold running water. Jamaica doesn't have oil and natural gas resources like Trinidad. No hot commodities to trade with the West."

"We get ripped off by the US, though," Violet said. "They don't pay a fair price for our resources."

"Yeah, but at least you're not dependent on strip mining and tourism to survive," he said.

Violet nodded and steered them back toward her mother's house.

"Besides," he said, "Trinidad was originally colonized by the Spanish. They came to stay."

Violet knew Trinidad was a Spanish word. And the

capital was called Port of Spain, after all. But she hadn't studied any Caribbean history past age thirteen. And she certainly hadn't learned any in the US.

"Spaniards built solid infrastructure in their colonies so they could settle comfortably," Nigel said. "At least they could send some of their men. But in Jamaica, they had one big house, and the rest was just slave quarters. The Brits didn't come to stay. Just to steal."

They were walking down the steps that led from a more elevated downtown part of the town to the neighborhood where Violet lived.

"Would you ever want to go back to Jamaica to live?" she asked.

He sighed. "I would if I could," he said. "But I have just the wrong amount of money. Enough that someone would shoot me for it, but not enough to get the kind of protection I would need."

"Protection?" she asked.

"Gated house," he said. "A few cars with bulletproof windows. Private security. Cash to fly back and forth to the States to get the things I can't get there."

"My aunt here lives in a gated community in the capital," Violet said. "But she doesn't need all that."

"Plus, I want to have kids someday," Nigel said. "I can see more of a future for them in New York than Jamaica. And there's plenty of Caribbean culture still managing to hang on in Brooklyn. But if I was from a place more like this?" he waved a hand, indicating the bustling outdoor market. "I'd be much more tempted to stay."

"I don't know," Violet said. "I've been thinking about it. I was so young when I left. Just assumed that everything in the US was better. Now I know that's a lie—some things are better, but some things are—"

She thought about the racism, and the narcissism, but the hardest thing was the way people in the US were just sort of . . . alone. No real sense of family or community, like back home. And they celebrated themselves for it.

"Still, I'm not sure I would want to move back home," she said. "But ask me in the middle of winter, and it might be a different story."

Nigel laughed.

"I can't really say where I want to settle, though," Nigel said. "I think . . . I mean, I know I want to have a family, but I guess it would matter a lot what my future wife wanted."

"What if your future wife didn't know what she wanted," Violet said. "Or was just . . . open to suggestion. What would you want?"

"I guess . . ." Nigel said. "I guess it's not about the land; it's about the people. We went from Africa to the Caribbean to New York. And we've made a new home in each land. So I guess I just need to be someplace with a critical mass of my people, and I can make it work."

"You ever think about living in England?" Violet asked.

"England is too damn cold," Nigel said. "Year-round. You gotta draw the line somewhere."

They walked up to Violet's house, and the door was locked. Her mother must have gone out to the store.

Violet fished her key out of her pocket. "What if your future wife had a father in England she wanted to get to know?" Violet asked, careful to avoid his eyes. "Would you be open to living there for a time?"

She opened the door, and the two of them stepped inside.

"If my future wife was there, with a bunch of West Indians," he said, "I could find home."

Violet closed the door behind them.

"Mom," she called. No answer. The house was empty.

She took a step closer to Nigel. He smelled of sweat and coconut oil and body soap that doubled as laundry detergent.

She put a hand on his chest, just below the collarbone.

"I've been wanting to do that ever since I ran into you on the train," she said. Her palm could feel the firmness of the muscle beneath his shirt. The tips of her fingers could feel the even harder surface of the bones where his ribs met. And her whole hand could feel the throb of his heart.

She looked up to his face, tilting her head back slightly.

He leaned down and kissed her. Softly at first, but then their tongues met, and he was pulling her close to his chest, his heart starting to hammer beneath her palm.

A moment later, she heard a car in the driveway and sprang apart from Nigel. She felt like a kid again, a feeling that maybe was made stronger by their visit to the Catholic school.

"Anybody home," her mother called, walking up the porch. "I bought some pone from Mrs. Andrews. I figured we needed something sweet now that your handsome Jamaican friend has left."

She walked in the door and saw both Violet and Nigel standing there. "Or hasn't left at all," she said, raising her eyebrows. "Good thing I got plenty."

Violet hadn't had pone since she was a kid. It was a gooey, dough-like dessert made out of cassava and coconut. The closest thing she'd ever had in the states was a butterscotch fudge dessert she'd had at a friend's house in high school. It was the same thick, sugary-sweetness, but the texture and flavor were all wrong.

Now that Violet was eating solid food, she was ravenous.

"So, Nigel," Violet's mother asked, "how long have you lived in the US?"

"Well, Mrs. Johnson, I'm around the same age as Violet," he said. "My aunt was teaching in Brooklyn and managed to get me into one of the local high schools. I didn't have papers for a few years."

"But you managed to get into a fancy college, and then you run off and join the circus?"

"I know it looks bad," he said. "But in my defense I will say that first, I sponsored my little brother and sister to come join me in the US. I mean, I did the corporate thing for a while til I got them settled, but it just wasn't me."

"And what did your parents have to say about that?" she asked.

"My mom was disappointed," Nigel said. "But what could she say? My siblings were in college. I invited her to come live in the US, but she can't stand the cold. She's happy enough in Kingston, as long as she can come to New York for her medical appointments."

"And I bet she schedules them in the spring and summertime," Mrs. Johnson said.

"Yes, ma'am," Nigel said. "And what about you? Were you disappointed that Violet became a makeup artist?"

"At first I was, but then she was doing so well," Mrs. Johnson said, "I couldn't complain. Then all this craziness happened. Thank God it's over."

Nigel turned to Violet. "Will you go back to doing makeup?" he asked. "Now that all this stuff with Teddy Hughes is going to be cleared up?"

"I don't know," Violet said. "I might—I might want to go to art school."

"Well, there's a permanent job for you at the Caribbean Circus if you want to stay," Nigel offered.

"And there's a permanent spot here for you if you decide you're tired of—what is it you Jamaicans say? That 'white man country,'" her mother said, standing up and picking up several of the dessert plates. "Now let me get out of here. I'm late for choir rehearsal."

"I'll do the clearing up," Nigel said, standing and taking the dishes from her.

"Thank you, Nigel," she said. "Don't let Violet overdo it. You know how she is."

Nigel promised, and she headed out.

"It's not like it'll kill me to lift a dish," Violet said.

"No, but it's obviously killing you to rest," he said.

She slipped into the kitchen. "Just let me wash a few of these dishes."

They heard the door close behind Mrs. Johnson.

Violet filled the basin with hot water and poured in some dish soap.

Nigel lowered the stack of dishes into the basin, and she plunged a cloth into the water. She gripped it tightly to wring it out and began to rub it in circles on the smooth surface of the plates.

"I think you missed a spot," he said.

"Just like a man to sit on the sidelines while a woman is doing some work and criticize, but not offer to help," she said, laughing.

"Oh, I plan to help," he said, coming up behind her.

"This is your idea of helping?" she asked.

"I don't want to take over or anything," he said, pressing up against her. He slid his arms down along her arms and took the plate in his hands.

"You see," he said. "You need to really scrub the plate . . ."

She laughed. "You're going to mansplain dish washing to me."

"Definitely," he said, putting his arms around her. "You just need to try my technique. You have to use a lot of water."

"Okay," she said. "Like this?" She sank the dish into the basin.

"Yes," he said. "Like that. Make it nice and wet."

She laughed again, and he pressed his hips against her ass, harder.

She gasped, and he began to kiss her neck, one of his hands sliding across her belly, pressing her hips back into him.

Her hands went slack, the dish falling into the basin. Water from the faucet ran onto her hands and down her elbows, trickling onto the stone floor.

He reached up and shut off the tap, his hand coming back to rest on the side of her face, his fingertips sliding down her ear, her jaw, her throat, her collarbone. He slid fingers into her shirt, the soft cotton of the tank top yielding to his insistent touch. He slid into her bra, and she moaned.

She twisted to kiss him again but let out a sharp moan with the sudden pain in her side.

"Oh God," he said. "Violet, I'm so sorry. What am I doing?"

She leaned forward and kissed him.

"You need to stop," he whispered. "You're still supposed to be on bed rest."

"I'll meet you halfway," she said. "Bed. But no rest." She slid her hands down the back of his pants and gripped his ass, pulling his hips in to hers.

"I can't," he said, attempting to back up, to pull out of her grasp. "I'm afraid I'll hurt you."

"Oh, but you can," she said. "I have an idea."

She went to the hospital bed and pressed buttons until she had the back upright and the footrest down. She put a few pillows behind her back. It was like a tall, cushy chair. She raised it as high as it would go, and her feet dangled above the floor.

"I shouldn't," he said.

She peeled off her tank top, then her bra. She slid out of her shorts and her underwear.

She sat naked on the bed.

"I can't come near you or I will devour you," he said, his voice hoarse.

"Take your clothes off," she commanded. He shook his head but removed his shirt, then his pants and underwear.

She needed him. Now. It was as if her entire life she had been waiting for this moment. No other thing mattered. Nothing else existed. It was only the two of them in this moment.

Once he was naked, they looked at each other. Her brown frame against the white hospital sheet. His long brown body outlined in the doorway.

There were scratches on her skin, as well as the white gauze bandage along her ribs.

The boil of desire she felt for him was like nothing she had ever felt before.

"What if I—"

"Just come here," she said, beckoning him. "Kiss me."

Slowly, as if walking through neck-deep water, he advanced toward the bed.

He leaned down and gently kissed each scratch, reserving the lightest, featherweight kiss for the gauze at her ribs.

She tilted her head back, and he kissed her gently at first, then more insistently. Her skin burned everywhere he touched, and it burned everywhere he didn't touch for lack of him.

He took both her breasts in his hands and caressed her. He kissed her neck, her shoulders.

She felt her skin flush, her heart beat hard. She was wet, unimaginably wet and hungry for him.

She reached down and wrapped her hand around his erection. He gave a deep groan, and she pulled him toward her.

"Come inside me," she murmured into his ear.

"But what if—"

She spread her legs and wrapped them around his hips. Insistently, with both hands, she guided him inside of her.

"Oh, God, Violet," he gasped.

"Oh, baby, yes," she breathed. As he slid inside her, she felt herself sink into the sensation of it, simultaneously more relaxed and more aroused.

"Start slow," she instructed.

His eyes rolled back into his head, as he rocked his hips gently back and forth.

She moaned. "See," she whispered hot in his ear, "I'm fine. I'm just—" She broke off with a sharp moan.

"Am I hurting you?" he asked.

"No," she breathed. "Just the opposite. Don't stop."

"Okay," he said.

She put her arms tighter around his neck, bracing herself against him. He thrust gently inside her, and she wrapped her legs around his hips.

He continued to thrust, and they found the rhythm.

"I don't know if I can—" he whispered. "I mean I'm about to—"

But before he could finish the sentence, her nails

were digging into his neck, and she was crying out in pleasure. His eyes widened for a second, as he gave himself permission to surrender to his own orgasm, and he thrust hard into her, moaning her name.

"Oh shit!" he said afterward.

There was a fresh line of blood seeping into the gauze the covered her wound.

She laughed. "I didn't feel any pain." She looked down at her side. "That's nothing to worry about. It was so worth it."

She kissed him deeply.

They were lying face-to-face in the hospital bed.

"I love you, Violet," he said.

A tear slipped from her eye and down onto the hospital sheet. "I love you too, Nigel."

Later that night, in Saint Kitts, a team of CIA agents circled the perimeter of the Hughes house. They moved in carefully, covering the front and rear entrances, and kept an eye on all the windows.

"On my signal," the commander said. The house was dark and quiet. The SUV was parked in the driveway, and no one had come or gone since they had put the place under surveillance. They had begun watching it with some of their local operatives thirty-six hours before, and the CIA team had arrived late the previous night.

Once everyone was in place, the commander gave the signal. CIA agents stormed the front and rear entrances. Members of the team stood outside to cover any possible alternative escape routes, and there was even an agent on the roof deck.

They trooped in through the downstairs, pointing guns and swinging bright flashlights. The living room was clear. They moved into the dining room.

"Clear!" an agent yelled.

Several agents trooped into the kitchen. An agent looked into the bathroom. Both were clear.

"Found something, sir!" an agent called from the master bedroom.

Several other agents piled in through the door.

On the bed, two body-sized lumps lay beneath a thick comforter. Even with the air conditioner on, they were beginning to smell.

"What do you have?" the commander asked.

The agent pulled back the sheet. He grimaced and set it back down. "Caucasian male. Fifties, maybe early sixties. Medium height and build. Female. Race unclear. Mid-twenties. Both shot through the head."

"Homicide?" the commander asked.

"Looks like a murder-suicide, sir," the agent reported. "He's still holding the gun."

Within hours, CIA technicians were combing the scene. They gathered thirty-eight pieces of evidence indicating, in combination with the blood spatter pattern, that the woman had been shot first while lying in bed. Then the man climbed into bed beside her, pulled the covers over both of them, and shot himself.

The next morning, Lily called her sister with the news.

Violet shuddered at the thought. "Are you sure she isn't the one who did the murdering and the suiciding?" Violet asked. "I never thought I'd say this about anybody, but I'm glad she's dead. That woman was fucking crazy." It was such a relief to imagine that she was no longer in any danger from that blade-wielding psycho.

"First of all," Lily said, "don't use the word 'crazy' that way. It reinforces the stigma against people with mental health challenges."

"Look," Violet said, "I'm sure she was a very disturbed person, and I don't like the idea of anyone meeting a violent death, but she tried to cause *my* violent death."

"Well, in happier news, how are things going with Nigel?" Lily asked. "I thought he was supposed to be back, but I heard he's still in Trinidad."

Violet was sitting at the dining room table. She looked around to make sure she wouldn't be overheard. Her mother was in the shower, toward the back of the house, and she wasn't sure where Nigel had gotten to. She whispered into the phone, "He's still here. Lily, I think I'm falling in love with him."

"What?" Lily asked excitedly. "Tell me more!"

"Hold on," Violet said. "I'm getting another call. From a 212 number. Maybe it's the FBI wanting to give me back my passport."

"Call me back!" Lily said, and Violet clicked over.

"Hello?" she said.

"Violet, it's me, Quentin," his voice came through the line, as familiar as a ghost.

"Quentin?" Violet heard herself say the name, but it felt strangely disconnected from her own body.

"Oh, baby, I'm so sorry. For everything. I was such a fool. I was just afraid," he said. "I'm sorry. Even my mother is sorry. I got the news about the FBI raid. I should never have put you through all of this. Can you ever forgive me?"

"Okay," Violet said, "I forgive you." Her voice felt completely disembodied, like she was on autopilot.

"Great, then the wedding is back on. We're gonna get you back up here as soon as possible."

His words felt surreal, like she was watching a video where the sound and the image weren't synchronized. She tried to object, but she felt like she was a beat behind, trying to get her voice to catch up with the action.

"But Quentin, I—" Violet began.

"I know," he said. "I spoke to Mrs. Hughes—Etta. She said you can't travel by plane. Because of the injury. But I'm sending a yacht for you. It'll completely circumvent the passport issue. The car should be there within the hour to take you to the harbor. Your mother still lives at the same address, right?"

"Yes," she said in a daze. "In Tunapuna."

"Oh, Violet," he said, "I'll spend the rest of my life making it up to you. I'll see you soon, baby. Sooner than you think. I gotta go, but I love you, Violet. I love you so much."

Even after Quentin hung up, Violet sat for a few moments with the phone to her ear, totally disoriented.

She snapped out of it only when her mother hustled in from the back of the house. "Who you talking to on the phone, sweetie?" she asked Violet.

"And, Nigel, don't just stand there in the doorway, love. Come on in."

Violet swiveled to see Nigel standing in the living room, just inside the door. His expression was a combination of shock and bitterness.

"Have either of you seen my keys?" her mother asked, bustling from room to room. "Of course, I can't find them on my first day back to work."

Slowly, Nigel walked in to the living room.

Violet set the phone down.

"That was Quentin?" Nigel asked.

"Oh, here they are!" Mrs. Johnson called from the kitchen. "Gotta rush. See you both later!"

They heard the back door open and close, then the sound of Mrs. Johnson's steps down the cement driveway and the starting of the engine. She put the car in gear, and they both listened to the sound swell as it passed the open front door and then retreated down the street.

"Were you expecting a call from Quentin?" Nigel demanded.

"No," Violet said. "He just—" She blinked. Finally taking in what had happened. "I need to call him back."

"Call him back?" Nigel asked, outraged.

"He said he would send a car for me," Violet said, shaking her head. "A yacht to take me back to New York."

"And you're calling him back to say what? You have an extra passenger?"

"No," Violet said, "I'm calling to say I don't want it."

Nigel's brow contracted in anger. "You didn't bother to say it the first time he offered?"

"I was caught off guard," Violet said.

"Caught off guard?" Nigel said. "No, Violet. Caught off guard is when you pick up the phone and it's a telemarketer with a 212 area code. Caught off guard isn't when your ex calls and offers to send a car and a yacht and you don't bother to say 'No thanks, Quentin, I'm home in the Caribbean, and I'm fucking someone else, so go shove ya raas yacht up ya yankee ass!' "

"Well, I wasn't exactly gonna phrase it that way, but that was gonna be the gist of it," Violet said.

"No," Nigel said. "I think you were caught off guard when I overheard you. I think you were ready to run back to Mr. American Dollars." He stood, balling and unballing his fists.

"No, Nigel, I don't—" Violet began, then stopped. "Why are you acting like this?"

"Me?" Nigel asked, beginning to pace back and forth across the small living room. "Why am I—? You know, that's a good question. Why am I acting like this? Why did I travel in a leaky-ass boat all the way to Trinidad for a woman who is just using me to pass the time til her raatid yacht can arrive to take her back into the arms of the man who was fucking her friend?"

"Well, at least he never talked to me the way you're doing right now," she said. As he prowled around the living room, the chest and shoulders and arms that had looked large and protective suddenly began to look formidable and threatening.

"Of course not," Nigel said. "I bet he spoke softly and carried a large stack of cash," he said, his voice creeping up to the edge of a yell.

"Nigel," she said, "please lower your voice."

"Lower my voice?" he asked, advancing on her, sarcasm dripping from each syllable. "You think this is the time to use inside voices?"

Violet felt scared. Was he going to hit her? How could she defend herself? She couldn't fight back because of her stitches. She pulled her knees up against her chest in the dining room chair.

"I'm sure Quentin would never raise his voice," Nigel sneered. "He would just treat you like shit." By the time he got to the word "shit," Nigel was definitely yelling.

"Yes," Violet said, wrapping her arms around her knees. She was basically curled into a ball. "Quentin did treat me like shit. He fucked up. And you know what? Now he knows it. And he apologized. But you know who else fucked up? Me. I fucked up when I mistook what I thought was your kindness for you just trying to get in my pants. Well, you got in. Congratulations. You wanted to take me back to the States as your prize? Well, that won't be happening. I wish I had let you get on that bus, but I didn't. That was my second mistake."

There was a sudden thudding sound. Violet started and tucked her head down between her knees.

Nigel's head whipped around toward the front door. Someone was knocking.

"Island Limousine Service," a man's voice said.

Violet blinked and picked up her head.

"I'll be right there," she called.

"You're going?" Nigel asked, mouth agape.

"I guess I am," she said. "I thought I had a reason not to, but I misjudged the situation."

"I don't fucking believe this," Nigel said and scooped up his backpack. He grabbed the doorknob and swung it open. The limo guy was totally startled, as Nigel pushed past him down the steps.

The driver stood on the porch as Violet packed her few belongings in a shopping bag. She recalled how it was with Quentin. She could buy whatever she wanted along the way.

She locked the door behind her.

"Next stop Port of Spain harbor?" he asked.

"I need to make a stop first," she said, directing him to her mother's job to say goodbye.

As they traveled down the main road, she saw Nigel sitting at the bus stop, and her heart clenched. She recalled their bodies crushed together, his hands on her, the intensity of the passion like nothing she'd ever felt before. But then she also thought of the rage she'd witnessed this morning. Wasn't it Lily who had told her Jamaican men were jealous? Hotheaded, controlling, and dangerous. She didn't want to get in deeper only to find out it was even worse than she thought.

As the limo sped away from the bus stop, she watched

him til he was just a speck, until he was just a spot in her vision where a speck used to be, unable to pull herself away until the road curved and he was only a memory.

After a tearful goodbye with her mother, the limo ride was a blur. Yet, when they docked in the harbor, she noticed she had unconsciously doodled a woman with nopal cactus leaves for hair on the corner of the receipt the limo driver had given her.

The yacht ride was a five-day blur, but with unexpected company. Quentin had hired a nurse to monitor her health and a wedding planner to get her preferences for cakes, napkins, invitations, decorations, menus, and place cards. She had her measurements taken and looked at an endless parade of dresses online. The yacht had a satellite internet connection. Quentin Skyped in a couple of times a day and at least once daily had a "very good friend" like Melissa Harris-Perry or Amy Goodman join him in what ended up being an ambush interview.

By the time they docked in Manhattan, there was a battalion of paparazzi, several news vans, and a helicopter waiting for her. The Ross family had used their abundant connections to smooth over any legal concerns with Violet having left the country illegally. They had stopped briefly in Florida for a custom suit and a hairdresser. By the time Violet arrived in New York, she looked ready for Fashion Week or a Broadway premiere.

In a dramatic entrance, Quentin fought his way through all the reporters and photographers to sweep her up in an embrace. They kissed, and he put passion into it, but she couldn't feel anything. Which made sense. Who could enjoy an intimate moment with a hundred flashes popping before her eyes along with the bright lights of video cameras and the drone of a helicopter overhead?

Behind Quentin was Glenda with an apology, followed by her former boss. Before she could even get into a limo to leave, a white horse rode up with a stuffy-looking British royal guard type, who had an apology from the royal family and the Delacroix wedding party.

The next day, she was all over the news. She was the hero in the case of the strip club mogul theft, and she was marrying a black millionaire. Glenda put her up in a deluxe hotel suite in Manhattan and staged a media circus.

One room for makeup and prep. One room for interviews. One room for Glenda and the publicist to take calls. The smallest room was where Violet slept—without Quentin—because Glenda thought that would look bad.

The latest reporter was a slight, blond woman from some tabloid magazine. They had all begun to blur together.

Violet sat on the cream-colored sofa in a cream-colored pantsuit. She felt like she was melting into the hotel furniture.

"So tell me," the woman said. "When you got off that plane in Saint Kites, were you thinking, 'I'm gonna single-handedly take down a major criminal'?"

"Saint Kitts," Violet said. "It's Kitts. Short for Christopher. And I wasn't single-handed. I mean, I was part of a team. My cousin Clive was in the harbor. And Serena Kostopolous from the Maria—"

"Did you know Violet smuggled the bloodstained bonds out in an inflatable plastic contraption she wore around her waist?" the publicist said. "Went in with it full of air, then out with it full of bonds. Can you imagine? Like Gwyneth Paltrow in that fat suit movie."

"That's so wild," the reporter said.

"Would you like to see it?" the publicist asked. "I can bring it out."

The plastic item was brought out. Violet complied with the request to try it on.

"It can't be inflated now, of course," the publicist said. "It was ruptured by the stab wounds. Thirty-five of them."

Violet could see the reporter writing down the number thirty-five.

Violet didn't know which she hated more, the basic questions she had answered dozens of times or the more invasive questions that some journalists asked. And in between interviews for press, radio, and TV shows, Violet had photo shoots for magazine covers.

There was a big *New York Times* feature that even included an interview with her mother. The publicist that Glenda had hired kept spinning Violet's triumph as a plucky bootstraps story of rags to riches, including her prep school, Harvard, and then some careful product placement of Facing Manhattan makeup. They did a ton of interviews through the Fourth of July holiday, which landed with headlines like MEET VIOLET JOHNSON, A CARIBBEAN FIRECRACKER! and IMMIGRANT RESCUES THE AMERICAN DREAM.

Things had slowed down for a moment, and Violet was sitting in the hotel room contemplating a text from Lily:

Friends coming over tonight. Hope you can make it!

Violet had another Skype interview with a UK publication that evening. She didn't want to do it, but she had agreed. She kept composing, then deleting apology texts to Lily. She was afraid they would come off like *I'm too important to go to your party.*

She was trying a third time to compose an apology when the publicist stormed in to the hotel suite. She was livid because the feature on Violet in the *New York Times* didn't get the prominent placement they had expected.

"We got bumped for this douchebag?" she demanded, waving a copy of the *Times.* The headline said CARL WILLIS TO STAND TRIAL IN NEW YORK.

Violet skimmed the article, which detailed how the aging Chicago R&B singer was being tried on several counts of sexual battery, statutory rape, and criminal confinement.

"Everybody knows he's a damn pervert," Glenda said, snatching up the paper. "Why is this even considered news?" She read from the paper. "Listen to this drivel:

> *Rap artist Thug Woofer has broken the code of silence among black male artists. "I'd stake my money that he's guilty. In fact, I already have. I was slated to do an album with him a while back, and I pulled out of the deal. It cost a lot to break that contract, but I couldn't look myself in the mirror if I worked with a man who treated young black women like that."*

"Nobody cares what a barely literate rap artist has to say," Glenda fumed.

"Well, I'm glad that he's gonna stand trial," Violet said. "And it's good that the media is giving it prominent coverage. I'm sick of rich and famous men getting away with whatever they want."

"Soapbox time is over," the publicist said. "You won't be saying anything like that in the interviews we have set up for tomorrow with black publications."

"Don't tell me what to say," Violet said. "If a reporter asks me about it, I'm certainly going to speak my mind."

"You know what?" Glenda interrupted with a high-wattage smile. "I think we've been doing too many interviews. Maybe it's time for Violet to take a little break."

"Glenda, what about—" the publicist began.

But Violet was already taking off her blazer. "I need to go," she said. "I haven't seen my sister. My friends. The outside of this hotel room." She texted Lily.

Yes. I'm coming. Where are you? Text me the address.

"Well, I didn't mean for you to leave, dear," Glenda said. "Just to take a break. Quentin is due here in a couple of hours."

"No," Violet said. "I'm going to Brooklyn. My sister is having some friends over." She looked down at her phone, and Lily had texted:

I'm at the One-Eyed King. About to go home on the subway.

"Sweetheart," Glenda began, "why don't you just move back in to the family apartment? It's much more convenient."

Violet shook her head and texted Lily back.

Stay put. I'll pick you up there in a Lyft.

"No, thanks," Violet said to Glenda. "I'm gonna stay at my sister's place tonight."

Violet looked around for her purse and realized that everything she had was given to her by the Ross family. Except her cell phone. She ordered a Lyft and walked out of the suite.

* * *

Violet walked into Lily's tiny apartment for the first time. The sisters had caught up on the ride over.

"It's really small," Lily said of her Bed-Stuy studio, "but it's all mine."

"I'm just sorry I've never seen any of your apartments before this," Violet said.

Lily sucked her teeth. "You didn't miss anything."

They walked up the dank staircase to the fifth floor, and Lily opened all three of the locks.

"Surprise!"

There was her whole crew: Etta, Serena, Marisol, Tyesha, and Jared. Behind them was a WELCOME BACK, VIOLET! banner. The five of them, plus the banner, took up most of the apartment.

Violet couldn't help it—she began to cry.

Lily put an arm around her.

"You all are the best people in the whole world," she said. "The best. I never could have done it without you."

And Nigel, she thought but didn't say. With these people, she knew they were in it to help her. Or to get their own money or lives back. Or to help the dancers' union. But Nigel had been trying to help himself to her.

"So, what's the update with the case?" Violet asked, when she had finally stopped crying.

"Well, the FBI was giving us trouble about the bonds," Serena said. "It seems there's some loophole for the wealthy about buying these particular bonds. Even if the money is shady, you can't confiscate them."

"But now that Teddy's dead, they're mine," Etta said. "In fact, the whole One-Eyed King franchise is mine."

"And Etta will be reinstating the 401(k) for the workers," Tyesha said, "with a setup that can't be looted."

"What about the bonds that were cut or bloody?" Violet asked.

Marisol scoffed. "Those rich people have never let a little blood keep them from their money."

Everyone laughed, and Lily got Violet a drink.

Violet sat down with Lily on the love seat, which opened out to become Lily's bed. There were three folding chairs, and that was it for furniture. Serena and Jared sat on pillows on the floor.

"Serena," Jared said, "how've you been? I haven't been able to catch up with you."

Serena smiled. "I know, right?" she said. "Things have been so crazy at work."

"I was thinking maybe—" Jared began.

"Attention, everyone," Lily said. "We need a group photo!"

They all crowded in. Violet had the fanciest phone, and the case had a little built-in tripod, so they set it up to take their picture.

The six of them crowded onto the love seat, laughing.

"Say 'victory,' " Lily instructed.

"VICTORY!" everyone said, and the camera took a burst of shots.

Lily recovered Violet's phone and looked at the photos. "These look great!" she said. "Except for this one where Violet's eyes are closed. You look like you're falling asleep."

Suddenly Violet's screen lit up with a photo of Quentin.

"Your fiancé is calling," Lily said and handed her sister the phone.

"Hey, babe," he said, when Violet answered. "Can I put you on with mom about wedding details?"

"Well," Violet said, a bit annoyed, "I'm with my friends right now."

"Perfect!" Glenda Ross's voice sang in the background. "We need to make arrangements for the bridesmaids."

"You're on speaker," Quentin added.

"Hi, Glenda," Violet said brightly.

"Listen, darling," Glenda said, "I just wanted to know if your friends are available for a bridesmaid's dress fitting tomorrow morning at eleven in Midtown. I know it's short notice, but it shouldn't take too long. Ladies?"

Violet told Glenda to hold on and muted the phone. "I am so sorry about this," she said. "I had no idea—"

"Don't worry, honey," Marisol said. "I can make it work. Does anyone have a conflict?"

"Nothing I can't move," Lily said.

The rest of the group nodded.

"Tell her I look terrible in peach," Jared said, and everyone laughed.

Violet unmuted the phone. "Okay," she said. "Eleven it is."

"All right, girls," Serena said. "See you tomorrow morning."

"Serena, can I—" Jared started.

Serena looked at her phone. "Sorry, folks, my Lyft is here. Gotta run."

And before anyone else could say anything, she'd dashed out the door.

But her Lyft wasn't there. The driver had canceled. And the next driver was ten minutes away. She was still in front of the building when Jared came out a few minutes later.

"Damn drivers," he said. "Let me walk you to the subway."

Serena shrugged. "Okay."

It was a beautiful evening. The sky was clear, and there was a cool breeze.

"This has been an amazing experience," Jared said. "I mean, at first I was like, this ruined my life. But maybe it was the best thing that could've happened to me."

"How so?" Serena asked.

"Before this," Jared said, "I was just the money guy. All I thought about was money. What it could buy me. If I had more or less than other people. If you had more money, I'd put up with you being an asshole."

"Was Teddy one of those assholes?" Serena asked.

"Definitely," Jared said. "But there were other guys in the office who had less money, and they had to put up with me being an asshole. That's just how it worked. Nobody cared about anybody. We were all just out for ourselves. And when I first came to work with Etta, I just wanted to get my old life back. Be that dog in the middle trying to claw my way up."

"And now?" Serena asked.

"Now my old life looks kind of fucked up," he said. "Really fucked up, come to think of it. Now that my name is clear, I sort of wanna start over. Re-evaluate all my priorities. You know, go on a vision quest or something crazy like that."

Serena laughed. "That's not what I was expecting."

"How about you?"

Serena shrugged. "This is my life. These are my folks. It's all part of my work at the clinic. The world is fucked up, but we're trying to make it better."

Jared nodded, and they walked along for a while without speaking.

"So, a bridesmaid again," he said. "You think one of these days you'll be the bride?"

"I don't know," Serena said. "For years, I didn't think about it. I was more living day to day, you know?"

"Not really," Jared said. "I've always been a planner."

"Do you plan to get married?"

"I always saw myself getting married," Jared said. "I mean, at first it was just for the tax break. But then, you know, now that I'm in my thirties, I would like that kind of companionship."

"And what did you do in your twenties?" Serena asked.

"I dated a lot," he said.

"I did too," Serena said. "In my early twenties, at least. How do you define a lot?"

"A few times a week," he said.

Serena nodded. "Same here," she said. "More or less. Any relationships?"

"A few," Jared said. "Mostly, I played the field."

"You have a type?" Serena asked.

Jared shrugged. "Not really. I like all different kinds of women."

"In my experience," Serena said, "people think they're a lot more open-minded than they are."

"Look," Jared said, "I don't really know how to say this. But I know that—I mean—er—Lee told me you were—or are—"

"That I'm what?" Serena asked, looking him directly in the eye.

"Trans—" Jared said. "I looked it up on the internet, and I know there's a lot of ways to say it wrong, so just give me a second to get it right." He took a breath. "That you are transgender. That you are a transgender woman."

"That's right," Serena said. Her jaw was tight. She was ready for him to fuck this up.

"Yeah," Jared said. "Which I'm glad she told me, because I like you. And I wouldn't have wanted—I mean, I was surprised, but not in a bad way. And I wouldn't want you to think—I mean, if you had been the one to tell me, and I had a surprised look on my face—that I was bad-surprised. It could be good-surprised."

"Good-surprised?"

"Am I doing this wrong?"

"Doing what wrong?" Serena asked. "Letting me know you know I'm trans? Okay, you know."

"No, Serena," he said, "asking you out on a date. Now that we recovered the money and had the welcome back party for Violet. This is the last time we're gonna see each other unless we decide we want to get together. And I'd really like to see you again."

They had arrived at the subway station. The two of them stood close together. They were about the same height—five foot six—but Serena was a bit taller in her heels.

Serena bit her lip. "I guess this is what good-surprised feels like."

He leaned in and kissed her softly, placing a gentle hand on her bare shoulder. When he pulled back from the kiss, they smiled at each other.

"So which way are you headed?" Serena asked.

"Into Manhattan," Jared said.

"I'm going to Queens," Serena said.

"Maybe I could ride that way with you," Jared suggested.

"You mean like go home with me?" Serena asked.

Jared's eyebrows rose. "Sure," he said. "I was sort of hoping things might go that way."

"It wasn't an offer," Serena said. "It was a request for clarification. I'm not that kind of girl. At least not tonight."

Eleven the next morning found Violet, Lily, Serena, Marisol, Etta, and Tyesha at an exclusive bridal shop in Midtown. A harassed young blonde handed them all flutes of champagne, and another young woman circulated through the different client rooms with trays of canapés.

Glenda was presiding. She had clearly been there for a couple of hours preparing and had had more than her share of champagne.

Several young assistants were measuring each of the women in the party. Glenda waved for the young blonde to bring out the bridesmaid's dresses.

The girl hung several ice-blue dresses on the clothes rack. "These are all a size too big, of course," the blonde said. "We'll do a custom fitting."

She ran around handing out the dresses. A size twelve for Lily. A ten for Etta. A fourteen for Tyesha. A six for Serena. A sixteen for Marisol.

"So," Glenda said, "not only was I a fool to ever doubt you, Violet, my dear, I was a fool to give up our wedding venue. Such short notice is always hard, but Labor Day is impossible. All of Manhattan was sold out."

Lily, Tyesha, and Marisol needed their dresses taken in significantly at the waist. The size six was way too big for Serena. The blonde went back to get her the four. It fit perfectly.

"But here's the good news," Glenda continued. "I managed to find a spot in Brooklyn. That borough is really on the map these days."

"On Labor Day?" Lily asked. "I don't know how you'll find a soca band during carnival."

"Soca?"

"It's basically calypso," Violet said, using the name for Trinidadian music that was better known in the US.

"A calypso band?" Glenda laughed. "No darling. We'll have no such thing. It's customary to have a string quartet for the wedding and a DJ for the party. We'll play something from your culture, too. How about 'Day-O' by Harry Belafonte?"

"Excuse me?" Lily began, but Violet put a hand on her arm.

"I don't think that song is really—" Violet began.

"Leave those little details to me," Glenda said. "Feel free to text a few suggestions to the planner."

Violet whispered to Lily, "Quentin's mom is gonna be incredibly bossy. Don't worry about her. Quentin will help solve all that later."

"Ladies, you look gorgeous," Glenda proclaimed, taking another flute of champagne and an oyster.

After the fitting, all the bridesmaids except for Lily said their goodbyes.

After Glenda walked them out, she came back into the dressing room. "I have a surprise for you," she said to Violet. "Your bridal dress is ready."

The assistant brought out a Dilani Mara custom gown.

The bodice was asymmetrical, like an ocean wave. It cinched at the waist and had a wide, full skirt. The fabric was luminous, with bit of opalescence, and tiny pearls were sewn in rows at the seams.

Violet gasped audibly. "It's stunning," she whispered.

"I'm so glad you like it," Glenda said.

Violet tried it on, and it truly was stunning. The

dozen measurements they had taken on the ship were not in vain, as the dress fit perfectly.

"Look at you," Glenda said. "A vision of loveliness. And these bridesmaids will also be gorgeous by the time we get these dresses altered. What happened to that nice friend of yours? Shelby, was it? She's not in the wedding?"

"She slept with your son," Lily said in a deadpan. "You didn't hear about that?"

Glenda's eyebrows rose. Apparently, she hadn't heard.

"Lily," Violet hissed at her sister to shut her up. "Quentin and I were broken up at the time. But she was still supposed to be my friend."

"Quentin is definitely a man in demand," Glenda said. "You're smart to hang on to him this time around."

"Quentin is the one who's lucky here," Lily said. "He should be hanging on to Violet."

"Well," Glenda declared, "I think my work here is done. The bride is gorgeous, and the bridesmaids are too, but not enough to outshine her. You girls can stay as long as you like. Help yourselves to more champagne or canapés, on us." She trailed out leaving a cloud of slightly cloying perfume.

The moment she left, Lily turned to Violet. "Are you sure you want to go through with this?"

Violet sighed. "Yes," she said, "I'm sure. I'm not marrying her. I'm marrying Quentin."

"Okay," Lily said, "if this is what you really want."

"It's what I've always wanted," Violet said. "As long as I can remember."

A week later, Violet was sitting on Quentin's couch. He had just gotten home, and they had ordered takeout from a nearby Italian restaurant. Violet was opening the containers when both of their phones signaled incoming texts.

Quentin grabbed a stick of garlic bread and looked at his phone. "Mom sent the seating chart," he said, talking with his mouth full.

Violet put down the compostable utensils and picked up her own phone. She blew up the image on her phone, searching for names she recognized. There were dozens and dozens of tables. She found a familiar name here and there. Friends of Quentin's. Relatives she'd met at family holidays. But nobody she was excited to see. Finally, in the back, she found a single table that had all her people. Lily. Tyesha and Woof. Marisol and Raul. Serena. Jared. Etta. Her people filled a single table of eight. The crew of friends she'd shared with Shelby had all declined to come.

"Babe," Quentin said, "this calzone is so good."

"What is it that I bring to this marriage?" Violet asked.

"What?" Quentin looked up from his plate.

"It's like I'm getting swallowed up by your family and your life."

"Violet," Quentin said, putting down his plate, "I know it's a lot. It could make anyone feel insecure. But that's what you bring to the table. You're just . . . genuine. I run with all these guys who are total sharks, you know?"

He poured himself a glass of wine. "My peers at the firm resent me because I'm the boss's son. They think my dad's gonna make it easy for me, but he's gonna make me work even harder so everyone knows I earned it."

He took a sip of wine and went on. "And these sharks are all trying to bring me down. They can't do it openly, so they stab me in the back. Try to make me look bad."

He gestured to Violet's phone, which still had the seating chart visible. "There are tables and tables of these assholes at the wedding," Quentin said. "Dad is inviting half the firm so the other half will feel left out. That's the water I'm swimming in every day. I need to come home to someone who's above all that."

He scooted closer to Violet on the couch. "I'm so grateful that I'll have a wife who doesn't have the morals of a sociopath and the ethics of a pimp, all wrapped up in an elite law degree and a designer suit."

He squeezed her arm. "That's why I flipped out when this stuff happened with the strip club king. It was the first time I'd ever had to doubt you. Not really doubt—I shouldn't have doubted—but even to question. I wasn't used to it. I was used to you being my rock. My moral compass."

Violet wasn't sure she wanted to be someone's moral compass. But that was what she wanted, wasn't it? For Quentin to see that she was loyal to him. And now he could see it. He saw her as even more upstanding than he was. But maybe something had changed through all this. Not just the night with Nigel, but all the lawbreaking, the change with her sister. She had lost her need to be the good one. She wasn't even sure what being good meant anymore.

"I slept with Nigel," she said. "When we were in Trinidad." The words just slipped out. As she said them, she realized she needed to know she wasn't just on some pedestal, some Pollyanna figure to him. She couldn't look at him as she said it. Her eyes were in the distance, looking out the window.

In her peripheral vision, she could see Quentin freeze. "You did what?" he asked.

"Just one night," she said. "You called the next morning."

Then he turned to her, his eyes wide. "I blame myself," he said. "I left you all alone to figure this out. Another man had to help you and not me. And yet, when I called, you chose me anyway."

He pulled her close to him. "I'm so sorry I abandoned you. And you still chose me."

As she sat in his embrace, she could feel his heart beating hard against her own chest. She recalled her intention to call him and tell him no. She wanted to let him know that she would have, if Nigel hadn't showed her such rage.

She was almost going to tell him, but he leaned in and kissed her. There was such tenderness and raw need. She felt something powerful: vindication, pity, the power of being on the other end of such wanting? She kissed him back, hard.

Later, as they made love, she could feel the power of the emotion between them. It was a different kind of intensity than she'd had with Quentin in years. A similar quantity of intensity to when she'd lost her virginity to him, but the emotional quality felt different. And all of it paled, somehow, in comparison to what she'd had with Nigel. But that kind of passion was for romance novels. In real life, nothing like that could be sustained. That kind of fire burned people to a crisp. What she had with Quentin? That was a love for a lifetime. She lay back on the luxurious sheets and let his hips press between her legs. She closed her eyes and let his stroking against her clitoris bring her to a climax.

"I love you, Violet," he whispered in her ear.

And as she came, she said it, too.

* * *

The whirlwind of the interviews had given way to the whirlwind of wedding planning. And just as that began to let up a bit, Violet got a call from Glenda's publicist.

"Violet, hello," she said in her honeyed voice. "I just heard from a literary agent who thinks you should write a memoir about this whole experience. Can I set up a meeting for you?"

"I—well, I guess so," Violet said.

She didn't like the agent. He seemed like a hustler, and worst of all, he obviously didn't understand the experience. He used words like "tropical backdrop" and "spunky."

But she did like the idea of writing a book. She began to do her own research about writing a memoir. She queried a few other agents, people who had represented other Caribbean authors. They were all excited about working with her. She asked about maybe including some of her artwork in the book. Most of them thought that wouldn't work, so she settled on the agent who said she'd try to find a publisher who could do it.

In the weeks leading up to the wedding, she found herself in a whirlwind of writing a book proposal, then sending it out to different publishers. The next thing she knew, there was an auction. They were fighting over her book. A book that wasn't even written yet.

One publisher was offering an advance of two hundred thousand dollars. But they didn't want artwork. They said they would consider an image of hers for the cover but wouldn't guarantee it. Another publisher was offering half that but would guarantee a cover. An art publisher was offering twenty-five thousand but promised a dozen full-color images in the book. How could Violet even decide?

"Go with whichever one will be more fun for you,"

Quentin said. "Money's no object here. I can easily support us both, so focus on what's going to make you happy."

Violet was tempted to go with the art publisher, but the agent disagreed. "Go with the big publisher," she said. "With an advance like this, they'll be committed to making the book a success. Then you can easily do a book of just pictures with any art publisher you want."

Violet decided to go with the big publisher. And the agent got the advance up to three hundred thousand dollars. For her story. It was amazing. Best of all, she felt like she was bringing her own prosperity to the marriage. Upon signing the contract, she got a hundred thousand dollars.

That night, she made a special dinner for Quentin. She set the dining room table and poured wine for them. She lit a pair of candles and arranged a flower centerpiece. In the middle of the flowers, she put the check.

She smiled at her handiwork as her phone signaled that she was getting a text from Quentin:

Working late. Sorry to cancel dinner.

Violet blew out the candles and slumped back into a chair. She called Lily and then Etta, but nobody was answering. Finally, she picked up one of the wineglasses and celebrated alone.

A few nights later, Violet stood in a crush of people against the back wall of the Nuyorican Poets Café. Lily was pressed into the crowd beside her. The show hadn't started yet, but attractive and stylish folks, largely black and brown, pushed through the throng and greeted each other.

Lily's hair was pulled back in an Afro puff, and she had on a bright green halter top and a kente cloth skirt. Violet was much more understated in a white silk tank top and jeans. Lily seemed to know everyone. She greeted various friends, introducing some of them to Violet, and just shouting to others across the room.

Lily explained that she was "sacrificing" tonight. Apparently, this was an integral part of a poetry slam, which was like the Olympics, only poetry. There were judges, and they needed to be able to calibrate their scores. So a sacrificial poet went first, someone who wasn't actually part of the competition. Their performance would be scored, and all other poets would be judged against that calibration.

A DJ was playing a bouncy nineties hip-hop instrumental, as the host stepped up to the mic, a chocolate sister with long dreadlocks.

"We're just about to get started," the host said. "It's packed in here tonight, so Lily Johnson, please make your way to the stage. Come on, now, people gonna have to make way for the poets."

Violet squeezed Lily's hand, as her sister made her way toward the stage at the far wall. As she crossed the room, she smiled and waved at several people. But then the grin died on her face, and she glanced anxiously at Violet.

Violet followed Lily's eyes and saw Nigel pressing his way into the crowd. She could feel her heart in her throat. She tried to press her body backward, to melt into the wall. But in an instant, he had also followed Lily's glance, and he saw Violet. The eye contact was like a punch to the chest. She looked quickly away, her eyes scouring the walls for an exit or a restroom sign, but the only way out was in Nigel's direction.

On the stage, the host was saying in a bright and warm voice, "Make some noise for the Nuyorican's own Lily Johnson!"

As the applause thundered in Violet's ears, Nigel pressed through the crowd toward her.

"Ninety-nine!" several members of the crowd yelled.

"Not tonight," Lily said. "Tonight, I wanna read a piece about Trinidad."

Nigel was only a few feet away now, pushing past a Latina with a blue-tipped afro.

"Trini posse!" someone yelled out.

"*West* Indian!" someone else yelled back.

Nigel slid into a nonexistent space beside her.

"Violet, I've been trying to call you, but your phone is disconnected," he said, his voice low. "And you wouldn't answer my emails."

Violet didn't trust herself to speak.

"I just wanted to apologize," he said. "For how I—"

"Apology accepted," she said in a rush, her voice tight.

From the stage, Lily bellowed "Port of Spain haunts me on this island, even in its half-frozen year."

"Can we talk?" Nigel murmured into her ear.

"I—" Violet said.

"After Lily's poem, I mean."

Violet shook her head.

"I just want a chance to—"

"I'm marrying Quentin on Labor Day," she said. "There's nothing to talk about."

Nigel frowned, and his face went tight. "That's not—" he began.

"Shhhhh!" hissed the Latina in the blue afro.

From the stage, Lily went on. "Manhattan streets filled with native and slave ghosts, an ancestral parade down Fifth Avenue like carnival."

Violet kept her eyes riveted on Lily, her own jaw tight, her body rigid.

"That's not what I—" Nigel whispered in Violet's ear.

"Can you take this conversation outside?" the blue Afro woman asked. "Some of us came to listen to poetry."

"Forget it," Nigel said in a low murmur. He turned and began to press his way back out of the café, little murmurs of "excuse me" and "sorry" in his wake.

Violet turned back to the stage. Lily's eyes were on Nigel's retreating back.

"And sometimes in Brooklyn summertime—" she was saying. But then she went quiet. Blinked. Shook her head. "Sometimes in Brooklyn summertime—" She looked up at the ceiling. "Fuck!"

Violet realized Lily wasn't reading from her notebook. She was reciting from memory. Or lack of memory.

The audience began to applaud and snap. "You got this, Lily," a voice yelled.

Lily took a deep breath, her face suddenly lighting up. "Sometimes in Brooklyn summertime, if I sprinkle sea salt on my tongue, I can taste the Caribbean—"

Lily found the thread of the poem and recited the rest without faltering again. But Violet didn't hear another word from her sister's lips. The only phrase that kept spinning in her head was Nigel's voice: *I just want a chance to . . .*

The host was back on the stage. "Okay, judges," she said. "I need those scores."

But the phrase kept rattling around in Violet's brain until it had no meaning anymore. Ijustwantachanceto. Ijus. Wanach. Anceto. Suddenly, nothing made any sense. Not the words in her head. Not the judges yelling out numbers with decimal points.

Not the host, sharing the final tally. "Looks like Lily scored high, but got that time penalty."

Lily pressed in by her side. "Are you okay?"

Violet shook her head, her eyes filling.

"Let's go," Lily said, taking her hand, pressing through the crowd toward the door.

"But your show," Violet said, as various people waved, nodded, and clapped her sister on the back on their way out.

"I'm here every week," Lily said, waving to the bartender as they approached the door.

From behind them, the first competing poet had begun. "Inside every catcaller is an insecure toddler, who wishes he was taller, insecure 'cause his dick is smaller."

The audience laughed.

"That's right, girl!" someone yelled.

The poet went on. "I used to be a staller, but now I'm a brawler, a consciousness installer with a 'fuck you' holler. I know my curves give you the urge to surge with words, but you can bury that commentary, and I'll sing the dirge . . ."

As they stepped onto the street, Violet held her breath, wondering if somehow Nigel would still be out there. But she only saw a knot of young white hipsters, smoking cigarettes.

In mid-August, Etta was throwing a party. Violet didn't really want to go. But she didn't want to stay at Quentin's place, either. He had been working late so frequently these days, and she couldn't face another evening alone in the house. Solitary nights like this, she used to call Shelby, and they would watch a favorite TV program together. They might hear each other breathing quietly on the phone during the show itself, then they'd talk smack about the characters during the commercials.

Shelby.

She'd had a persistent sense of heaviness and loss since she'd come back from Trinidad. Her sister had suggested that maybe she was grieving over the loss of her best friend. It made sense. She and Shelby had shared so much; they'd shared their college years, vacations, apartments, and then—behind Violet's back—they'd shared a man.

Since Violet's return, she'd tried to watch her favorite show with Lily and Etta, but they talked smack during the show itself. It just wasn't the same.

A text came in from Lily:

Meet me downstairs in 5. Do you have your costume on?

Etta was throwing a theme party. Violet had bought the costume but couldn't bring herself to put it on. She texted Lily back:

In my purse. Coming down now.

She threw on a loose cotton tank dress and headed down to join her sister in the Lyft.

Half an hour later, the two of them were ringing the bell at Etta's house. Lily had on a lightweight trench coat.

Etta came to the door with a drink in her hand, wearing nothing but lingerie. On her head was a small black top hat that tipped at a rakish angle, with a mesh veil covering one eye.

"Welcome!" she said. "To the merry widow party."

As she swung the door open, Violet could see that all the women inside had on similar lingerie, bustiers with garters and stockings attached, skimpy or thong underwear, and high heels.

Serena came up and hugged them both. She had on a blood-red ensemble. Her high, full breasts were held up in strapless lace cups, and the peplum ruffle just below her navel flared over narrow hips.

As the two Trinidadian sisters stepped in the door, Lily opened her trench coat to reveal electric turquoise lingerie.

Etta whistled at the sight of her, and Serena handed each sister a flute of champagne.

"Violet, where's your outfit?" Etta asked. "I figured you'd just get something extra while shopping for your wedding night underthings."

"See?" Lily said. "I told you to change in the back of the Lyft."

Listlessly, Violet pulled a handful of black lingerie from her purse.

"It's okay," Etta said. "I won't force you to wear it."

"But the invitation said costumes were mandatory," Lily said. "How come Violet gets a pass."

"Because," Etta said. "without Violet, I might be a widow, but I certainly wouldn't be merry."

"And you definitely wouldn't be the sole owner of the One-Eyed King," Serena said. She turned to Violet. "Did Lily tell you Etta's gonna let the workers turn it into a cooperative?"

Lily grinned. "Okay, Violet. I'll forgive you for breaking the dress code." She turned to Etta. "And I like the hat." Her voice softened. "How was the funeral?"

Etta shook her head, but the hat and the veil stayed stuck in place. Violet figured the hat must be pinned into Etta's mane of curls.

"It was so strange," Etta said. "It took so long til they finally released the body and sent it back to New York. At the funeral home in Queens, his relatives were all there. They were all patting my hand and offering sympathy for my loss." She chuckled mirthlessly. "But I realized I'd been grieving him since that time he tried to double-cross the strippers. After that, I kept going through the motions, but my love for Teddy died that day. When he ran off, I was pissed, and I was hurt, but I wasn't really crushed, you know? Now that he's dead and buried, I'm ready to move on."

Lily downed her champagne. "You won't be alone long if you keep dressing like this."

Etta laughed. "We'll see," she said. "I don't think I'll ever get married again. Marriage sucks ass." She turned to Violet. "Sorry, honey. At least mine did. Yours can only be better."

Etta adjusted her breasts in the bustier. "Maybe in the future I'll just have a bunch of young lovers."

Lily grinned, looking her up and down. "You'd make a good cougar."

Suddenly, a blast of house music began in the living room just past them.

Several lingerie-clad women shrieked and clacked onto the dance floor in tall heels.

Violet felt a bit overwhelmed with all the noise and energy and skin.

On the far wall of the living room was a string of the foil letters generally used to spell out things like "Happy Birthday." It read: WE GOT THE MONEY BACK, MOTHERFUCKERS!

"Where's the restroom?" Violet asked.

Serena steered her to a door in the hallway past the dining room and kitchen.

Violet thanked her and headed for the bathroom to put on her lingerie. As she made her way through the house, all around her were gorgeous women chatting and laughing. They were certainly sexy, but what made them particularly attractive was how they all looked jubilant.

In the doorway between the dining room and the kitchen stood two women—a brown-skinned Latina and a girl with tattoos peeking out from her cleavage. The pair of them screamed across the house.

"Lily! What took you so fucking long to get here?"

"Come do some victory shots with us!"

Violet finally found the bathroom and closed the door behind her.

She pulled out the lace top with garters. She dug in her purse for the matching undies and the stockings, still in the plastic package. Holding the top up to her body, she didn't feel sexy or merry and certainly not victorious.

Violet felt trapped. She didn't feel comfortable keeping her dress on. And being the only person wearing clothes would make her feel too self-conscious.

But could she stand around half naked at a party with a bunch of strangers? Strange women, she reminded herself. Friends of her sister's. Women whose money she'd helped recover. What were her other choices? Go somewhere by herself? Go back to Quentin's lonely apartment?

She downed the champagne and drew her dress off over her head. Maybe she could pull this off. But she'd be needing a few of those victory shots.

Chapter 11

Labor Day dawned muggy and golden, with streaks of clouds in the sky that made for a vibrant sunrise.

Violet had been awake for hours, her stomach filled with butterflies. She woke up at Lily's apartment. She had wanted to stay with Lily the whole time, but the space was tiny, and Lily got annoyed with all the wedding-related calls.

Again, Glenda had offered to put Violet up in the family's apartment, where she'd stayed before, but Violet declined. She preferred to stay at Etta's for the weeks between her return from Trinidad and her "big day."

She spent weekend nights with Quentin, but they hadn't made love more than a few times. Often, when they started to fool around, the phone would ring with a call from his mother or the planner, wanting to discuss some detail about the wedding. By the time they had gotten off the phone, the mood was ruined.

And mornings weren't an option, because Quentin was up early to get work done in the office. He had to close several big deals before they took off on their honeymoon.

The night before the wedding, Glenda had offered a hotel suite at the Brooklyn Gardens, but Violet just wanted to be with her sister. The two of them slept in the double fold-out love seat. Lily snored gently all night. Violet found it comforting—reminiscent of when they were kids. But she only dozed. Tomorrow night, everything would be different. She'd move in with Quentin, live in Manhattan, and be the younger Mrs. Ross. But, first, they'd be off on their honeymoon.

He'd surprised her with a change of plans. They were going to Paris. Violet had never really been particularly excited about Paris, but it was supposed to be the pinnacle of romance, and they had deluxe accommodations. How could she say no?

There were times when she would watch Quentin across the room. He would be talking to a client or colleague. He appeared so powerful. It had always been a quality she found incredibly attractive, but it seemed somehow different now.

During the times that they had made love, she enjoyed the physical pleasure, but it didn't feel the same.

"He cheated on you," Etta said. "Yeah, yeah, you were technically broken up, but you know what I mean. I had to forgive Teddy more than once. It takes a while to come back from betrayal. But your guy is no Teddy. He's a keeper. Just give it time."

It was true: the betrayal still stung. Quentin had apologized. Violet had watched as he'd deleted Shelby's number. He had cried in her arms and begged her to take him back. To love him again.

A honeymoon in Paris couldn't hurt. And she would

have a lifetime to forgive him. With all the pleasures of being the young Mrs. Ross.

She couldn't lie to herself, though. She did think of Nigel, sometimes. A lot. Compared Quentin to Nigel. But that was just a fantasy. Like comparing your boyfriend to Superman or Prince Charming. Real life wasn't like what she had had with Nigel. Traveling halfway across the world to rescue her. Safecracking. Maybe he had saved her life, but the fact that he had even come showed how inappropriate and unbalanced he was. Almost a stalker. Yes, of course, their one night together had been intense and unforgettable. But the shadow side of passion is obsession. She was better off without him. Quentin was the one who could offer her a life. A good life.

Three hours later, Violet stood in front of the full-length mirror in the gorgeous Dilani Mara dress. It had taken her and Lily nearly an hour to travel across Brooklyn because so much of the borough was blocked off for the West Indian Labor Day parade. In fact, the wedding venue was right along the parade route.

"So are you ready?" Lily asked.

Ready? Violet didn't feel "ready" as much as she felt at peace. She had made her peace with the fact that Quentin had cheated—she would find a way to forgive him. She had made her peace with the fact that she now knew what passion was, and she wouldn't have that in her life. It just wasn't worth it. She'd even made peace with the idea of getting married without her mother in attendance. Her heart condition meant that she couldn't fly, and it was the peak of hurricane season in the Caribbean.

She had cried when she'd gotten the news that the yacht captain thought it would be too dangerous. There were a couple of big storms. They could try to avoid them, but once they were underway, there was no way to predict whether the storms would change course.

"Maybe it's a sign," Lily said. "Maybe this wedding just isn't meant to be."

"No," Violet said, drying her eyes. "It's just another obstacle I'm not going to let get in the way of my dream."

So Violet was a calm bride. She let Lily insist that she have some toast and tea for breakfast. She kept drinking water every time Etta handed her the bottle. She was doing her own makeup, though. Glenda Ross didn't like that.

"What?" Lily asked. "She afraid you'll draw a Trinidadian flag across your face like it's the world cup?"

Etta laughed, but Violet barely cracked a smile. She sat there solemnly in her slip and a push-up bra, in front of the lighted mirror they had brought in. Her hair was up in rollers.

Violet drew the tiny black brush across her eyelid as Serena rushed in, breathless and late.

"So sorry," she said. "The traffic was crazy. I stayed over at Jared's house on the Upper East Side."

"I see you, Serena," Lily said. "Making your move on the money man."

Serena grinned.

"What a shame that the only day they could get was Labor Day," Tyesha said. "All our crew from Manhattan is hitting major delays."

"A shame?" Serena said. "More like a coup. For the Ross family, at least."

"What are you talking about?" Lily asked.

"You all don't know?" Serena asked.

"Know what?" Tyesha asked.

"Jared says it's common knowledge that the Ross

family is in tough financial straits," Serena said. "This is perfect to help them rebrand beyond their elite Manhattan circles."

"Are you serious?" Lily asked.

"It's a brilliant move," Serena said. "You saw the guest list. All the Who's Who of Brooklyn is invited today."

"Violet, are you hearing this?" Lily demanded.

Violet had just put on the dress and was looking at herself in the three-way mirror. She looked like she was standing in a luminous cloud.

"Hearing what?" Violet asked, looking over her shoulder.

Serena repeated what she had said.

Violet's eyebrows rose as she listened. After a moment, Violet turned and walked purposefully out of the room. Lily trailed after her.

In the hallway, Violet ran into Etta. "Have you seen Quentin?" she asked.

"You can't go see him now," Etta said. "It's bad luck."

"Something's gonna be bad, all right," Lily said.

Violet hiked up her gown and strode down the stairs. She looked in the ballroom and the three different rooms behind it. She knocked on the door of his suite, Glenda's suite. She kept going til she found Quentin in the hotel bar with his friend Dale from work. They were both in tuxedoes.

"Babe," he said, "you look—amazing. But what are you doing here?"

"I'll tell you—" Lily began.

Violet put a hand up. "Lily, let me handle this." Unlike her sister, Violet was calm. "Quentin, is it true your family is in financial trouble?"

"What?" Quentin asked. "Just before you take me for

richer or poorer, you want to make sure that it's for richer?"

"Are you calling me a gold digger, Quentin?"

"That's not what I said," Quentin stammered.

Dale ran a hand through his sandy hair. "I'll leave you all to sort this out," he said, and left the bar with his drink.

"Are you saying Violet is a gold digger?" Lily said, tilting her head to the side.

"Lily, maybe you should stay out of this, too," Quentin said.

"Oh, so now you want me out of this," Lily said. "Me and all the Brooklyn street cred I represent. Now that Trump has made it hard for even the black millionaires, you want to rebrand in a little darker color? How dare you accuse my sister of being a gold digger. When you're the one who dumped her and cheated when things got even the slightest bit difficult. And she's the one who stood by you. After all that, you're the one who needs her. And you aren't even man enough to admit it. Pathetic little—"

Violet turned to her sister. "Please, Lily. Enough." She turned back to Quentin. "Just be honest with me. Is it true?"

"Listen, Violet, I'm sorry," Quentin said. "It's just a little economic bump in the road. I didn't want to spoil the beginning of our life together with a bunch of financial bad news. I love you. I want to marry you. The financial drama's not important."

"I don't want our wedding to be part of some Brooklyn dog and pony show," Violet said.

"It's not like that," Quentin said. "We can imagine it's just the two of us. And starting tomorrow, it will be. A week in Paris."

"I don't want to go to Paris," Violet said. "I want to go to Trinidad. I want—I want my mother to see me get married."

"We tried," Quentin said. "But the hurricanes—"

"But planes are still flying," Violet said. "Let's catch the next plane to Trinidad. Let's get married in my home. With my mom. Lily will come, right? We don't need to marry this whole financial empire. Let's just marry each other."

Violet waited to see a spark in Quentin's eye, but it wasn't there.

"Okay, if that's too much, then let's just go to the justice of the peace here in New York," she pleaded.

Quentin shook his head. "If you didn't want this, you should have said something before," Quentin said. "Now everyone's here. We owe them a wedding."

"My sister doesn't owe your family anything," Lily said. "I've held my tongue up til now, but I'm done. I see your mother and her publicist. Here Violet was, risking her life to get back into your good graces, and your mother has this publicist spinning it to the benefit of your family. Do you really even love Violet?"

"Of course I do," Quentin said. "I'm marrying her."

"In this spectacle," Lily said, "but not in private. That's how you rich boys like to do it. Intertwining the fortunes. The millionaire and the spunky immigrant heroine. But I'll bet you still have your side pieces."

"Side pieces?" Quentin asked, incredulous. "I don't have any side pieces."

"Sorry," Lily said. "Is that too ghetto? Is the proper term 'mistress'? Maybe even the lovely debutante Shelby is still on the scene."

"That is uncalled for," Quentin said. "Just because

you're a stripper and see the worst of how some married men act—"

Violet cut Quentin off. "No need to get—um—whorephobic about it." She turned to her sister. "But it's true. I saw him delete Shelby's number from his phone."

"Oh, really?" Lily said. "Quentin, let me see your phone."

"Fine," Quentin said.

Lily flipped through his contacts. Sure enough. No Shelby.

"Violet," Lily said. "What's Shelby's number?"

Violet rattled off a 347 prefix cell phone number.

"What are you gonna do, call her?" Quentin said. "Come on. Give me back my phone." He reached for it, but Lily pulled it out of his reach.

"Did you say the last four digits were 2463?" she asked Violet.

"Come on, Lily," Quentin said. "Don't call Shelby on our wedding day. Just give me the phone."

"Oh, I'm not gonna call her," Lily said. "I'm gonna look up her number."

Quentin froze.

Violet looked at him, incredulous.

"Funny," Lily said. "Quentin seems to have a contact named 'Front Office' with that same number. A lot of calls back and forth with the front office. And that night you got your book deal? Sat at home alone with the dinner you cooked for him? He'd gotten a call from 'Front Office' at 4:41PM."

Violet could feel her face flush with rage.

"And texts, too," Lily said. "A text earlier this week to 'Front Office' saying, 'On my way!' "

Violet never took her eyes off Quentin but slowly

reached for the engagement ring and slid it off her finger.

She stared into Quentin's face. His mouth was open, but what could he say?

Violet shook her head. She held the ring up and opened her fingers.

Quentin began to reach for the ring, but she let it drop. It hit the marble floor with a *plink!*

"Fuck!" he said. "Violet—"

Violet turned abruptly. She and Lily walked toward the front door of the hotel as Quentin scrambled around on the floor looking for the ring.

Violet hiked up her skirt and walked through the hotel's sliding glass doors, out onto the street. Lily was close at her heels.

Marisol was just walking in. "What's going on?" she asked, as the two of them swished past.

"Quentin's a dick, and the wedding's off," Lily called over her shoulder, rushing to keep up with Violet.

"Oh fuck," Marisol said. "I'll tell the girls."

At the foot of the hotel steps there was a police barricade, and the parade was in full swing. A contingent of dancers went by, whinning to the latest soca jam with power strips in their hands. They were everywhere at the parade, a silent protest against the NYPD beating of a teenage girl from Haiti. During her incarceration, she had been beaten with a power strip. She had lost the sight in one eye and was still in critical condition. It had been proven that she'd been arrested in a case of mistaken identity.

Violet plunged into the milling crowd on the sidewalk, oblivious to the revelers, the music, the power strips, the police. The crowd parted for her. In the massive-skirted white dress, she looked like a performer late to get on her float. Lily rushed after her. But her blue bridesmaid dress garnered no special recognition.

"Violet," Lily called. But between the music from multiple floats, live bands, the DJs, and the crowd noise, she couldn't be heard.

Lily elbowed harder, pissing off several folks to the point of cursing her and attracting a few unwelcome hands on her ass. She usually would have turned around and done her own cursing, but she needed to catch up with Violet. Finally, she got close enough to grab the lacing on the back of the bodice.

"Slow down," Lily said. "Where are you rushing so fast?"

"The Caribbean Circus is back there," Violet said. "I can't see Nigel."

"Why not?"

"I can't get my heart broken twice in one day," Violet said.

"I thought you loved Quentin," Lily said.

"I thought so, too," Violet said. "I mean, I did. I used to. I've been trying to convince myself that this new feeling I have for him is still love, but I think I was just clinging to an old dream. Maybe if none of this had happened, I could have married him and been happy. But even if he wasn't still messing with Shelby, something's changed. I haven't been the same since my night with Nigel."

"Then why did you come back with Quentin?"

"Nigel got so angry," Lily said. "And over nothing. It scared me, so I just left."

"You never told me that," Lily said. "You haven't wanted to talk about Nigel at all."

"He was yelling," Violet said. "He was clenching and unclenching his fists. I was scared he was going to hit me."

"Did he?" Lily asked. "Did he even come close?"

"No, but—"

"You never had a West Indian boyfriend before, have you?" Lily asked.

Violet shook her head. "There was another American boy in prep school—he was white. And then only Quentin since college."

"Jamaican men in particular are famous for their tempers," Lily said. "You just have to figure out if he's the type who's hotheaded but loyal and solid, or if he's the type who's angry and dangerous. I've dated both types, so I know. Nigel is hotheaded but solid. Was it some kind of jealousy thing?"

Violet nodded. "Quentin called, and I just sort of froze. I didn't tell him no. I was just too stunned."

Lily's eyebrows rose. "Nigel thought you were going back with Quentin?"

"I was calling Quentin back to tell him no, but Nigel just lost it."

Lily shrugged. "Then you need to get in his face and give him a reality check. Tell him some shit like, 'You are my man, not him. So sit in that damn chair and watch me call Quentin on the phone and tell him to shove his yacht up his ass because my new man loves me up so good, I might never come back to the US.' And dare Nigel to say some shit to you after that."

"That's exactly what I should have done in Trinidad," Violet said, her face puckering. "I should have given him a chance."

"You were scared," Lily said. "Believe me, I know how scary Jamaican men's tempers can be. Some of those badjohns are straight-up abusive. Why do you think I jumped ship in Manhattan that time?"

"But now I'm sure Nigel hates me," Violet said, her

voice cracking. "And it's not just like I've slunk off into the sunset. I've been all over the news. He thinks I'm getting married to Quentin today."

"And I ran into him last week," Lily said. "He's still in love with you. He wouldn't tell me what happened in Trinidad, but he blames himself."

"Do you think I still have a chance?" Violet asked.

Lily looked up the street at the tall Caribbean Circus float. "Let's find out."

She took Violet's hand and pressed through the crowd.

It was hard to move against the people on the sidewalk. Violet's giant skirt was slowing them down. The crowd bottlenecked at one point, and the two sisters got separated. Lily looked back and couldn't find Violet in the sea of brown faces.

But there was no way Violet could miss the Caribbean Circus float. It had the name written in golden letters across a deep green arch that was almost black. From the center of the arch hung a trapeze, where a lithe young man was swinging in a bright turquoise unitard.

Violet got separated from Lily because somehow her dress was caught. She leaned down to loosen it but couldn't seem to. What had it hooked on? She backed up a bit to see where it had snagged, but there was too much foot traffic. Finally, she just pulled up the train and yanked it free, with a ripping sound. She prepared to press forward toward the Caribbean Circus, when she felt an arm gripping around her and a knuckle at her throat.

Suddenly, it was as if she was transported back to a moonlit night in Saint Kitts, though she felt cement instead of dirt beneath her feet and the sky was bright with sun. But the blade was the same, as was the hissing voice. Chloe.

"You thought you could take my man's money?" Chloe said. "You thought you could take the money but leave me the man? I didn't want his ass without any money. He was no use to me anymore. You really thought I would let him kill me and then himself? It'll be ages before they figure out that bitch in the bed wasn't me. If they even bother to investigate. Just like they'll never figure out it's me who killed you at the parade today."

Violet didn't dare move, but she looked from side to side with her eyes. Against the nearby barricade was a black woman cop, her shoulders bouncing in time to the music. She was just out of arm's reach.

"Sure," Violet said. "You slit my throat. But that police officer would notice."

Chloe made a growl of irritation. Keeping her arm around Violet's chest, she lowered the knife carefully so that it was at her back.

"Start walking," Chloe hissed in Violet's ear and pressed her away from the cop.

But Chloe was trying to walk her in the opposite direction of the way the crowd was going. They couldn't seem to move.

The parade was flowing toward them. The first in the series of Caribbean Circus floats headed their way.

Now it was Lily on the trapeze in the arch. The skirt of her bridesmaid's dress was torn into strips, and she had put on a pair of booty shorts underneath. She hung from the trapeze with one knee, her body arching under it and her other leg extended over her head. She was looking around, trying to spy a large white dress. But her sister's body was pressed between the revelers.

The only thing visible was Violet's dark head and brown shoulders, blending in with the rest of the crowd.

Nigel stood on the back of the float, scanning the crowd for Violet. Lily must have told him she was coming. He was dressed as the ringmaster. He wore a top hat that was crowned with a giant crow's head.

Violet didn't dare speak or lift an arm or hand to signal him. Besides, even a waving arm would be hard to notice in a crowd where everyone was grabbing something to wave. So Violet just stared at him as hard as she could. Her eyes burned into him.

Nigel had on a tuxedo coat, no shirt, and knee-length pants. She was careful to focus on his face and not that giant raven hat, which looked like some omen of death. No. She was not going to die. Her eyes searched for Nigel's eyes. Some part of her had already been dead, had been sleepwalking through life. But not anymore. She was determined to live through this. To live. She felt the knife pressing at her back, slicing through the fabric of the dress, pressed just hard enough to cut through silk, to scratch her skin. She ignored the sibilant voice in her ear, hissing threats—promises—of a death at knifepoint for trashy island bitches who didn't know how to keep their hands off her man.

"And you thought today was gonna be your wedding day," Chloe sneered.

Violet had almost forgotten. Of course. That was how Chloe had found her. The wedding. The story of her daring robbery. It was in all the papers. She felt tears sting her eyes. Her vision swam. Just another reason she had made the wrong choice with Quentin.

"Violet!" she heard someone calling her name above the crowd. It was Nigel. His voice, strong from projecting with those groups of loud kids.

Violet's vision sharpened, and she actually saw him.

He jumped down from the float and pressed his way toward her.

Chloe was oblivious to him, lost in the tale of bloody revenge she was spinning in Violet's ear.

Nigel approached, his brow furrowed. Had he seen the fear on her face? Violet kept her eyes wide and glanced to the right, where Chloe's chin pressed into her shoulder.

Nigel's mouth opened, then closed again. He gave a subtle nod and looked away from the two women.

"Officer!" he called. "Excuse me, officer! I need help!"

Chloe was on her guard now, retreating behind Violet.

Shifting his body to sidle between people in the crush of bodies, Nigel slid next to Violet. The cop pushed through the crowd to where Nigel was standing.

"What's going on?" she asked, then barked a command into the radio at her neck for backup.

The crowd gave them a few inches of space.

Nigel grabbed Violet around the waist.

"This woman has a knife," he said, pulling Violet toward him with a jerk.

Chloe let out a howl of rage and swung the knife after Violet. She sliced across Violet's forearm but stabbed the officer in the shoulder.

The crowd pressed backward, away from the altercation, but there wasn't room to move. Both cuts were shallow, but the officer's uniform was cut, and a small stain spread into the dark fabric, coloring the navy to black.

Violet's cut was a bit deeper and bleeding more openly on exposed skin.

A pair of cops materialized behind the stabbed officer.

"Officer assaulted!" one of them called into his radio, as his partner and the stabbed cop jumped on Chloe, twisted the knife away, and wrestled her to the ground.

"No!" Chloe screamed. "You need to arrest these bitches tryna take my man and my money!"

"Are you okay?" Nigel asked. "Should we call an ambulance?"

"I just need to get away from her," Violet said.

Nigel leaped over the police barricade onto the street and lifted Violet over. The two of them jumped onto one of the last Caribbean Circus floats.

"Let me see if we have a first-aid kit," Nigel said.

The two of them climbed down into the bottom of the float, which was made out of an old boat. He handed her a paper towel, which she pressed to the wound. He looked for a better bandage but couldn't find any first-aid supplies.

"It's not that deep a cut," Violet said. She reached down and ripped the front of the Dilani Mara dress, the relatively clean part of the hem, and wrapped her arm. Then she tore a length of tulle from the back of it and tied it even tighter.

"Are you okay?" he asked. "What happened?"

Violet shook her head. "I don't even want to talk about it."

They sat there awkwardly, Violet cradling her arm.

Nigel surveyed her in the torn and bloodied dress.

"So," he said with a hopeful half smile. "I take it you didn't get married.

Violet shook her head no, but she couldn't help the tears from falling. He scooted over to her and encircled her in his arms. She collapsed into him and let the storm come, heaving and sobbing against the silk of his tuxedo jacket and the moist skin of his bare chest.

And then, just as she thought she was spent from the

crying, something stirred inside her. A hunger like she'd never felt before. The recollection of their night together, but also the tears that had cleansed away the last of Quentin, the last of the good girl, the nice girl, the girl trying to fit, trying to sand away the Caribbean from her tongue, her hips, her hair. She didn't want to be the girl to please; she wanted to be pleased. She wanted the pleasure of Nigel with the raucous calypso music in the background.

The wedding dress had seemed to have too much fabric before, and it was a nightmare as the pair of them pulled at the layers to get them out of the way.

He stripped off his pants and boxers, and knelt between her thighs. He couldn't see in all the layers of tulle but let his hands guide him.

He smoothed his fingers along the insides of her soft thighs, letting touch direct his progress. He found her lips and lifted the fabric to duck his head under. He buried his face between her legs, kissing from her pubic hair down through the opening of her lips. He placed a tiny string of kisses down her closed lips, then slid his tongue in, and she cried out.

"Come inside me," she moaned. "Please, don't make me wait."

Her voice was lost in the loud music and noise of the crowd. But Nigel heard it.

He pushed the layers of white fabric aside and brought his hips up to hers.

"I love you, Nigel," she breathed in his ear. "I'll never let you go again."

"Oh, God, Violet," he said. "I didn't think I'd ever—" But he couldn't finish the thought, because she had pulled him inside her, as her body opened in welcome.

The soca music throbbed outside the float, the crowd

was raucous as the float rolled forward along the street. But inside the bottom of the boat, time stood still. All the two of them could feel was the press and thrust of their bodies and the insistent and increasing pulse as the pleasure intensified.

She came first, howling like never before. The first time she'd ever let herself be loud. She just didn't care who heard, but, of course, in all the noise, no one heard.

And then Nigel came, his own staccato moans in a discordant rhythm with the calypso music all around them. Like when two floats playing music got too close to each other.

And then, the two of them just lay pressed together for a moment. The skin of her shoulder somehow managed to find the skin of his chest, despite the silk tuxedo jacket that hung halfway off his shoulders, the bodice they hadn't managed to undo, and the layers of crushed white tulle between their hips and bellies.

Yet they grinned at each other. Amazed and satisfied.

Violet felt her lids drooping, and she dozed.

When she woke up, it couldn't have been more than a quarter hour later, but she felt suddenly shy. She began to crawl around the small space and found her underwear. She pulled it on while sitting, and then she struggled to push all the fabric of her skirt back down.

The movement woke Nigel. He got up and wriggled back into the jacket. He found his boxers and pants and put them on, all while kneeling.

Above them, they saw the reflection of flashing police lights on the float.

Nigel scooted over to sit next to her. "Should we do

anything about that crazy woman in the crowd?" he asked. "That was Chloe, right? Wasn't she supposed to be dead?"

"They'll probably figure out her identity when they fingerprint her," Violet said. "But I'll call in later to be sure."

"Why don't you call now?" Nigel asked.

"I don't have a phone," Violet said.

"So did you just walk out of your wedding?" he asked.

"It wasn't really my wedding," Violet said laughing. "I was just a prop."

She moved her arms stiffly, like a mannequin, and a line of red showed through the makeshift tulle bandage.

"I—are you okay?" he asked. "I got carried away. Baby, I would never intentionally do anything to hurt you."

She looked up into his eyes. "I wasn't so sure about that in Trinidad."

He shook his head. "I know," he said. "Can I tell you how many times I've regretted that moment? How many times I've replayed that conversation in my head? How many times I've berated myself for not listening to you?"

He took both of her hands in his. "When I finally cooled off, I was able to put myself in your shoes. How you might have just been frozen. In shock. You had been through so much. I was jealous. No, really, I was insecure. I have always felt like a big, awkward, foreigner next to guys like Quentin, with their smooth accents and their designer suits. I get transported back to being some kind of fresh-off-the boat misfit in high-water, hand-me-down pants."

Violet blinked. "I know how that is," she said. She realized that she had felt the same way around Quentin. At least at first. And his love for her had felt transcendent. If he could accept her, desire her, then she was okay. His eyes had been the American mirror she had craved since the day she landed in Boston.

"I know you said you forgave me that night at the Nuyorican," Nigel said. "But if you could really forgive me, open your heart back up to me, I swear I'll be a good listener from now on."

"You think I haven't opened my heart to you after I opened my legs to you?" Violet said, laughing.

Nigel grinned. "I didn't want to make any assumptions," he said. "You know how you millennial women are. Maybe it was just . . . I don't know . . . a hookup."

Violet shook her head and laughed harder.

"Come on," he said. "Let's get some air."

Then he took her hand, and they climbed up from the bottom of the boat and blinked in the bright daylight. The pair of them stood up on the back of the float, a blood-spattered bride with black dripping eyeliner and a raven in a tuxedo. Violet looked at him and then down at her dress and began to laugh again.

People on the street waved to them, and they found themselves waving back. She lifted her injured hand to wave, and it smarted. She cried out in pain, but then just kept laughing.

"Are you okay?" he asked.

Violet nodded, unable to stop laughing.

"It's not funny," he said. "We should probably get you home."

"I'm not going anywhere," she said. "This is where I belong. With you. With my people."

"Violet!" She heard someone call her from the float ahead, and she turned around.

On the float was Lily, hanging down and facing

them, her ankles wrapped up in the side ropes of the trapeze.

"What the hell happened to you?" Lily asked.

Violet could only laugh, tears streaming down her face.

"Seriously," Lily asked. "Are you okay?"

But Violet couldn't stop laughing. She bent double with the force of it. She laughed so hard it hurt the wound in her side, which was still healing, but she couldn't stop. In between the gasps for air, she managed to squeak out the word *yes.*

She looked out into the sea of brown faces, bright costumes with twirling power strip cords, hips and feet dancing to the loud music.

She was alive. Her body shook with the laughter and relief and joy of it.

"This is—" she rasped, holding her side. "This is the best I've ever been."

Keep reading for a sneak peek at

SIDE CHICK NATION

And get in on more heists with

THE BOSS

And

UPTOWN THIEF

Available now

from

Aya de León

And

Dafina Books

Prologue

Water flooded the storage space as Dulce slept. It seeped through the metal slats in the pull-down door. It pooled on the concrete floor. It rose around the mattress where Dulce was sleeping. Although not exactly sleeping, more like in a stupor or a spell from the cocktail of rum and marijuana. It dulled her hearing, so she didn't startle with the shrieking winds and battering rain, and thudding of broken branches against the building. It dulled the panic she would have felt—alone in a storage space where she was living illegally. In a hurricane. And nobody knew she was there.

Water seeped up, turning the mattress into a giant sponge. Soon her back was wet. The criss-cross of her racerback tank top, the cotton shorts. The moisture seeped up into the fabric, even above the surface of the water she lay in. Inch by inch, the line crept up her feet, her beautifully painted blue toenails, the sides of her arms and legs, hips, and torso. It soaked her hair, destroying the remains of the blowout she'd been trying to conserve. She had sweated out the roots, but the tips of her hair had stayed somewhat straight, even in the humidity. She'd kept it up in a ponytail over the last few days, so the ends didn't erupt into tight curls from the sweat on her back and shoulders.

But now, the water rose just above the mattress, soaking her hair, and it bloomed into springing curls all around her head.

Still she slept.

It wasn't until the water seeped into her ears that her body moved at all, beyond the rise and fall of her chest. Her shoulder flinched with the moisture tickling her ear canal, but it didn't wake her. First one side, then the other, as her head was slightly tilted on the mattress. No pillow. But then both ears filled and the tickle was gone. Her body stilled again in sleep. The now full canals dulling the howls of the storm.

The flooding outside was anything but gentle, yet the water could only seep in through the slats in the metal door, the crack at the bottom above the cement floor. So the water level rose slowly. It crept up gently along her neck, her jawline, her cheekbone. The water sidled up tenderly, like a lover.

Dulce slept, like a maiden awaiting a prince, awaiting a kiss.

Yet she slept on when the water first touched her lips. Only when it began to seep into her mouth, did she truly stir. The water, pooling in the back of her throat and making it impossible to breathe properly now. The prince had come. The rescuer on his horse. The discoverer. The pimp.

She flashed back in the choke of the water. She recalled his hands around her throat, the bruising press of fingers against skin and muscle and tendon and windpipe. As the floodwater of the hurricane trickled delicately into her throat, her body recalled the more searing pain of constricted breath. The scrabbling panic of asphyxiation, her heart hammering frantically, as if it needed to escape her body in order to survive. Then the half blackout, feeling her body slump to the floor, the wince with the sharp press of his boot toe, as he delivered a single kick to her hip.

Her hip was soaked now in the floodwater, the left hip. Her pelvis was tilted slightly, and her left side pointed down toward the sodden mattress. The right hip was slightly raised, the bone jutting above the waterline like a disappearing island, as water pooled between the tops of her thighs.

Yet she could feel that the real threat was at her throat. Again.

Like that other time her pimp had sent one of his thugs to kill her. The man had a knife at her throat, as a few dozen women and some of their kids looked on in horror. She recalled standing out on the icy Manhattan ground in bare socks, numb with terror, unable to feel the freezing concrete beneath her feet. Again, the press at her throat. The knife threatening not only skin and muscle and tendon and windpipe, but now her carotid in jeopardy, as well.

More water trickled into her throat, and she coughed weakly, her gag reflex still kicking. And it was with the gagging that part of her old brain began to realize her life was in danger. Some fight or flight response activated her tongue, dragging it into action to spit some of the water out.

Her life was in danger. Like the time after she'd been fool enough to go back to her pimp. And he'd thrown her against the wall. Paint and plaster crashing into her back and shoulder like a drunk driver. When she staggered to her feet, he'd choked her. His thick fingers more insistent than ever this time, despite her own hands, gripping his wrists, digging her fingernails into his skin, trying in vain to open the vise of his oppositional thumbs. Yet it was her own grip she could feel loosening and she began losing consciousness.

That had been Dulce's breaking point. The moment she decided to leave him for good. Or rather, she passed out fearing she might die, but deciding to live if she found she had a choice.

That same resolve woke her inside the storage unit.

She sputtered to life coughing through a burning throat. In total darkness, completely soaked. Her body sluggish with the alcohol and disoriented with the marijuana and the residuals of rum. She tried to lift her head, but her hair was unexpectedly weighted down with water.

Slowly, through the chemical fog, she rolled to her side. As if in slow motion, she dragged an arm beneath her side, propping herself up on one elbow, her mouth just above the water line.

She coughed hard and gagged, suddenly vomiting. Yet the retching made her a bit more lucid. Even in the total darkness, she was able to orient herself, to make sense of the bizarre combination of mattress and moisture, screaming winds and crashing thuds.

Storage space. Hurricane. Flooding. Fuck.